Total Madness
Grips the Western Seaboard!

Six days after Pearl Harbor, a Japanese sub-
marine surfaces off the American coast.
Southern California goes on military alert. Los
Angeles is blacked out.
And lunacy prevails ...

1941

A wild outrageous comedy set in the world of
bobby socks and zoot-suits, padded shoulders
and military-issue bellbottoms.

1941

A story of paranoia, disaster – and craziness on
a monumental scale.

COLUMBIA PICTURES
AND UNIVERSAL PICTURES PRESENT
AN A-TEAM PRODUCTION OF
A STEVEN SPIELBERG FILM

1941

starring

Dan Aykroyd	Tim Matheson
Ned Beatty	Toshiro Mifune
John Belushi	Warren Oates
Lorraine Gary	Robert Stack
Murray Hamilton	Treat Williams
Christopher Lee	

DIRECTOR OF PHOTOGRAPHY
WILLIAM A. FRAKER, ASC
SCREENPLAY BY
ROBERT ZEMECKIS & BOB GALE
STORY BY ROBERT ZEMECKIS &
BOB GALE AND JOHN MILIUS
MUSIC BY JOHN WILLIAMS
PRODUCED BY BUZZ FEITSHANS
EXECUTIVE PRODUCER JOHN MILIUS
DIRECTED BY STEVEN SPIELBERG

Bob Gale

1941

ARROW BOOKS

Arrow Books Ltd
3 Fitzroy Square, London W1P 6JD

An imprint of the Hutchinson Publishing Group

London Melbourne Sydney Auckland
Wellington Johannesburg and agencies
throughout the world

First published 1979

© Bob Gale, Robert Zemeckis and the A-Team Inc. 1979

Set in Intertype Times

Set, printed and bound in Great Britain
by Cox & Wyman Ltd, Reading

ISBN 0 09 922150 0

For CUS and all the gang

About this book

Although *1941* is based on actual incidents that took place in Southern California during the Second World War, in many cases the truth has been modified, embellished or completely thrown out the window in the interests of drama, entertainment, cheap sensationalism and getting a few laughs. To those readers who prefer hard facts to drama, entertainment, cheap sensationalism and a few laughs, we respectfully suggest that you read the *Encyclopedia Britannica*, the World Almanac or the Manhattan telephone directory instead of this book. To those readers who have decided to continue with us ... don't say we never told you so.

Acknowledgements

I would like to thank everyone associated with the production of the motion picture *1941* for their vast creative contributions to the film and consequently to this novelization, including the actors, the crew and the entire production staff. I would especially like to thank my cohorts in crime, Robert Zemeckis, Steven Spielberg and John Milius, without whom none of this could have happened. And, special thanks to my wonderful secretary, Mary Anne Porlier, for her perseverance through the whole mess.

*For those who didn't know
or have simply forgotten ...*

On 7 December 1941 the Naval Air Arm of the Imperial
Japanese Fleet, in a surprise attack, struck the United
States Naval Base at Pearl Harbor and hurtled an un-
suspecting America into World War Two. American
citizens were stunned, shocked and outraged at this
treacherous attack. On the West Coast, paranoia gripped the entire population as panic-stricken citizens became convinced that California was the next target of
the Japanese Forces. Major General Joseph W. Stilwell,
Commander of the Army Third Corps, was given the
responsibility of defending Southern California. Army
and Marine Units, half-trained and ill-equipped, were
mobilized. Anti-aircraft and Coast Artillery defence
batteries were manned and made ready. Civilian Defence
operations sprang into action. For the first time since
the Civil War, American citizens prepared to defend
their homeland against an enemy whose first assault
was expected anywhere, at any time, and in any force ...

Part One

DAY

1

Her name was Anne Barton, but that wasn't important. What was important was that Anne Barton was a member of the Northern California Chapter of the Polar Bear Club. Polar Bear Club members are quite frequently regarded as out of their minds by the rest of the world because they find pleasure in such activities as frolicking around nude in sub-freezing temperatures and skinny-dipping in icy waters. Indeed, Anne Barton had been a member of the Polar Bear Club for two years, ever since she was eighteen, and most of her friends regarded her as out of her mind. What was about to happen to Anne Barton on this cold morning of 13 December 1941 would only reinforce her friends' opinion of her.

Every morning at daybreak, Anne Barton drove her late model Hudson to the Pacific for her morning swim. The attack on Pearl Harbor six days ago and the nation's entry into the war had done nothing to change her habits. And so, as usual, this Saturday morning she drove out along a rock jetty that extended into the ocean, several miles from the community of Big Sur. This was *her* spot, far enough away from civilization to be lonely, secluded and private – this was important, because Anne Barton enjoyed swimming in the nude and did not fancy the idea of having spectators around for the ritual.

The coast was shrouded in fog. The sky was grey, the sea was grey, the very air was grey. Anne Barton couldn't care less. Just as long as the water's cold, she thought. Of

13

course, she knew it would be. She stuffed her golden hair under her bathing cap and climbed out of the car, taking a deep breath of the cold, moist, grey air. She could hear the cawing of several gulls, but couldn't see them – it was too foggy. Visibility couldn't be more than fifteen yards. She wiped the sleep out of an eye, then ran for the end of the jetty, throwing off her terrycloth robe on the way. The cold air felt wonderful on her perfect pale skin. Had anyone been there to watch, they would certainly have been taken with her ripe, lithe, lovely figure, made even lovelier by the surreal quality of the fog and the sea. But there was no one there to see her – that is, not yet. Anne Barton dived into the ocean.

There was nothing so invigorating as a plunge into forty-degree water as far as Anne was concerned, nothing! Freezing cold showers were enjoyable, bathing in icy water was stimulating, but a plunge into the cold Pacific was by far the best! Anne thought that there might be only one thing better – a plunge into the Arctic Ocean! A year ago, she had thought sex might be better, having had nothing to go on but the testimony of two of her more experienced girlfriends. But that was a year ago, and since then she had had experiences with three different men. None of them made her feel as good as old King Neptune did every morning. And so she gave herself completely to the good old King, letting him work his magic on every part of her body, from her face and the back of her neck, across her shoulders and over her breasts, stimulating her nipples like nothing else could, continuing down her abdomen and hips, and then between her legs, letting his cold, cold fingers inside her to work their wonders. She purred with pleasure.

She had backstroked quite a distance from the jetty, as was her custom, and her car had nearly vanished in the fog. But no matter, she could find her way back blindfolded. She lifted one leg high out of the water, letting the cold air make it even colder, and then did likewise with the other leg. She executed a perfect surface dive, lifting both of her legs out of the water, all the time imagining herself to be Esther Williams, movie queen of the water ballet. Her head broke the surface and again she sighed with pleasure. She floated on her back, completely motionless, allowing the calm sea to rock her gently.

Suddenly the ocean wasn't calm any more – she felt currents below her and turbulence around her – the water around her began churning and air-bubbles erupted all over. Anne Barton was too frightened to scream – countless thoughts flashed through her mind as she tried to make sense of the situation: a freak storm? A whirlpool of some sort? A shark attack? Oh, God, not a shark attack! She imagined drowning, she even imagined herself dead as the water became increasingly violent. But what she didn't imagine, what she couldn't have imagined, in fact, what no one in their right mind could have imagined, is what happened: a black steel shaft broke the surface and rose up out of the Pacific, right between her legs. Anne Barton didn't know what it was, nor did she have much time to think about it, because in moments she felt herself rising out of the ocean along with the black shaft. Without thinking, she grabbed the shaft to gain her balance – now, the water was even more turbulent. And then, Anne Barton was completely lifted out of the Pacific Ocean by the periscope and conning tower of an Imperial Japanese submarine!

She gripped the periscope tightly for dear life – shivering not from cold but from fright. After several moments the turbulence and upward movement stopped: the submarine had completely surfaced. Anne Barton looked down, eyes wide with terror. She couldn't let go now – it would mean a fall of some twenty feet to the hard surface of the deck below. And so she remained there, with baited breath, wondering what would happen next. She didn't have long to wait. In moments she heard the sound of grating metal: the hatch was unscrewing! Anne Barton was certain that whoever was about to come out would spot her ... and then what? Would she be captured? Interrogated? Tortured? Murdered? She closed her eyes tightly, then opened them again as she heard the creaking of metal which was the sound of the hatch being thrown open. Below she could see a man in a blue uniform climbing on to the deck. She did not know that this was the uniform of the Imperial Japanese Navy, nor that the man was the Commander of the submarine. All she knew was that he was Japanese, and that he hadn't spotted her yet. She prayed to God that she would get out of this alive!

Commander Akiro Mitamura of the Imperial Japanese Navy and Captain of Submarine I-19 had a serious problem: he was lost. As he climbed out on to the deck of his vessel and found everything shrouded in fog, he realized that his problem was not about to be solved by the sighting of land formations or by calculations based on the position of the sun. However, he did not let this realization affect his dignified, military manner – it was simply another setback, perhaps one of too many setbacks, but nevertheless, a problem to be dealt with in a calm, logical fashion.

The war had not been going well for Mitamura or the crew of his submarine. They had repeatedly missed out participating in any of the recent glorious victories of the Emperor's forces in the Philippines, Guam or at Pearl Harbor. In fact, Submarine I-19 had not tasted battle once since it left Japan many weeks ago. Furthermore, there were serious problems with much of the navigational equipment on board. Mitamura knew that despite these problems, he could not return to Japan until he had accomplished something of value for his country. To do otherwise would not only dishonour himself but dishonour every member of his crew . . . and death would be preferable to dishonour.

Therefore, Commander Mitamura had made up his mind that he and his men would be the first members of the combined Imperial Forces to attack the coast of the United States of America. For the past two days, he had been maintaining an eastward course. And now, he was certain that they were somewhere within American territorial waters. But where exactly, he did not know.

Commander Mitamura had one other problem on board his submarine: Naval Lieutenant Wolfgang von Kleinschmidt of the Third Reich. Lieutenant von Kleinschmidt was on board as an observer for the German Navy, as part of an experimental programme designed to improve relations and promote understanding between the Axis nations. As far as Mitamura was concerned, the programme was a failure. It was beyond him how Germany could be so successful in its conquest of Europe with officers like Lieutenant von Kleinschmidt at the helm. If only von Kleinschmidt would cease his constant dissertations on the superiority of the Master Race. . .'. Mitamura wished that some day the Emperor would declare war on Germany so that he could show these Nazis just what he thought of their 'Master Race'.

Lieutenant von Kleinschmidt squeezed through the hatch and followed Commander Mitamura on deck. Von Kleinschmidt was tall: six foot five inches tall to be exact, more than a head taller than the tallest Japanese seaman on board. His manner was cold and aloof, and his greying hair gave him an aristocratic appearance. He cursed in German as he had been wont to do of late, damning his luck to have been put aboard a vessel full of heathens and commanded by a fool. The curse did not escape the ears of Commander Mitamura, nor had von Kleinschmidt intended it to. Mitamura was fluent in German, just as von Kleinschmidt was fluent in Japanese, but it was seldom that either man spoke the other's tongue in conversation. It was a point of honour to both of them.

Following von Kleinschmidt was the Captain's Mate, Ashimoto, a stocky, serious man, and Ito, the young Navigator, who was quite the opposite. Ito was constantly playing jokes on other members of the crew, many of which back-fired on him and had got him into trouble several times. The Nazi and the two Japanese officers followed their Commander on to the bridge. Mitamura raised his binoculars, but they only served to magnify the dense fog rather than cut through it. He barked at his Navigator in Japanese,

'Ito! What is our position?'

Ito hastily opened his map of the California coast and indicated a point not far from Cambria, California.

'I estimate we are about here, Captain.'

Mitamura nodded, his face betraying no emotion. Von Kleinschmidt took a look for himself and reacted with horror.

'Captain, we must turn back at once!'

He protested in German, 'We are far too deep in American territorial waters!'

Mitamura eyed von Kleinschmidt as any brave man would eye a coward. 'Lieutenant,' he said in Japanese, 'your position on board as an observer gives you absolutely no prerogative to question my orders. It is my intention to destroy something on the American mainland – something honourable. For this reason, we shall proceed towards Los Angeles.'

Von Kleinschmidt smirked. 'Ha! What do you expect

to destroy in Los Angeles? American naval vessels in Los Angeles Harbor?'

Now it was Mitamura's turn to smirk. 'There are no American naval vessels in Los Angeles Harbor. Our Imperial Forces have already destroyed the American Navy, six days ago at Pearl Harbor.'

Ashimoto's expression turned to sudden concern as a horrible thought occurred to him. He spoke quietly to Mitamura. 'Captain, do they have anything honourable to destroy in Los Angeles?'

Mitamura had not even considered this. He had assumed that in a city the size of Los Angeles there must certainly be something worth destroying. But as he thought about it, he was no longer sure. The assuredness on his face turned to doubt. And Ito's expression also became grave as he desperately tried to come up with an answer.

Suddenly Ito jumped up. 'Hollywood!' he cried with joy. 'We can destroy Hollywood!'

Mitamura and Ashimoto looked at Ito, then at each other, hope and purpose lighting both of their faces. Mitamura smiled laconically and nodded his approval of Ito's idea. Hollywood, he thought. Why not?

But von Kleinschmidt shook his head and scowled. 'Hollywood is inland,' he said smugly.

Mitamura's patience was wearing thin. He slowly turned to face the Nazi and stared straight into the German's eyes for several long moments, never blinking. 'Ito,' he said, never taking his eyes off von Kleinschmidt, 'set a course for Hollywood.'

'Yes, sir,' replied the Navigator with a smile.

'You are a fool, Captain,' said Lieutenant von Kleinschmidt. 'Even if we forget the fact that Hollywood is inland, far beyond the range of your torpedoes or your deck cannon, even if you could attack Hollywood, what

19

purpose would it serve? Hollywood has absolutely no military value.'

'Lieutenant,' answered Mitamura, 'the tactics of war comprise more than simply destroying an enemy's ships. We must also destroy his will to fight, by striking fear into his soul. True, a blow struck at Hollywood would serve no military purpose. However, it would greatly demoralize the American spirit.'

'Those are intangible concepts, Captain. War means seizure of territory and the subjugation of conquered peoples. That is what our Reich has been doing in Europe. You speak of psychological victories. What sort of psychological victory would it be for us to die in American waters?'

'We shall not die, Lieutenant. We shall attack the United States and return to Japan with honour.'

Von Kleinschmidt grunted with disgust. 'This crew will never find Hollywood,' he muttered. 'They will probably never find their way back to Japan, either.'

'We shall see, Lieutenant. We shall see.' Mitamura turned to his crewmen. 'Prepare to dive.'

Ashimoto repeated the order into the intercom, then he and Ito hurried off the bridge towards the open hatch on deck. Von Kleinschmidt remained standing on the bridge. 'After you, Captain,' he said in his best Japanese.

Mitamura smiled. 'After *you*, Lieutenant,' he replied in his impeccable German.

Von Kleinschmidt returned the smile. 'No, Captain, I insist. After you.'

'I insist, Lieutenant. After you.'

The two of them stared at each other for a long moment, their smiles masking their total contempt of one another. Finally, von Kleinschmidt's smile turned into a scowl and he stepped down from the bridge, muttering another German curse. Mitamura's expression turned to triumph and he followed. Both officers proceeded through the main hatch into the submarine, leaving Ito on deck to batten the hatch. Already the I-Boat was beginning to submerge. Ito dropped through the hatch, went partway down the ladder and then reached up to close the hatch. Suddenly, Ito froze, his face turning white in shocked amazement. He found himself looking up at a beautiful nude woman perched on the ship's periscope, the twin cheeks of her buttocks quivering. Ito let out a scream – 'A I E E E E E !'

Anne Barton looked down and saw the face of the Japanese Navigator looking right at her – she screamed too!

Ito continued to stare, his eyes brightening. His expression turned to joy as he realized that the vision before him must be an omen. One word formed on his lips, an English word. 'Holly-wood!' He said it again. 'Holly-wood!' He raised his arms and began chanting it, over and over again. 'Holly-wood! Holly-wood!'

The submarine continued to submerge. Water began pouring over the main deck, and then into the main hatch. Ito was completely oblivious to it, even though the water was freezing and it was pouring all over him. Below, Captain Mitamura was attempting to retract the periscope, but he was unable to turn it. He couldn't understand it – it felt as if there was something on the other end preventing it from moving. Then he felt cold water splashing around his ankles.

'Ito!' he yelled.

The Captain and several other crew members ran to the main hatch through which gallons and gallons of the Pacific were pouring. Ashimoto and another crewman grabbed Ito's legs and began pulling on them. Ito wasn't even aware of this – he just kept staring up at the vision before him, completely transfixed. The Japanese crewmen gave another mighty tug and Ito came plummeting through the hatch, soaking wet! The force of the rushing water slammed the hatch shut, and Ashimoto scrambled up the ladder to seal it tight.

Two seamen picked Ito up off the floor and attempted to shake him to his senses. Captain Mitamura stepped forward, dumbfounded by Ito's conduct and especially nonplussed at the strange smile and idiotic expression on his face. 'Ito!' he yelled. 'What's the matter with you?'

'Holly-wood!' Ito replied. 'Holly-wood!' He was still grinning.

Mitamura slapped him several times across the face.

'Holly-wood!' said Ito.

As soon as the periscope touched water, Anne Barton was swimming for shore. Had there been someone timing her, she would have officially set a new world record for speed. But Anne Barton wasn't thinking about world records, or speed or anything else besides getting to her car and getting to a telephone.

A minute and a half later she was at a 'phone – a public telephone by an abandoned bait shop at the other end of the pier. Somehow she managed to get a nickel into the slot and dialled the operator.

'Operator. May I help you?' came the voice.

'JAPS!' screamed Anne 'J A A A P P P P P S S S S S !'

Anne Barton had been a member of the Polar Bear Club for two years, and most of her friends thought she was out of her mind. Now they were sure.

And somewhere in the Pacific, Japanese Submarine I-19 headed south for Los Angeles.

2

To call Malcomb's Cafe of Los Angeles, California a 'greasy spoon' diner would be an understatement – it was far more than a greasy spoon. It was a greasy fork, a greasy knife, greasy cooking utensils, greasy plates, greasy tables, a greasy kitchen and a greasy floor. It was owned and operated by a greasy old man, and if you asked him, he'd tell you he had an eighteen year-old 'greaser' washing dishes for him and waiting on tables. Whether Wally Stephans was literally a 'greaser' in the true sense of the ethnic slur – which is to say that he was of Mexican descent – couldn't really be said. Wally Stephans was an orphan, and he didn't know who his real parents were. He was certainly dark, and quite good-looking, but he could easily be of Italian background. Whatever his racial origin, Wally didn't worry about it; and it wouldn't have mattered anyway because Old Man Malcomb would have called him a greaser even if he had been of pure Swedish stock. Old Man Malcomb considered anyone who was constantly in trouble with the law a greaser, and Wally Stephans certainly fitted this definition. By the most usual term, however, Wally would be called a juvenile delinquent. He had been released from Reform School just two weeks ago, having spent two months there for attempted car theft and property destruction. But now Wally had decided to give up his life of crime. He had good reason to; he had met Betty Douglas.

Betty Douglas! The one name, the one face that was

constantly on Wally's mind. Wally had hung an eight by ten photograph of her above the sink so that he could look at her while he was scrubbing plates, as he was doing now. He read her signed inscription for the zillion-and-third time: 'Wally, I'll be waiting for you when you get out. Love Betty.' She had sent him the picture while he'd been in the reformatory, and it was her words that had kept him on good behaviour for those months. And now tonight, at long last, he would be going out with her.

They had made the date several weeks ago when she had come to see him one visiting day. Betty had told him how much she enjoyed dancing and Wally had said that he enjoyed it too, even though he had never danced before in his life. And the next thing he knew, they had made a date to go to the annual Christmas Dance at the Crystal Ballroom this very night. Five weeks later, when he was released from the reformatory, Wally realized he had a problem. Not only could he not dance, but he didn't have a decent suit to wear or a dime in his pocket. So he got a job slinging hash at Malcomb's Cafe, and started taking dancing lessons. Of course, he couldn't afford to take lessons at a dancing school, so instead he would sneak behind the screen of a nearby movie house and dance along with Fred Astaire. Whenever he got thrown out, he would go to any of a number of dance spots in Hollywood and watch the jitterbuggers tear up the floor doing the 'Lindy Hop'. Now Wally felt that he could go to a dance and not feel embarrassed . . . at least not by his dancing. His clothes were another matter, but Wally had this bet covered too – he had the suit already picked out, and sixty dollars in back pay coming to him today. As soon as he got off work, he would be off to the department store. Yes, Wally figured he had it made. He couldn't wait to see Betty tonight . . . or for Betty to see him.

'Wally, I still can't believe you fell for the dame who sent us up the river.'

Wally turned upon hearing the voice to see the grinning face of his best friend, Dennis DeSoto, who had just entered the kitchen through the back door. Wally had met Dennis years ago in Elementary School, and they had continued through schools together: Junior High School, High School and Reform School. Like Wally, Dennis was eighteen; unlike Wally, Dennis had blond hair and blue eyes.

'She didn't send us up the river, Dennis,' replied Wally. 'You did!'

It was a subject Wally and Dennis argued about constantly: who had really been responsible for their stay in the reformatory? They both knew that the fault was equally theirs, but they still enjoyed blaming each other for blowing up Mr Douglas's car. They had sneaked into the Douglas garage late one night, with the idea of 'hot-wiring' the car and going out for a joy-ride. Wally, however, had forgotten to bring a torch, so Dennis had to light matches in order that Wally could see what he was doing under the bonnet. Unfortunately, there had been a leak in the car's fuel pump and Dennis accidentally dropped a match in the vicinity. And that was how Wally met Betty: the explosion awakened the entire Douglas family and brought them all out to the garage.

Wally stared dreamily off into space, replaying that night over again in his mind, especially that moment when he first saw Betty. He thought about how romantic it was to have fallen in love by firelight, even if the fire was from a burning automobile.

Suddenly, his reverie was interrupted by the voice of Old Man 'Pops' Malcomb, who was out working at the counter. 'Have you got them pots clean yet, like I told you?'

Wally had completely forgotten about the pots. 'Almost, Pops!' he lied. Wally looked over at Dennis who was helping himself to some bacon off the grill.

'Hey, did you come here to help me or to screw around?'

'Sure I'm gonna help you, Wally. You asked me to help you, didn't you? And I'm your best friend, ain't I? But you don't want me to starve to death, do you?'

'Come on, Dennis, you gotta gimme a hand with these dishes!'

Dennis looked with disgust at the mountain of filthy plates piled around the counters, and then gazed into the sink full of dirty dishwater.

'You want me to put my hands in that? I'd rather stick 'em in the toilet at the ball park! I'll tell you what: you wash 'em. I'll throw 'em to you!'

'I'll tell *you* what,' replied Wally. 'Go out there and put a nickel in number sixteen.'

'Sure, Wally,' agreed Dennis, who proceeded to stand there and simply watch as Wally scrubbed dishes.

It was almost a full minute before Wally noticed that Dennis hadn't moved an inch. 'Well? What are you waiting for?' he asked.

'You gotta gimme the nickel.'

'You cheap bastard!'

'Hey – what do you want for free?'

Wally shook his head, knowing not to expect anything else from Dennis. All they ever did was argue with each other, just for the hell of it, of course. Wally tossed Dennis a nickel. 'Don't spend it on the way!'

Dennis hurried out into the lunch-room where the Rock-Ola 'Monarch', 1938 model, stood shining in the corner. The jukebox was the newest thing in the cafe, and the only item in the whole place which could not be described as 'greasy'. Dennis dropped the nickel in, pushed number sixteen, and watched the Smythe mechanism swing the 78 r.p.m. disc on to the spinning turntable and the tone arm drop on to it. The horns of the Glenn Miller Orchestra blared out the swinging strains of the band's biggest hit, 'In the Mood'.

Old Man Malcomb looked up from the counter in time to see Dennis scurrying back into the kitchen with a load of dirty dishes. The old man scowled, pushing back his American Legion cap with one hand and scratching his pot belly under his soiled T-shirt with the other. 'God-damn greasers,' he muttered to himself.

Wally started washing the dishes in time to the music, and dancing as well. 'Why not practise?' he figured. He flipped a plate into the air, spun around, and caught it back-hand, then wiped it dry and tossed it on to the shelf, never missing a beat. As he whirled around, he saw Dennis enter with the new load of dishes. Wally gave him a nod, and Dennis started tossing them to him, always keeping time with the tune. Wally scraped the remains of food into the rubbish bin and dropped the plates into the dishwater.

'Fill that order while you're at it,' said Wally, tossing Dennis a clean coffee-cup. Dennis filled it with hot java, then caught another cup and filled it too.

'Two eggs, sunnyside up,' called Wally, and Dennis cracked the eggs on to the grill, getting more shell in them than not. Wally tossed him a clean plate.

'It's still dirty,' said Dennis, throwing it back to him. But Wally was executing a spin-out and wasn't there to catch it – the china crashed to the floor and shattered to pieces.

'You'd better get your mind off that dame and back on the job, Wally, or we'll never get outta here.'

'Just keep slingin' the hash, Dennis. Nothin's gonna keep me from being at that dance tonight!'

Dennis had heard all this before, but he was still sceptical. 'The hell you say! They probably won't even let you
in. That Crystal Ballroom's a class joint.'

Wally grinned at his pal. 'Hey, I'm a class guy! It's
like I been saying, I got the prettiest girl in the world, I
been teachin' myself how to dance, and that sixty smackers I got coming to me is gonna buy me the sharpest set
of drapes this side of Alvarado Street.'

'Sixty smackers?' said Old Man Malcomb. 'You're
gonna get a smack in the kisser if you don't quit farting
around back here.' The Old Man had just entered, pissed
off as usual. He glared at Dennis. 'I thought I told you
to stay away from here.' Then he saw the broken plate on
the floor and the sorry state of affairs around the rubbish
bin. He looked at Wally. 'Look at this mess!' The old man
pulled a completely intact fried egg out of the bin. 'Look
at this egg! There's nothin' wrong with this egg! You're
throwing away perfectly good food!' He threw it on the
grill. 'You can reheat that and serve it to them boys out
there. What kinda place you think this is?'

'It ain't the Brown Derby!' cracked Dennis.

The old man snarled at him. 'What are you? A smart-
ass? I suppose you jailbirds had it better in Reform
School!' He turned on Wally now. 'And you, you damned
hoodlum, all the time prancin' around back here like a
trained jackass!'

'Hey, come on, Pops —'

'Don't call me "Pops"! I ain't your Pops!'

'Pops, I was just practising for the dance tonight.'

'You can't dance. I seen you dance – you can't dance
worth spit!' The old man spat a huge piece of phlegm
on to the grill. It sizzled into steam.

Now Dennis interceded. 'Pops, take it easy on him.
He's in love!'

The old man scowled again. 'Love? Love my ass!' He

took the picture of Betty off the nail above the sink and looked at it. Was Wally imagining it, or was there a hint of approval on the old man's face? The old man studied the photograph, looked at Wally, then back at the photo, as if imagining the two of them together. He shook his head. 'When are you gonna remember which side of the tracks you came from, boy?'

Wally stared at the old codger for a moment, then grabbed the picture away from him. Before he could tell Malcomb what he thought of him, a voice hollered out from the lunch room.

'Hey! How about some more coffee out here?'

Wally grabbed the coffee-pot and hollered back. 'Comin' right up!' Wally gave his employer another look and then, with total defiance, danced his way out of the kitchen, keeping in perfect step with the music. Old Man Malcomb was not pleased.

The customer who had hollered for more coffee was Chuck 'Stretch' Sitarski, and he was a Corporal in the United States Army. Sitarski was twenty-five years old, well built, and quite handsome. He was also a trouble-maker with a psychotic temper, who hated the Army with a passion. Whenever there was work to be done, Sitarski could always figure a way to get out of it. He was a brilliant bullshit-artist, and it had been through the use of this talent that Sitarski had attained the rank of Corporal.

Sitarski was seated at a table with the four other members of his tank crew, who were all picking over the remains of a rather miserable breakfast. For the past few days, they had been delivering anti-aircraft guns around town, assisting in the massive effort to prepare Los Angeles for a defence against a possible Japanese air raid. It was a job which Sitarski hated, but then, he hated just about every job in the Army.

Sergeant Frank Tree, Tank Commander and leader of the group was, as usual, talking about the war and military history. 'Talking' was actually not the right word – Tree was running off at the mouth. He had a proclivity for making speeches, and the war was his favourite subject. Also, as usual, his men were completely ignoring him.

Frank Tree had been in excellent spirits ever since the United States had declared war on Japan. All his life, Tree had wanted to participate in a war and fight for America. At the age of five, Tree had decided to make the Army his career. At the age of seven, he could recite the United States Constitution from memory. By twelve, he had memorized all specifications and statistics on every weapon currently in use by the United States military forces. At sixteen, with a picture of George Washington taped to his heart, he ran away from his home in Vandalia, Illinois to enlist. He lied about his age – the only lie he had ever told in his life – and got in. Now, at the age of twenty-five, he was the commander of his own tank, nicknamed 'Lulubelle', after his mother, Lulubelle Mary Tree. And Frank Tree couldn't wait to ride 'Lulubelle' into combat.

Wally Stephans danced over to the five soldiers, coffeepot in hand, still keeping time with 'In the Mood'. 'Stretch' Sitarski gave Wally a look that could kill flowers, taking special notice of Wally's loud Hawaiian shirt which carried the words, 'Souvenir of Pearl Harbor, Hawaii', on the back.

'What's eatin, you, kid?' asked Sitarski with disgust. 'You got ants in your pants?'

Privates Reese, Foley and Quince, the other soldiers at the table laughed at Sitarski's joke. They always laughed at Sitarski's jokes – it kept them on the good side of Sitarski's frequent fits of insane rage.

Wally shrugged off Sitarski's remark with good humour. 'Hey, I'm just practising some dance steps.'

'Oh, yeah?' retorted the soldier. 'Dance steps, huh? You got something to be dancing about, bud?'

'Maybe I have,' said Wally, coolly, picking up some of the dirty dishes off the table.

Sitarski decided he didn't like Wally at all. 'Yeah, well, there's a war on, pal, and I want to know why you're not in uniform. I want to know what you're doing dancing around tables. Why aren't you in the Army?'

Wally looked at him with the slightest hint of a smile. 'Because I don't take orders from nobody, that's why.'

Sitarski wasn't about to let any punk kid talk to him like that. 'So you're a tough guy, huh?' Sitarski stuck his foot out and kicked Wally's leg out from under him. Wally went down, dropping the coffee-pot and breaking all of the dishes he had picked up. He fell headlong into another table, landing on its edge, thus catapulting the remains of food on it back at the soldiers. Pieces of egg, bacon, toast, and a half-full bowl of oatmeal went flying, all narrowly missing the Army men. But the bowl of oatmeal flipped over in mid-air and spilled all over Wally!

Sitarski burst out laughing; Quince, Reese and Foley followed suit. Sergeant Tree just shook his head. Then Sitarski noticed that a tiny speck of egg had splattered on the sleeve of his uniform. His laughter abruptly turned to wild-eyed rage.

'Why, you little son-of-a-bitch,' he screamed at Wally. 'You got egg on my uniform! I hate eggs! I can't stand eggs!'

Sitarski had become a psychopathic maniac. He jumped to his feet and grabbed Wally by the shirt. Wally, however, wasn't about to let Sitarski bust his jaw – he put up his fists, ready to defend himself. But before any punches could be thrown, Sergeant Tree had leaped to his feet and separated the two. This was the one kind of behaviour that Tree could not tolerate.

'Can it, Sitarski!' he yelled. 'Save it for the Japs!'

'For cryin' out loud, Sarge, look at this stooge!' Sitarski pointed at Wally. 'Anybody who wears a shirt like that is asking for it!'

'He's an American, Sitarski,' replied the Sergeant, 'and if there's one thing I can't stand, it's seeing Americans fighting Americans. I won't stand for that, not here, not anywhere, and especially not while we're at war.' Tree took a breath and looked at his men. 'All right, you foul-ups, you've had your chow, now move out!'

The three Privates headed for the door. Tree picked up the bill. Sitarski looked at him, then again pointed at Wally. 'You're not gonna tip him, are you, Sarge?'

Tree gave the Corporal a stern look. Sitarski knew what that meant, and he headed for the exit.

Wally wiped the oatmeal off his shirt and faced Tree. 'That's all right. I don't need your tip.'

'I think you do,' said Tree, too politely. 'Get rid of that shirt. It's in bad taste.' He threw a two-dollar note on the table and walked out.

Wally sighed, then turned around to clean up the mess. He found himself facing Old Man Malcombe who was totally irate.

'You're fired!' he screamed.

'But Pops,' Wally protested, 'it wasn't my fault! I was tripped!'

'You're bad for business. Now scram!' The old man shoved Wally towards the door.

'Pops – wait a minute – look – I'll pay for the busted dishes.'

'Damn right, you will!' shouted the old man as he shoved Wally again. 'I owe you sixty dollars, and I figure them busted dishes is worth seventy-five. You owe me fifteen!'

'You can't do this to me, Pops – I'll do anything! I'll work Sunday – I'll work for free – anything – as long as I get that sixty bucks! I've gotta have that new suit!'

Malcomb grabbed Wally by the ear and literally dragged him to the door. 'The only way you're gonna get a new suit is to steal one! Now you get outta here and don't ever come back!' Malcomb threw open the door and gave Wally a good swift kick in the arse. He went sailing across the pavement and into the gutter. As he climbed to his feet, he saw a truck with a 40 mm Bofors anti-aircraft gun hitched to it pulling away from the kerb. Corporal 'Stretch' Sitarski was riding on the rear of the gun, taking a swig from a bottle of beer. Again Sitarski's eyes met Wally's.

'Hey, tough guy!' shouted the soldier with derision. He threw the bottle at Wally – Wally ducked, and the bottle shattered against the wall behind him. Sitarski laughed as he rode off down the street.

Now Dennis came running out of the cafe. He watched as the Army truck disappeared around a corner; then he looked at Wally and shrugged. 'Well, easy come, easy go.'

Wally looked at a bill posted on the wall advertising the big jitterbug contest which would take place at the Crystal Ballroom that night. Meyer Mishkin, a talent scout from the RKO Movie Studios would be the judge, and first prize was a movie contract. Wally turned to Dennis. 'You think this is gonna stop me?' Wally shook his head, answering his own question. He seemed quite sure of himself. 'Nothing's gonna stop me from dancing with Betty tonight!'

3

Betty Douglas was seventeen years old. She was a sweet, lovely girl with perfect blonde hair, soft eyes, and a ripe figure, and she was very clean. She was the type of girl that any young man's mother would be proud to have as a daughter-in-law. She was, of course, a virgin – the idea of 'going all the way' before marriage had never even crossed her mind. That's how clean she was. That she could be attracted to somebody like Wally Stephans came as a surprise to her, to say nothing of her family. On the surface, it seemed that Wally was exactly the wrong kind of boy for her. After all, he was a juvenile delinquent. But below the surface, there was something inside him that was incredibly attractive, something that stirred certain feelings within her which she couldn't put into words. And she knew there was a core of decency in him. Wally fascinated her, and she had been looking forward to their date for a long time. She had had to keep their date a secret from her family, especially her father, who didn't approve of Wally at all. This was understandable since Wally had blown up the family car. But the car had been replaced, and Betty was willing to forgive and forget, even if her father wasn't.

But now, Betty Douglas was worried. From the way things were shaping up, it appeared she would have to break her date with Wally tonight. However, she had to make sure, and so she hesitantly raised her hand, waiting to be recognized by the woman at the front of the room.

Betty Douglas was among some three hundred girls, aged sixteen to twenty-two, who were seated attentively on folding chairs in the main ballroom of what used to be the Crystal Ballroom Dance Hall of Hollywood. The Crystal Ballroom had just been taken over by the United Service Organizations, or USO, and was being converted into a recreational facility for servicemen. All of the girls here had volunteered to become USO Hostesses, and were here this morning for the 'get acquainted' session, in which they were instructed on the duties and responsibilities of USO Hostesses. Betty had had no qualms about signing up. Like all the students in her high school, she had been shocked by the Japanese attack on Pearl Harbor. Her patriotism had been stirred, and she was ready to do anything she could to help in the war effort. When her best friend, Maxine Dexheimer, had told her about the USO, Betty decided it was her duty to volunteer. Betty's father had been delighted that she was so eager to do something for her country, and had readily signed the permission slip.

Maxine Dexheimer's reasons for becoming a USO Hostess were slightly different from Betty's. Maxine was short and chubby, and her social life left much to be desired. When she had heard that the basic responsibility of a USO Hostess was to entertain men in uniform, she became very interested in the programme. When she had heard that the likely ratio of men to women would be five to one, she immediately went into heat! Of course, she had given her parents all of the standard patriotic reasons why it was vitally important she should become a USO Hostess – for God and country, and to keep the world safe for democracy. She had finally convinced them to sign the permission paper. All the while, Maxine was dreaming about handsome soldiers, dashing sailors, and debonair marines. And tonight she would dance with all of them.

The woman at the front of the room was Miss Fitzroy of the USO. Miss Fitzroy was a middle-aged, stern woman, and in her full dress USO uniform, she seemed to be the embodiment of the same qualities that made up the huge poster of Uncle Sam that hung behind her. She could have been Uncle Sam's wife.

Miss Fitzroy had been lecturing the girls for the past twenty minutes, and had now opened the floor to questions. She spotted the nervously waving hand of Betty Douglas and her eagle eye read the name from the USO name-tag Betty had been issued. 'Yes, Miss Douglas?'

Betty swallowed hard. She felt like a fool, being the only one here to raise her hand. She could barely get the words out. 'Do you mean . . . I mean, did you just say . . . uh, I mean, I don't know if I understand . . .'

'Speak up, girl! Out with it!' snapped Miss Fitzroy.

Betty blurted it out. 'Are you saying that we won't be allowed to dance with civilians tonight?'

'That is correct, Miss Douglas,' replied Miss Fitzroy. 'You will *not* be allowed to dance with civilians. In fact, civilians will no longer be admitted to this facility. A week ago, this was the Crystal Ballroom. Today it is the USO Crystal Ballroom for servicemen only!

'Remember those words, girls: for servicemen only. Because as a USO Hostess, each and everyone of you is now for servicemen only. Forget about civilians. Forget about your civilian boyfriends – if you want to dance with them, get them to join the Army or the Navy or the Marine Corps. Servicemen, girls – that's why we're here!'

Miss Fitzroy emphasized the remark with her pointer, then began to pace deliberately back and forth across the stage.

'Remember, what we are doing goes far beyond any foolish adolescent infatuation with the opposite sex. These servicemen are involved in the serious business of

36

defending our country. And it is our duty, our patriotic duty, to keep their morale at the highest possible level. Therefore, I don't want to hear any talk about precious morality. That is a luxury you do not have in wartime. *Morale* – that's what's important! If you think you're saving yourself for 'Mister Right', just remember that he may never come along, and all those boys you turned a cold shoulder to may end up on the end of a bayonet.

'I'm not saying it's going to be easy. You will have to smile at men to whom you'd never give a second glance in peacetime. You will have to make polite conversation with men whose minds are in the gutter. You will even have to dance with men who are repulsive to you.'

As if to give credence to Miss Fitzroy's words, Betty noticed that a wall of faces was pressed against the large plate-glass window at one side of the ballroom. Every face was male, and every male was in uniform. And most of them were behaving like savages and lower primitives. Betty could faintly hear their grunting and catcalling through the window, and could clearly see their sandpaper complexions and horrible tongues hanging from their open mouths, dripping saliva. Obviously, they had come to 'check out the merchandise'. Betty gulped.

Miss Fitzroy continued. 'But a month from now, when that young man is crawling across some blood-drenched battlefield in a place with a name you can't pronounce, the one thing that may keep him going when life is at its darkest hour, the one thing he may be thinking about is the time he spent with you . . . here . . . at the Hollywood USO Club.'

Miss Fitzroy paused, gazing out over the faces of her girls. All of them were deadly silent, serious, attentive. After the appropriate dramatic pause, Miss Fitzroy quietly resumed. 'I trust you will make it a pleasant memory for him. Dismissed.'

There was a thunder of folding chairs as three-hundred-odd girls all stood up at the same time. Betty turned to Maxine and indicated the window with the faces pressed against it.

'I don't know if I'm going to like dancing with those guys.'

Maxine gave her a look. 'Maybe you'd rather dance with a Jap?'

'I'd rather dance with Wally.'

'Betty, you heard what she said. They won't even let Wally in here. So forget about him. Anyway, guys in uniform are much cuter. We're gonna have a great time tonight! That's what you should be thinking about.'

But Betty couldn't think about that. All she could think about was Wally. 'Maxine, do you think anybody would mind if I didn't come tonight?'

Maxine couldn't believe what she was hearing. 'Are you nuts? That would be desertion. You'd be a traitor. And believe me, nobody would ever want to associate with a traitor. They'd probably kick you out of school. And your father would kick you out of the house. You can't back out now, Betty. This is war!'

Betty sighed. She knew Maxine was right. She remembered what Miss Fitzroy had said earlier: 'The world is changing, girls, and we have to change with it. It's wartime, and we all have to make sacrifices.' So Betty would just have to break her date with Wally. Maybe he would understand. Then again, maybe he wouldn't. Betty shook her head, wondering why the Japs couldn't have waited one more week to bomb Pearl Harbor.

4

Death Valley, California
High Noon

Business was slow this morning at Eloise McCracken's Death Valley Gas Station and Diner. That was usual. Business had been slow yesterday morning, and the morning before that and the morning before that. Business had also been slow yesterday afternoon. Business was slow all the time here. That was just the way it was. Somebody had once told Eloise McCracken that the reason her business was so slow was because no one would want to stop at a place with the word 'death' in its name. That person was an idiot. The real reason that business was slow was because Eloise McCracken's Death Valley Gas Station and Diner was in the desert, out in the middle of nowhere. And business is bound to be slow when there's no one around. The old state highway carried little traffic, and most of that drove past without even slowing down. But Eloise McCracken didn't care. She was sixty-one years old, and had spent thirty of those years right here, sitting outside in an old rocking-chair in the shadow of her building, always ready to pump gas. As far as Eloise was concerned, things were just fine the way they were.

Her brother Dexter minded the kitchen and general store inside, and spent most of the day chewing the fat with three or four of the locals who came by every day because they had nothing else to do. Eloise never could figure out what it was they talked about. Nothing ever happened here, so there was never anything to talk about.

But all of that was about to change. . . .

Eloise McCracken was rocking back and forth in her chair as she always did. Her dog, who answered to the name of George, was sleeping on the ground beside her as he always did. Several chickens were wandering around, pecking at sand and pebbles like they always did. And the usual assortment of lizards were crawling around like they always did.

Then something happened. The lizards stopped crawling. The chickens stopped pecking. And George the dog stopped sleeping. He awakened with a start, suddenly aware of something, and raised an ear to listen. Eloise McCracken stopped rocking, turning a curious eye to George. The dog sensed something, something in the air.

Eloise looked around, trying to figure it out. Then she heard something. It was a faint buzzing sound, like a bee, and it was getting steadily louder. Eloise looked for the source. She knew there were no bees out here, in fact, no insects of any kind. The buzzing sound was getting still louder – louder than any insect. It was an aeroplane, of course! Eloise looked up at the sky and saw a black dot gettting bigger and bigger. Just an aeroplane, passing overhead, she thought. But no! the 'plane was dropping, coming towards the horizon ... in fact, it was coming towards the highway! The aeroplane was actually going to land! It was going to land on the highway!

Eloise stared in disbelief as the 'plane descended. At first she thought it was a crop duster, forgetting that there were no crops at all in a radius of seventy miles, let alone crops that needed dusting. Then she realized that she had never seen a 'plane of this type before. It had a single engine, and unless she was seeing things, she was positive there was some sort of mouth painted on the nose ... a mouth with sharp teeth.

The 'plane was coming down at a very steep angle of descent, maybe too steep! It was now only a few hundred yards away, and couldn't be more than thirty feet off the ground, now twenty. It barely cleared the electrical lines strung across the highway. Turbulence from the engine began blowing sand and dust everywhere, and George covered his eyes with his paws. Eloise spat dirt out of her mouth and squinted, raising an arm to her forehead to protect her face from the grit. She wasn't about to avert her eyes – if this 'plane was going to crack up, she sure as hell wasn't going to miss it! Eloise was certain the pilot wasn't going to make it; after all, no man in his right mind would try to land a plane at an angle like that, going at what must have been 85 m.p.h.

However, the pilot was not in his right mind. The 'plane was only eight feet above the surface of the highway, and it looked like the propeller was going to eat cement. Suddenly, at the last split second, the nose jerked up and the two front wheels slammed down on to the road; then the entire aircraft bounced up into the air again. The tyres hit the highway again, and again the 'plane bounced. It bounced for at least a hundred yards until there was no more bounce left.

Eloise could not believe her eyes. The 'plane was actually pulling up at the petrol pumps. She covered her ears – the engine noise was deafening – and watched as the aircraft stopped with the engine still running. Yes, indeed, there was a red mouth with sharp white teeth painted on the nose of this green aeroplane, like a shark's mouth. And there were machine-guns mounted in the wings. This was a warplane! It was a Curtis P-40 War-hawk to be exact, a one-man fighter 'plane. The wing-mounted machine-guns were fifty-calibre, and the markings on the wings and fuselage belonged to the United States Army Air Corps.

Captain Wild Bill Kelso, United States Army Air Corps, shoved the sliding glass canopy back and leaped out of the cockpit on to the wing, pulling out his Army-issue ·45 automatic pistol at the same time. He was ready – ready for anything! He glanced around quickly, trying to determine whether anything was ready for him. Nothing was. But of course, nothing was ever ready for Wild Bill Kelso!

'Wild Bill' was not a nickname. It was Captain Kelso's actual Christian name. Wild Bill had nearly killed his mother three times before he was born, by kicking in the womb. When he was born, it wasn't necessary for the delivery doctor to spank him to start him breathing and crying. Wild Bill Kelso had come into the world screaming at the top of his lungs! His mother took the ten pound five ounce bundle into her arms. (She couldn't call him a 'bundle of joy', because he certainly wasn't that.) She took one look at his face, then shook her head. 'I was going to name you Charles,' she told her screaming infant son. 'But I guess I'm going to have to name you Wild. That's what you are, so that's what I'm going to call you: Wild Bill Kelso. And I expect you to live up to that name.' It was one of the few things in his life which Wild Bill Kelso actually did as he was told to do. He lived up to his name. At the age of three, he shattered his mother's eardrums living up to his name. At seven, he drove her into the State Mental Institution living up to his name. At twelve he caused his father to blow his brains out living up to his name. Perhaps after all, his mother had given him some bad advice.

Captain Wild Bill Kelso was now twenty-eight years old, and one look at his face was enough to tell you that he was still living up to his name. With his wild eyes and crazed expression, he was about the most maniacal pilot in the history of the United States Army Air Corps. And in his leather flying jacket with his silk scarf and aviator cap, Kelso was the archetype of that classic American figure, the hotshot flier. In fact, not only was the pilot hot, but the aeroplane was 'hot' too: Wild Bill had stolen it two days ago!

Wild Bill surveyed the area again. He rubbed his two-day growth of stubble and blew a big puff of smoke out of his Dutch Masters. He spotted Eloise McCracken on her rocking-chair and jumped off the wing, grabbing his crotch as he approached her.

'You got a bathroom here?!?' he screamed at the top of his lungs.

Eloise was still too astonished to answer. George, however, was not. He immediately started barking at Kelso.

Kelso aimed his ·45 at the animal. 'Shut up, ya crazy mutt!' George took one look at the gun and shut up. Wild Bill looked back at Eloise. 'What's the matter with you, lady? Are you deaf? I gotta go to the bathroom!' Kelso rubbed his groin, trying to hold it in.

Eloise stood up slowly, then pointed in the direction of the rest-room. 'Around the back,' she said, her words barely audible over the P-40's engine.

Kelso ran towards the bathroom, then stopped suddenly and turned around. 'And put some gas in there,' he yelled, pointing at his 'plane. 'Ethyl!'

Eloise nodded, pulled the hose from the Ethyl pump and approached the aircraft. Then she realized she didn't know where the fuel tank was. She started to ask the pilot, but it was too late – he had already disappeared into the toilet. Well, never mind, she'd find it herself.

Wild Bill emptied his bladder, then came running out of the toilet. Eloise had found the fuel tank in the wing, shoved the hose in and locked it into the 'on' position. The level in the pump began to drop as Ethyl poured into the P-40.

Inside the Diner/General Store, Dexter McCracken and his three patrons watched through the windows with

43

incredulity. Suddenly the door burst open and Kelso rushed in, brandishing his pistol.

'Everyone stay where they are!' shouted the Captain. 'This is an Air Corps Alert!' The terrified patrons raised their hands and stood perfectly still. Wild Bill looked around the place, then grinned as he spotted a partially eaten ham-and-cheese sandwich on a plate in front of a ratty-looking man. He grabbed the sandwich, then looked at the men. 'Now you listen to me,' he said urgently. 'My name is Captain Wild Bill Kelso, United States Army Air Corps, and you remember it! I ain't had no food or water in two days, but I intend to be the first American to shoot one of those little monkeys down!' He waved the sandwich in the air. 'That's why I'm taking this. I'm taking this in the name of God and country and motherhood!' He shoved the entire sandwich into his mouth and swallowed it, whole. 'And apple pie, too!' he added as he spotted a wedge of it behind the counter. In a flash, he had crammed the huge slice down his gullet, leaving a good deal of it on the outside of his mouth as well. 'And I'm taking some of these as well,' he explained, as he helped himself to chocolate bars which he proceeded to eat, wrappers and all. Then Kelso grabbed the coffee-pot from the pot-bellied stove and poured scalding java down his throat. He looked at Dexter. 'You seen any Japs around here, pal?'

Dexter shook his head. 'What would Japs be doin' in these here parts?'

'Don't you know?' thundered Kelso. 'The sneaky little bastards tried to bomb San Francisco last night – two squadrons of 'em! I've been trackin' 'em ever since, but I lost 'em somewhere over Fresno. They could be anywhere by now!'

'Well, sir,' replied Dexter, 'I heard on the radio this morning that there weren't any 'planes over San Francisco last night. The whole thing was just jittery war nerves.'

Kelso couldn't believe it. He began breathing in short, quick snorts, like a bull preparing to charge. His fury was building and the fires of rage were burning in his eyes. 'You heard that on the radio?' he asked with as much restraint as he could muster.

'Yes, sir, on that radio right there,' explained Dexter, pointing to his thirteen-year-old RCA on the shelf behind the counter.

Kelso took one look at the radio, then levelled his automatic and blasted it to smithereens. 'I say your radio's wrong!' he shouted. 'I say there's Japs!'

A man with a face like a frog looked up from his plate of spaghetti and meatballs. 'Hell, mister, I don't even know what a Jap 'plane looks like!'

Kelso glared at the man for a moment, stunned at his colossal ignorance, shocked that this man could actually be an American. 'You don't know what a Jap 'plane looks like, huh?' Kelso grabbed the frog-faced man by his shirt and shook him. 'Well, I'll tell you what it looks like! It's got big red meatballs painted on the wings, just like the rising sun. I'll show ya!' Kelso took a forkful of spaghetti and meatballs and flung it at the window: sure enough, it splattered into a crude representation of the Japanese battle flag. 'That's what it looks like!'

Suddenly, Kelso did a double-take. Through the window, he saw his 'plane starting to move away from the fuel pump, all by itself, with no one in the cockpit. 'Holy shit, I gotta go!'

Wild Bill charged out of the Diner, knocking over Eloise who was running in to tell him what was happening. Kelso ran out just in time to see the hose jerked out of the fuel tank of his departing 'plane. The hose was still locked on, so Ethyl began spewing out all over the ground. The pilotless P-40 headed for the open highway, picking up speed. Wild Bill didn't know how or why this could be happening – perhaps the running engine had somehow jerked the 'plane into gear. Whatever, he didn't have time to think about it. He chased after his aeroplane, screaming like a maniac. 'Stop that 'plane! Stop that 'plane!' Wild Bill raised his pistol and fired a warning shot into the air, thinking it might slow the aircraft. It didn't. Instead, the shot severed an electrical line directly above, and the live wire dropped right into the huge pool of petrol that was getting bigger and bigger. The petrol immediately caught fire, and flames quickly engulfed the pumps. A tremendous explosion followed seconds later, and Eloise McCracken was out of the petrol business!

But Kelso was totally oblivious to the havoc and destruction he had left behind him. The only thing that mattered to him was his Warhawk, and now he was gaining on it. Faster he ran, faster and faster, closing the gap between himself and the wing of his craft from several yards to several feet, until finally he lunged and grabbed the wing. He pulled himself up, and jumped into the cockpit. Then he jerked forward on the joystick and the P-40 lifted up into the desert sky. Wild Bill Kelso laughed insanely. Once again, he had lived up to his name!

5

The Central California Coast

12.22 p.m.

Commander Akiro Mitamura stood at the periscope of his submarine and gazed through it. He was looking at a foggy, tree-lined coast, and he was not pleased. He angrily turned to his Navigator, who stood nearby along with the Mate and Lieutenant von Kleinschmidt.

'Ito!' barked Mitamura. 'This is not Los Angeles! You assured me we were facing Los Angeles Harbor!'

Ito was just as confused as the Captain. He consulted his navigational charts once again, then checked some of his own calculations against the compass. Everything seemed to be in order except ... Ito banged the compass several times with his hand. The compass started spinning around continuously, never stopping for a moment. 'Captain,' said Ito, 'it appears we are lost. The compass is still not functioning properly.'

Mitamura glanced at the compass himself, and grunted with disgust. 'All of the navigational equipment on this vessel is inoperable,' he complained. 'This is what happens when we use imported products instead of those made in Japan.' He turned to von Kleinschmidt to vent his frustration. 'Lieutenant, what kind of submarine did your government sell us?'

'The navigational instruments on this vessel are the finest Swiss-made,' replied the German smugly. 'The problem is with your crew. Even children in the Hitler Youth learn by the age of ten how to properly operate and maintain a device as simple as a compass. I would

47

suggest you return to your homeland, Captain, and leave the American continent to our superior Reich Navy.'

Mitamura had to summon every ounce of restraint within him to keep from striking the Nazi for such an insult. 'We shall not return to Japan until we have attacked the American mainland and destroyed something honourable,' said Mitamura with total resolve. He turned to Ito and Ashimoto. 'Ito! Ashimoto! Take a landing party ashore and determine our exact position.'

Ito and Ashimoto nodded and saluted. Mitamura gave the order to surface.

Von Kleinschmidt was flabbergasted by the ridiculousness of Mitamura's plan. 'You are insane, Captain,' the Lieutenant told him. 'Your men will be spotted!'

'These men are the descendants of Ninja Assassins,' said Mitamura with pride. 'They will not be seen.'

Mitamura was correct. Ito, Ashimoto and five other seamen made it to the shore in the sub's launch without detection. From there, they made it to a deserted Christmas tree plantation several hundred yards away without detection. They had called upon every trick of stealth known to the Ninja to accomplish this. However, Ito's plan for further movement across land without detection did not come from Ninja lore, nor from any Japanese traditions. Ito's plan was based on something he had seen in an American movie – a short comedy featuring the Three Stooges. Ito's plan was that the entire group would disguise themselves as trees. Each of the seven had taken a Christmas tree and, with a few careful strokes of their knives, cut away enough branches to enable each man to stand inside the tree. Thus, they could walk along the road in search of a mileage marker or some sign indicating their position, and at the first sound of an approaching car, freeze steady, and become merely a clump of trees by the side of the road.

And so it was that seven evergreen trees trotted along a deserted stretch of the Pacific Coast Highway, some 200 miles north of Los Angeles, in search of a road sign that would tell them that. Unfortunately, none of the Japanese had much understanding of the English language. Ito and Ashimoto could understand a few words if they heard them, but only Captain Mitamura and Lieutenant von Kleinschmidt could read English. Therefore, Mitamura had given Ashimoto a piece of paper with the words 'Los Angeles' and 'Hollywood' written on it so they could take particular note of any road sign with either one on it. In addition, Mitamura had ordered them to copy down any other sign they spotted in case it contained a clue to their location.

They heard the sound of an approaching car and all of the trees froze in their tracks. A 1936 Ford Coupe whizzed by without paying the slightest attention to the clump of trees. Ito smiled: his idea was working brilliantly!

About a quarter of a mile down the road, the Japanese sighted their first billboard. It was highly visible because it stood in the middle of a wide clearing amidst quite a number of tree stumps. In fact, it appeared that the area had been cleared quite recently. The billboard had a picture of a log cabin and a pine tree on it and read, 'Pinewood Motor Lodge, 49 miles.' The Japanese approached it, and Ashimoto consulted his piece of paper. He immediately noticed the repetition of the characters 'wood' in 'Pinewood' and 'Hollywood', and shouted excitedly. 'Hollywood!' he cried.

Ito came over to him and glanced at the piece of paper for himself. 'No, not Hollywood,' he told Ashimoto, pointing out the differences between the words. None the less, Ashimoto proceeded to copy down the billboard's English characters in the hope that his Commander could make sense of it.

Once again, they heard the sound of an approaching vehicle. The 'trees' separated according to the pattern of the tree stumps, and froze. An old pick-up truck heaved erratically around the bend. It was loaded with evergreen trees, exactly the same kind of trees that the Japanese were using as camouflage. The truck zipped past the seven trees, then suddenly screeched on its brakes and backed up to them. Ito noticed the lettering on the side of the truck: 'Hollis Wood, Christmas Tree Sales.' He didn't understand what it meant, but he certainly recognized the first two words! Hollywood! Ito was sure that the man inside this truck must have something to do with Hollywood!

Hollis P. Wood of course had nothing whatsoever to do with Hollywood, other than the fact that 'Holly' Wood was his nickname. In fact he had never even been to Hollywood, and had no intention of ever going. Wood was a grizzled, pot-bellied farmer who turned to tree poaching every year around this time, because he could make a nice piece of change selling Christmas trees. He ran the tree-plantation from which the Japanese had stolen their evergreens. Wood had been on his way back not only with more trees, but also with his big cathedral radio so that he could listen to the war news, when he spotted the trees in the clearing. Wood squinted at the seven trees from his cab and stretched his head. He was a bit drunk – Wood also operated his own still and was never without a jug of moonshine – but that still didn't count for what he was seeing. 'Well, I'll be doggonned!' he muttered out loud to the trees. 'Now where d'you little bastards come from? I coulda swore I cut y'all down the day before yesterday!' Wood thought about it some more, then shook his head. 'Well, you ain't gonna get away from ol' Holly, that's for sure!' Wood took a snort from his jug, grabbed the two-bladed axe off the floor of the cab and staggered out of his truck and over to the nearest tree. Had Wood been a little less drunk, he might have noticed that there was a Japanese sailor hiding within. But his brain was buzzing, and Wood thought he was simply walking over to a perfectly ordinary tree.

Wood licked his lips, spat on one hand, spat on the other hand, belched, then spat on the axe blade. He took a firm grip on the handle, wound up and let loose with a mighty swing – but the 'tree' leaped two feet into the air and the blade whizzed harmlessly underneath! Wood was stunned beyond all words! He stared at the tree for several moments in disbelief. He knew he was a little tipsy, but hell, he had chopped down other trees when he'd been a lot drunker than now. Finally he shrugged. Those other trees had been a lot bigger than this one, so obviously he must have missed the trunk altogether. Well, if at first you don't succeed. . . .

Wood spat on his hands again for an even better grip. He had been so absorbed in this particular tree that he failed to notice that another tree that had previously been fifteen feet behind him was now only two feet behind him! Wood wound up for his second swing, swung the axe back – and could go no further. Something had grabbed the end of the axe! Wood turned: that 'something' was a tree with human arms! Wood's mouth fell open, his eyes bulged out and his hands fell away from the axe handle. He figured he must either be dead drunk or in the middle of a nightmare; of course, he was neither. And now Wood beheld an even more incredible sight: the five other trees were all moving towards him . . . and not just moving, but walking! They actually had feet! 'Jesus Palomino!' Wood cried aloud. 'Walking trees!'

He tried to run, but the trees surrounded him. And if that wasn't enough, they were now all talking in Japanese! Wood decided that he was just going to have to force his way through and knock the damned things over. He attempted to butt his way through, but a tree grabbed him by the arm and judo-flipped him through its branches. Wood landed on his back with a resounding thud. Before he could climb to his feet, another tree delivered a clean karate chop to the base of his neck. Wood dropped to the ground unconscious.

'We must take the prisoner back to the ship and let the Captain interrogate him,' Ito told the others. 'He is our one certain link with Hollywood!'

The other trees grunted their approval, and began the arduous task of bearing Hollis P. Wood and all of his possessions back to Submarine I-19.

6

The department-store Santa Claus had just asked the excited little boy sitting on his lap what he wanted for Christmas.

'I wanna machine-gun!' shouted Billy, with a big smile.

Santa laughed. 'Ho, ho, ho! And what would you do with a machine-gun, Billy?'

Billy's eyes brightened. 'Kill the Japs!' he exclaimed.

Billy's mother turned her face away in embarrassment, but Santa saw nothing to be embarrassed about. 'Good boy, Billy! You're a very good boy!'

Billy hopped off Santa's lap and rejoined his mother, and both of them disappeared into the crowd of Christmas shoppers. Although Christmas music played over the store's sound system and holiday decorations were everywhere, the mood in this May Company department store was not entirely of the holiday spirit. The spectre of war loomed over everything, and there was an underlying tenseness in the air.

Wally Stephans was very much aware of this tenseness as he pushed through the morass of shoppers, with Dennis DeSoto at his side. Wally had made up his mind that he was going to have his new suit, regardless of the fact that he had no money. He had talked Dennis into helping him, but now Dennis seemed nervous and hesitant as he followed Wally towards the Men's Department.

'I don't know about this,' said Dennis, glancing around. 'These people don't seem nervous enough.'

53

'Are you kidding me? They're nervous as hell! Take a look at that!' Wally pointed to the Sporting Goods Department where some twenty men were practically fighting each other as they rushed to purchase shotguns and rifles. It appeared that the store's entire stock of guns would be gone in another thirty seconds.

Then Wally noticed a grim-looking huddle of people in the Radio Department crowding around an Emerson Cathedral Model. He pulled Dennis along with him as he moved closer, straining to hear what everyone else was listening to. He could just make out the emotionless voice of the newscaster:

'. . . reported that two squadrons of Japanese 'planes flew over the city of San Francisco last night. US Army General John DeWitt confirmed the sighting and attacked sceptical city and police officials who believed the incident to be nothing more than a case of war nerves. When asked why no bombs had been dropped on San Francisco, DeWitt replied "I don't know why they didn't drop any bombs. But I wish they would have dropped some bombs. Then maybe the people of this city would realize the seriousness of the danger we face." '

A middle-aged woman looked at the crowd of people around her, eyes full of fear. 'They bombed Pearl Harbor, and now they're going to bomb here. They bombed Pearl Harbor and now they're going to bomb here!' She started yelling it. 'They bombed Pearl Harbor and now they're going to bomb here! Oh, God, oh my God!' And with that she fainted.

Wally and Dennis exchanged a look. 'They look pretty nervous to me,' said Wally. Then he hurried off to the Men's Department. Dennis caught up with him.

'I still think we shouldn't rush into this, Wally.'

Wally was searching through the suits on the rack, looking for the particular one he had seen here last week.

'Quit worrying, would you? All I'm gonna do is borrow a suit. I'll give it back on Monday.'

'Listen,' said Dennis, 'I know where you can get a swell suit – free – and there's no risk.'

Wally looked at Dennis for a moment, not understanding. Then the meaning became clear, and Wally shook his head. 'Dennis, I hope you're not thinking what I think you're thinking . . .'

'We could join up together, Wally, you and me! We'll go fight the Japs! Think of it. Instead of stealing cars down on Alameda Street, we could steal Hirohito's private limousine out of Tokyo. We could be heroes!'

'I'm not joining the Army,' Wally said definitively. 'In the Army, you gotta take orders, and I'm sick of taking orders. I been taking orders my whole life. From now on, nobody's pushing me around. And as far as the Japs go, well, I don't have to join the Army to fight the Japs. Believe me, when they land at Santa Monica Beach, I'll be there waitin' for 'em!'

'But those uniforms, Wally – dames are falling for uniforms. I've been noticing. Take a look over there.'

Wally looked where Dennis was pointing. A very homely soldier was walking through the store with an incredibly gorgeous girl on his arm. Wally couldn't believe it. What could a knock-out like her see in a joker like that . . . unless it was the uniform? He considered this, then dismissed it, turning back to Dennis, shaking his head. 'It's gotta be his sister.'

Now Wally found the suit he had been looking for: a charcoal-coloured zoot-suit with red pin-stripes and a wide-brimmed hat to match. He pulled it off the rack and proudly showed it to Dennis. 'Forget about those uniforms, and get a load of this! Now this is a set of threads! It's got a reet pleat, a stuffed cuff and a reave sleeve! And with these padded shoulders, it all works to give you the "drape shape"! With this on, it won't matter if I can't dance a step – I'll look like the king of swing!' This was true: the zoot-suit had originally been designed with jitterbugging in mind. The trousers were 'pegged'; that is, they wrapped tightly around the ankles, so that you wouldn't trip over them on the dance floor. And the overlong jacket gave the wearer striking lines, exaggerating every move.

Dennis nodded his approval. Who wouldn't want to wear a suit like that?

'Here – take this.' Wally handed Dennis the package he had been carrying around with him in the store. It was about the size of a hat box, and wrapped to look like a Christmas gift. But it wasn't a Christmas gift. Dennis took it reluctantly. 'I'll meet you in the dressing-room,' said Wally. 'I've gotta find a decent shirt.'

Wally walked away. Dennis started to say something, then decided it was no use arguing. He went into the dressing-room.

Wally picked out a purple shirt and a wide black-and-red tie. Just as he was heading for the dressing-room, he was intercepted by a salesman. The salesman was an effeminate, superior type and he gave Wally the once-over not bothering to disguise his disdain at the sight of Wally's grease-splattered Hawaiian shirt. 'Can I help you, young man?'

'Sure,' replied Wally. 'Just as soon as I put these on.'

Wally strode confidently into the dressing-room where Dennis was pacing around like a caged animal. With Wally in there, he didn't have room to pace. The wrapped package sat on the floor. Wally quickly changed into the splendiferous zoot-suit.

'I still say we should think this over,' said Dennis.

'There's nothing to think over!'

'Well, what about Betty? What's she gonna think if

she finds out about this? You told her you were going straight.'

'What's she gonna think if I show up at that dance looking like a degenerate slob? She's the only reason I'm doing this, Dennis. I'm crazy about her! She's the first decent thing that ever happened to me!'

'Well, what if we get nabbed? Then what?'

Wally gave Dennis a look. 'The only way we're gonna get nabbed is if you screw up!' Wally donned the zoot jacket, then looked at Dennis once more, this time completely seriously. 'Don't let me down, Dennis. I'm counting on you.'

Wally came out of the dressing area and walked over to a triple mirror.

He looked at himself and grinned: it was a near-perfect fit. He adjusted the hat and twirled his long watch chain around, as was the custom among zoot-suiters. Then he tried a few jitterbug steps. Boy, did he look great!

The salesman stepped over and cleared his throat a little too loudly. Wally ignored him. 'That's a very fine garment,' the salesman said. 'It's very expensive, you know.'

Wally started to perspire. Was this guy on to him? Regardless, he had to play it cool. Wally didn't even look at the man. 'What's that supposed to mean, bud?'

'It means that I couldn't help noticing the clothes you were wearing before.'

Wally turned on the salesman with sudden outrage and spoke very loudly. 'Are you accusing me of not having enough dough to pay for this? What kind of a clip-joint are you running here, Mack?'

Several heads turned to look at the source of these words, and the salesman turned red. He suddenly became quite humble. 'I beg your pardon, sir –'

Wally interrupted, 'You beg my pardon? You'd better

beg my pardon! I oughta walk outta here right now! I oughta report you to the manager of this store! He must have really been scraping the bottom of the barrel when he hired you!'

'Please, sir, there's no need for all that. I apologize. Please – wait here, let me get my tape-measure.' The salesman hurried off. Wally heaved a sigh of relief. Then Wally glanced over at the dressing-rooms. What was taking Dennis so long?

Inside, Dennis was all thumbs as he worked at ripping open the 'Christmas package'. Finally he managed to get the wrapping paper off.

Wally looked at himself in the mirror again, but actually wasn't paying any attention to his image. His head was pounding, sweat poured from his skin . . . what the hell was Dennis doing in there? Wally looked around nervously, then saw the salesman returning with his tape-measure. Wally closed his eyes. Dennis must have screwed up. Yeah, Dennis must have turned yellow and now . . . but wait! Was it his imagination or was Wally hearing a siren? Yes – a siren! It was getting louder and louder! Wally looked around the store. Everyone else was hearing it too. People stopped in their tracks, looking around, looking at each other, trying to figure out what it meant, and where it was coming from. The salesman looked around, swallowing hard. He was very frightened. Even Santa Claus and the little girl on his lap weren't sure what to think. But Wally knew what to think: Dennis had come through!

Dennis, in the dressing-room, was the source of the sound. He was cranking the hand-operated siren that had been wrapped in Wally's package. He and Wally had swiped it from an ambulance an hour ago, after Wally had come up with this idea. Since the signal for an air raid was a long continuous wail, Dennis kept on cranking, harder and harder. The noise was ear-splitting!

Wally kept looking around the store, barely managing to keep from laughing at the nervous reactions of the shoppers. What a wonderful diversion this was going to be! The salesman looked at Wally, and Wally looked him straight in the eye.

'Air raid,' said Wally, calmly.

The salesman's eyes opened wide in stark, raving terror and his face turned completely white. He screamed at the top of his lungs, 'AIR RAID! AIR RAID ! ! ! !'

That was it – the spark that ignited the powder keg. The cry spread through the department store like a brushfire. 'Air raid!' Everyone was yelling it. Shoppers ran madly about, running into each other, knocking over merchandise, going completely berserk. Women screamed, little children burst into tears. The entire store became pure pandemonium. A man broke into the glass-protected Fire Alarm, threw the switch, and a loud clanging bell added to the noise and hysteria! Another man smashed the glass storage case in the Sporting Goods section and started passing out ammunition to every man with a gun!

Wally was astonished at the magnitude of the panic. He stood dumbfounded, staring in disbelief at the insanity he had created. He had expected some hysteria, but hadn't dreamt of a reaction of this scale! Dennis came running out of the dressing-room, without the siren, and was nearly trampled under. He managed to find his way through the madness to Wally's side. 'You were right, Wally,' he yelled, trying to make himself heard over the noise. 'They *were* nervous!'

'Yeah, I'll say!' replied Wally. 'And if one little siren can do all this, I'd sure hate to see what would happen in a real air raid!'

The store Santa Claus came running past, wearing a

Civilian Defense armband, helmet and a gas-mask. He was brandishing a ·45 automatic pistol and screaming at the top of his lungs, 'Take cover! Take cover!'

Wally and Dennis couldn't believe what they were seeing. 'Well, at least we know one thing,' said Wally. 'They're not gonna miss this suit! Let's get the hell outta here!'

And they did.

7

Captain Loomis Birkhead, United States Army, had seen a lot of action since the war had broken out: there had been Jane Baxter, Margaret Davis, Laura Sanderson, Louise Foster, and several others whose names Birkhead couldn't, nor cared to remember. The name of the action right now was Madeline Hayes, and the place was in the back seat of Captain Birkhead's staff car which was parked on the tarmac of an airfield in Long Beach.

Captain Birkhead was thirty-one, very handsome and probably the smoothest operator in the armed forces. In fact, he would be the first to tell you so, assuming you were male. Captain Birkhead was also an aide to General Joseph W. 'Vinegar Joe' Stilwell, the General who was currently responsible for the defence of Southern California. General Stilwell was on his way to this particular airfield to inspect aircraft and to address an assemblage of reporters. Since he was late, Captain Birkhead had decided to make the most of the available time, and so he had generously volunteered to give Madeline Hayes, girl reporter, an exclusive story on Army equipment. Miss Hayes seemed to be getting a lot out of it, too.

Unfortunately, just as Birkhead was about to get to the most exclusive part, he was disturbed by a rap on the car door made by his driver, Private Laurance DuBois.

'Captain Birkhead,' DuBois called. 'General Stilwell's arriving now!'

Sure enough, Birkhead could hear the sound of an

approaching motorcade. Madeline Hayes immediately pulled up her stockings, grabbed her shoes, threw open the car door, and started out. Birkhead tried to pull her back in.

'Madeline, what are you doing? I'm not finished yet!'

'Sorry, Captain,' answered the lovely reporter, 'but if that's General Stilwell, I've gotta get my story!' She pulled herself away from him and began walking towards the reviewing stand where the other reporters were gathered.

'But I was just giving it to you!' he called. If she had heard him, she gave no indication. 'Shit!' he muttered under his breath. Private DuBois handed Birkhead the mirror he always kept in the car for such emergencies, and the Captain proceeded to button his shirt and straighten his tie. 'I'll tell you, DuBois,' he sighed, 'being a General's aide has its advantages and its disadvantages. Why couldn't the old man have been a few more minutes late?'

DuBois pushed his glasses back on his nose and attempted to offer a humble explanation. 'Well, sir, it's wartime. We all have to make sacrifices.'

'Yeah, I suppose,' mumbled Birkhead without much enthusiasm as he pulled up his trousers.

'This isn't the state of California,' said General Stilwell as he stepped out of his car. 'It's the state of insanity!' Major-General Joseph W. Stilwell was fifty-eight years old, and he felt as if he had aged five more years during the past five days. Every hour was a barrage of 'phone calls, messages, and telegrams, each one more idiotic than the next. For example, the Coca-Cola company had requested troops to guard its bottling plant, for fear that Japanese saboteurs would attempt to slip poison into California's supply of the soft drink. Earlier this morning someone had reported a Japanese submarine in the Great Salt Lake of Utah. And on and on and on.

At this moment, General Stilwell was probably the sanest man on the west coast. His superior officer, General John DeWitt, was apparently seeing Japs in his soup, judging from the ridiculous and irresponsible statement he had issued from San Francisco this morning in which he confirmed the 'sighting' of Japanese 'planes over the city last night. In addition, DeWitt had assigned Stilwell a bodyguard of twelve men armed with Thompson sub-machine-guns to protect him against enemy assassins. In fact, the one thing that was keeping Stilwell from falling prey to all of the madness around him was the knowledge that it would only be a matter of weeks, perhaps days, before he got a real assignment: an Army to command in battle – in Europe, he hoped. Until then, all he could do was to try to keep the people of California calm, to instil confidence in them, and to at least make everything appear organized. And that was quite a job.

Stilwell's physical bearing was helpful in this. Although not a particularly imposing man, Stilwell carried himself with an authority and confidence which instilled respect. His hair was grey on the sides and cut extremely short there, and he wore standard Army-issue wire-rimmed glasses. Stilwell rarely smiled, and it was this constant sobriety which had earned him the nickname 'Vinegar Joe' during a tour of duty in China. Stilwell despised pomposity and never asked anything of a soldier that he wasn't willing to endure himself. If a column of his men had to walk twenty miles, Stilwell would walk with them. He was a soldier's General, a man with little patience for bureaucratic bullshit, a man who said what he meant and meant what he said. General Joseph W. Stilwell was one of the finest Generals in the United States Army.

Accompanying Stilwell was his new secretary, lovely

Donna Stratton. Donna was twenty-seven, blonde, and very well built, a fact that her conservative grey suit with the maroon trim enhanced. Her manner was generally cool and detached, but beneath this exterior was a steamy sensuality that even Stilwell was aware of. Right now, her perfect blue eyes sparkled with excitement as she gazed at the various 'planes parked on the tarmac. Stilwell wasn't sure about his new secretary. There was something about her which was, well, a little strange, something that Stilwell couldn't quite put his finger on. However, he had no time to dwell on this because no sooner had the three of them stepped out of Stilwell's staff car, than the General was promptly inundated with more messages, reports and papers from military and civilian couriers. Stilwell glanced through some of them as they walked past a DC-3, reading aloud.

' "Request troops for guard duty." "Request troops for guard duty." "Request troops for—" Christ! What do these people think the Army is – a private security-guard service? How are we supposed to train troops to fight this war if we put all of our infantry on guard duty?'

Stilwell wasn't expecting an answer to his question, but Donna assumed he was asking her. 'Gee, sir, I really don't know,' she replied.

Stilwell gave her a look, then leafed through several more of the requests. 'Standard Oil wants troops! The Southern Pacific Railroad wants troops! The Department of Water and Power wants troops! Lockheed wants troops! The Harbor Department—'

But Donna interrupted him with sudden interest. 'Lockheed? Is that Lockheed Aircraft, sir?'

'That's right,' said Stilwell. 'Lockheed Aircraft.'

'Don't they build 'planes there, sir?' Donna asked with great urgency.

Stilwell was rather bewildered as to why Donna would

be asking about this. 'Yes, they do,' he replied.

'Well, 'planes are very important for the war effort, sir,' she stated, as if Stilwell didn't know.

'I know they're important, Donna. But so are all the rest of these requests. Have you got a special interest in airplanes or something?'

'Yes, sir,' Donna nodded eagerly. 'I think they're exciting!'

Stilwell shook his head. Yes, indeed, there was something strange about this young woman.

Captain Loomis Birkhead ducked around the side of his car to avoid being seen by Stilwell as he walked past, but immediately went back for a second look: Birkhead had just seen Donna. Amazed recognition lit his face. He turned to DuBois. 'Good Christ, is that the old man's new secretary?'

'Yes, sir. She was transferred in from G-2 this morning. Not bad, huh?'

Birkhead couldn't believe his eyes. 'Not bad!? She's a goddess, DuBois! A goddamn goddess! That's Donna Stratton! I knew her back in Washington. She's got this thing for airplanes like you wouldn't believe – used to be, what do you call it, one of those waitresses on an airplane – a stewardess!'

'One of those real high-flying types, huh, sir?' DuBois asked, hoping Birkhead would elaborate in intimate detail.

'No,' explained Birkhead, 'this is like nothing you've ever seen before. She's got 'planes on the brain!'

'You must have really scored big with her, huh, sir?' DuBois was still very eager for the details.

'I'd rather not discuss it,' Birkhead answered curtly.

DuBois could not believe what he was hearing. It could only mean one thing. 'You mean . . . you struck out, sir? You??'

Birkhead cleared his throat. 'Well, let's just say I bunted foul. But I think this game's about to go into extra innings!' Birkhead peered over the top of the car and kept his eye on Donna.

Stilwell and Donna, followed by the dozen armed bodyguards, continued along the tarmac towards the terminal building. They were joined by Lieutenant Bressler, another Stilwell aide.

'All right, Bressler,' said Stilwell, 'where are these reporters I'm supposed to talk to?'

Bressler pointed out the reviewing stand where a speaker's platform fitted out with radio microphones had been set up. 'Over there, sir. But I think you'd better read this telegram first.' Bressler handed it to him. 'It's from Colonel Maddox, sir.'

Stilwell reacted with alarm. ' "Madman" Maddox? What does he want?'

'Uh, troops, sir,' replied the Lieutenant.

'Troops?!?' exclaimed Stilwell with astonishment. 'He runs a practice bombing range out in Barstow! That's in the middle of the desert! What could he possibly need troops for?' Stilwell opened the telegram and read it aloud. ' "Request emergency troops. Invasion imminent. Suspect hidden Jap airfield in Pomona alfalfa fields." ' Stilwell sighed. 'A Jap invasion in the middle of the Mojave Desert.' He shook his head. 'Well, I blame myself. I put that lunatic out there. I thought it was the one place where he'd stay out of trouble. I should have put him in front of a firing squad after that stunt he pulled down on the border with that armoured cavalry division. He almost got us into another war with Mexico. But, there was nothing else I could do, not with his brother having all those political connections in Georgia.' Stilwell turned to Bressler, addressing the problem at hand. 'Tell him to hold his position. I'll have to send somebody out there later. Where's Birkhead? He was supposed to have my lunch out here.'

'I'm sure Captain Birkhead's around somewhere, sir,' answered Bressler.

Donna turned white upon hearing this name. 'Birkhead? Not Loomis Birkhead. . . ?' she asked the General with extreme trepidation.

'Yes, Loomis Birkhead,' said Stilwell. 'He's my aide. You know him?'

Donna stuttered. 'Well, I – uh – uh—'

'Of course you know him,' said Stilwell, answering his own question. 'Every woman in the War Department knows Loomis Birkhead.' He turned to Bressler again. 'Let's talk to these reporters.'

Stilwell and his entourage passed another DC-3 and headed towards the reporters gathered at the reviewing stand. All, that is, except Donna. For as they passed the DC-3, Donna spotted the B-17 parked adjacent to it and stopped dead in her tracks. Donna had never seen the four-engined long-range strategic bomber except in pictures, and it was even more incredible than she thought it could be! Her eyes opened wide and a tingle of excitement ran through her whole body. This was without a doubt the greatest 'plane she had ever seen! Suddenly Stilwell, the Army, her job, the war – everything else in the world vanished: there was only the B-17. She licked her lips and glided towards it, almost as if she was floating.

Stilwell was completely oblivious to this.

Birkhead was not. He nudged DuBois, grinning a schoolboy smile. 'What'd I tell you DuBois? That 'plane's attracting her like a magnet!'

He started to go after her, but DuBois grabbed his

arm. 'Are you sure you want to go through with this, sir? Remember what happened to the General's last secretary. . . !'

Birkhead remembered, all right, but immediately dismissed that sordid affair from his mind. 'This is different, DuBois. I've got to have her. My reputation is at stake.'

DuBois let go of his arm and Birkhead purposefully walked towards Donna and the B-17.

Donna Stratton caressed one of the 'plane's propeller blades slowly, lovingly and suggestively. Her breathing was low and heavy, and she seemed to be glowing. She was in heat. Captain Birkhead quietly crept up behind her and watched for a few moments. Truly, Donna was one of a kind! Finally he grinned widely and stepped forward.

'Well, well, well,' he laughed. 'If it isn't Donna Stratton! After all this time! How long has it been?'

The heat abruptly turned frigid. 'Not long enough,' she retorted.

'Aw, come on, Donna, you're not still sore, are you?'

'Yes,' she replied with an icy smile. 'In a number of places.'

Birkhead chuckled. 'Same old Donna! Always so . . . so whimsical! Why don't we kiss and make up? Whaddaya say?'

'Same old Birkhead. Always so . . . subtle.'

Birkhead was not put off in the slightest. 'Say, I've got an idea! Why don't we go out for dinner tonight? We've got a lot to talk about.'

'What could you and I possibly have to talk about, Captain?' she asked cynically.

Birkhead looked her straight in the eye. 'Airplanes.'

She gulped. She couldn't hide her reaction. And Birkhead saw it in her eyes. Now, if he could only keep her interested.

'I seem to recall you always had a keen interest in aircraft,' he continued. 'Take this B-17 for example. A woman like you is bound to appreciate a 'plane like the 17. After all, it's big. It's the biggest one here. Big . . . and long.'

She started to move away from him, but he followed her as she walked around the 'plane. 'And you know what else, Donna? It's got a lot of range. You know what I mean by range, don't you? I mean it can stay *up* for a long time. A *very* long time.' He slapped the side of the fuselage. 'And it's built firm. It has to be firm and solid because of its tremendous forward thrust. And when it delivers its payload . . .' he dropped his voice to a whisper, '. . . devastating!'

Donna turned to him and laughed. He laughed too, elated to have finally broken through her icy exterior. 'Captain Birkhead, let's get something straight,' she said with a bright bubbling smile.

'Please do,' he replied buoyantly.

With a frightening abruptness she turned to frozen granite, and her words came cold and terse. 'I don't like you. I don't like the way you act. And I especially don't like your immature sexual innuendos. The B-17 happens to be the most valuable strategic long-range air bomber in the United States Army Air Corps, and I would appreciate it if you would treat both it and myself with a little bit more respect!'

Birkhead's mouth fell open in stunned shock and for several moments he was utterly speechless . . . completely taken aback. No woman had even spoken this way to him before. Well, actually women *had* spoken to him this way before, but they had never meant it. Now, for the first time in his life, Birkhead had experienced Absolute Zero – a woman who could make Antarctica seem like the tropics. 'I'm sorry, Donna, I didn't realize you felt that way,' he said, backing away from her, afraid to say anything more. He backed right into the open hatch in the underbelly of the fuselage, banging his head into solid steel. He howled in pain and muttered a curse as he discovered the open hatch. 'Goddammit, when I went to flying school we were taught to secure these things.'

The comment did not go past Donna unnoticed. She looked back at him with sudden interest as he slammed the hatch shut. Without warning, spring had arrived and the ice was melting fast. 'Loomis,' she said warmly, 'you never told me you went to flying school!' She glided towards him, and he wasn't sure what to say, what to do or what to think.

'Huh?' he stammered.

Donna was becoming a flash flood of sexuality. She moved very, very close to him. 'I didn't know you were a pilot,' she smiled. 'Can you fly the 17?'

Birkhead still couldn't account for the sudden rise in temperature. 'Well, actually, I only logged a few hours in a little Beechcraft before I got kicked out – I mean, kicked upstairs and became the General's aide. . . .'

'But can you fly the 17?' she asked again eagerly.

'Well, no, I don't think I could—' Before he could even finish the sentence, he detected the immediate cold snap, and Donna Stratton became crystal clear to him. 'Oh – you mean the B-17!' he exclaimed, as if he had misunderstood. 'Can I fly the B-17? Well, hell, it's a 'plane isn't it? It's got four wings and a propeller, hasn't it? A 'plane's a 'plane! If you can fly one, you can fly 'em all! Sure, I can fly a B-17!'

The heat-wave was back on again. 'And I thought you were just making a play for me,' she apologized. 'I didn't realize you had a serious interest in strategic bombers.'

Birkhead grinned. 'Oh, my interest is very strategic!' He glanced around to make sure no one was watching,

70

then opened the hatch again. 'How'd you like me to show you the cockpit?' he offered. She nodded excitedly. He gave her a boost up through the hatch and then followed for his first look inside a B-17.

General Stilwell's press conference had been going on for several minutes. Stilwell recognized another reporter. 'Sir,' he asked, rising, 'would you comment on the two squadrons of Jap 'planes that flew over San Francisco last night?'

'There were no bombs dropped in San Francisco last night,' stated Stilwell definitively.

'Then you're suggesting, sir, that there were no 'planes?' replied the correspondent.

'Young man, if you were going to fly two squadrons of 'planes five thousand miles to a port city in an enemy nation, wouldn't you bring a few bombs along?'

There was some mild laughter from the group. As usual, Stilwell had a way of boiling things down to the obvious by using plain, ordinary common sense. 'What happened in San Francisco last night was a simple case of war nerves,' explained the General. 'Nothing more.'

But the reporter still wasn't satisfied. 'But, sir, General DeWitt swears there were Jap 'planes last night. He suspects they were on some sort of reconnaissance mission.'

Stilwell realized that this reporter wanted to believe that the Japanese had buzzed San Francisco last night, no matter what the facts were. It was a dangerous state of mind, but lately it seemed to be the rule rather than the exception. 'If General DeWitt is going to be seeing Jap 'planes,' said Stilwell calmly, 'he'd better shoot a few of 'em down. Then we can all see 'em. Next question, please.'

Madeline Hayes stood up. 'What about this city, General? What precautions have been taken in case the

Japs try to bomb us?'

'That's a good question, young lady, and I hope that everyone here will give it special attention. First let me say that the possibility of the Japs bombing us is at best remote. However, we are installing anti-aircraft batteries all over town, just in case. In addition, we have a vast network of Civilian Defense volunteer aircraft-spotters keeping a constant vigil. They report aircraft sightings to Interceptor Command Headquarters, which is the nerve-centre for the defence of southern California.

'Interceptor Command constantly receives reports about every airplane in the sky. They know which 'planes are supposed to be up there, when and where. In the event that a sighting comes through which cannot immediately be identified by Headquarters, we go to a condition yellow as a precaution. Usually these turn out to be 'planes which are slightly off course. However, if the unidentified aircraft continues its course, and attempts to identify it fail, we go to a condition blue. If the situation persists and radio contact cannot be established with the aircraft, we go to a condition red, the red alert.

'During a red alert, air-raid sirens will sound. All citizens must then extinguish all lights. The area must be completely blacked out. I understand that the Los Angeles City Council has just passed an ordinance that will make any citizen who refuses to turn out his lights during an air raid subject to a five-thousand dollar fine. I heartily endorse this action. Of course, we will have assistance from the utility companies in this as well. It is possible that they may shut your lights off before you do.

'At the same time, the Army will move into action. Searchlight crews will man carbon-arc lamps of 800 million candlepower to scan the sky for enemy aircraft. All troops in the area will be put on alert, and gun crews at the anti-aircraft batteries will stand at readiness.'

Stilwell added one more aside under his breath. 'I hope.'

Birkhead ushered Donna into the cockpit of the B-17. Her eyes danced with excitement as they took in every incredible detail of the controls and instrument panels. Donna wished that she was airborne. It had been so long since she had last been in flight, and she was desperate for the experience again. Because it was only while in flight that Donna could really let go of herself. Only in flight could she really feel like a woman. The first time Donna had ever climaxed with a man had been in an aeroplane. She was seventeen, and he was a pilot, and it had been the most wonderful experience of her life. In her dismay, she discovered that she was unable to experience these same sensations on the ground, not with a pilot, nor with any man. And so Donna became a high-flying girl. She began to hang around airports, flirting with pilots and navigators, promising them anything for a ride in an aeroplane. She became a stewardess for United Airlines and for two years had the time of her life, until a flight official caught her in the act with a married pilot in the cockpit of a DC-3 on a New York to Chicago run. Donna was blackballed from the airline industry. And so, it was back to pick-ups at airports and Army Air Corps bases.

'This is where the pilot sits,' explained Birkhead, showing her the seat. 'Now you just sit right here and get nice and comfortable.' He helped her into the seat.

If only they could take off right now, thought Donna. But she knew that was impossible with General Stilwell a mere stone's throw away. But perhaps if she used her imagination, and if Birkhead helped her ... well, what did she have to lose?

'You know, Loomis, when I was a little girl, I used to sit in my father's big chair, close my eyes, and imagine what it would be like to fly.' She closed her eyes, hoping he would take the hint.

'Well, why don't we do that right now!' he exclaimed.

Donna smiled to herself. Birkhead wasn't as dumb as she thought.

Certainly not. Birkhead didn't know much about 'planes, but he knew plenty about women and he could certainly recognize when one was getting hot. And Donna was pretty hot right now.

'Now keep your eyes closed,' he said, kneeling beside the pilot's seat, 'and imagine the powerful engines starting up ... va - rooommmmmm! Va - rooommmm-roooom-rooommmm! That's engine number one.' He continued with his sound-effects. 'There goes engine number two. Number three. And that was number four.' He began to shake her chair. 'Can you feel those vibrations?'

Her breathing was beginning to get heavier. 'Yes,' she smiled.

He shook the chair a little harder. 'Are your engines starting up?'

'Yes,' she exclaimed, really starting to get into it. 'They're starting up!'

'Am I cleared for take-off?' he asked.

'You're cleared!' she replied.

He moved closer to her. 'Now imagine we're taxiing – taxiing down that runway, accelerating faster, and faster, and faster ... and then ... lift off!' He unbuttoned her bottom jacket button.

'I don't feel any thrust,' she remarked.

'Don't worry, you will,' he said confidently. 'We're airborne now, and climbing, higher and higher.' Birkhead could feel himself getting hard. 'Ten thousand feet,' he said, unbuttoning her next button. 'Fifteen thousand feet,' and he unbuttoned the next button. He was delighted to see that she had no blouse on underneath. 'Twenty thousand feet,' he proclaimed, but he couldn't get the last button undone. 'Twenty thousand feet,' he continued, 'we're cruising at twenty thousand feet . . .' He couldn't get that last button undone. It was stuck on a thread in the buttonhole. 'Still cruising at twenty thousand, at the incredible speed of two hundred and fifty miles per hour . . . can you imagine that, Donna? Are you with me, Donna?'

Her breathing was very heavy and excited. 'Yes, Loomis, yes! I'm with you! I'm with you!'

Try as he might, Birkhead just couldn't get that last button unhooked. Finally he yanked on her garment to get it undone, and in so doing gave her quite a jerk.

'What was that?' she asked, worried.

'Oh – just a little turbulence! We hit an air pocket! Nothing to worry about!'

She relaxed again. He waited a moment for her breathing to get heavy again.

'How are we doing, Loomis?' she wondered.

Birkhead opened her jacket and gazed at the purple lace bra which uplifted her firm, well-formed breasts. 'Objective in sight,' he said, trying to control his own building excitement. 'We're right on target!' He began to unbutton his own tunic, then moved towards her. 'Bank a little to the left,' he suggested.

Donna reached for the steering control with her right hand and turned it as she moved to the left.

Outside, the aileron on the left wing lowered, causing the workman who was standing on the wing, refuelling the 'plane, to lose his balance and fall.

'Let's ease down towards the target,' said Birkhead, moving closer to her. Donna followed orders by pushing in on the steering control. Outside, this caused the elevators to drop, and a workman who was standing on one to wash the tail fin slipped off and fell!

'Peering down the bombsight,' said Birkhead as he looked into her cleavage. 'There it is!' He reached behind her to unfasten her bra. 'We open the bomb-bay doors. . .'

Donna's hand unconsciously went to the bomb-bay door switch and pushed it to the 'open' position. Outside, the bomb-bay doors fell open and revealed a huge 500-pound bomb in the bay, armed and ready!

Birkhead removed her bra, completely unaware that Donna's hand was on the bomb-release switch. He began to move his face towards her lovely breasts. 'Approaching target . . . almost there . . .' Donna gripped the control tighter, waiting for the proper command. 'Here we go,' continued Birkhead, ' . . . and . . . Bombs Awa—'

'HEY!' screamed a workman through the hatch. 'Quit screwing around in there!'

The yelling completely destroyed Donna's fantasy and her hand fell away from the bomb-release switch as she abruptly returned to the world of reality. 'Mission scrubbed,' she sighed, pushing Birkhead away from her.

Birkhead was nearly in shock. To be frustrated by two women in less than an hour was more than he could take! 'Now, Donna,' he protested, 'don't be hasty!'

She shook her head. 'Sorry to have to bail out, Loomis, but it just doesn't work on the ground. I should have known better. I tried it once in a simulator, but it was no good there either. We've got to be airborne.' She got up and was about to leave the cockpit, but Birkhead grabbed her arm.

'But we were almost there,' he pleaded. 'We were right over the target area!'

'Sorry, Loomis, it just won't work. Leave me alone.' She shook her arm free of him, but he immediately grabbed it again.

'Let me try it again!' he begged. 'I'll use a different

flight plan. We'll dive bomb Tokyo!' He started making sound-effects, but Donna didn't want to hear about it.

'Let go of me, Loomis, please!' she demanded, struggling to get free of him.

Several hundred yards away from the aeroplane, General Stilwell was in the process of answering the final question of the press conference. 'Let me say one final thing about bombs,' he was saying. 'The eventuality of an air raid on Los Angeles is highly unlikely. However, speaking for myself and my entire staff, we are doing everything humanly possible to defend this city against an enemy attack. . . .'

Donna continued to wrestle with Birkhead, trying to loosen his grip on her arm.

'You can't do this to me, Donna!' he exclaimed. 'You don't know what I've been going through today!'

Donna was really starting to shove him hard as her anger increased. 'Loomis,' she said threateningly, 'my father was an amateur boxer, and he taught me how to defend myself. Now you get your hands off me, or I'll show you what I learned!'

But Birkhead wasn't about to let her go. 'Donna, just calm down,' he implored.

Without any further ado, she socked him in the eye with a tremendous right hook! Birkhead went reeling backward into the cockpit instrumental panel and fell right on top of the bomb-release switch!

At the same time, Stilwell was concluding his remarks: ' . . . and I can assure you, there will be no bombs dropped here!' he said unequivocally.

At that moment, the 500-pound bomb dropped out of the B-17 bomb-bay, clanged on to the tarmac and began rolling straight towards Stilwell and the reporters. Soldiers and civilians scattered like rabbits in every direction. The bomb continued to roll, picking up speed, on an inevitable course towards the reviewing stand. Stilwell, Bressler, and several reporters took cover under a DC-3. And then came the explosion; it was colossal! The fireball was blinding, the blast was ear shattering, and the concussion was extraordinary. The entire reviewing stand, chairs, speaker's platform, everything was blown to smithereens!

There was a long, long moment of silence as the smoke cleared. Everyone had got out in time, so no one had been injured. In fact, the total damage done had been minor, especially compared to what could have happened. Stilwell and Bressler exchanged a glance and they both sighed with relief. So did the reporters. One of them turned to Stilwell.

'You were saying, General,' he remarked, 'that no bombs would be dropped here.'

'I meant Jap bombs,' Stilwell replied dryly.

8

Hollis P. Wood marched proudly, defiantly, across the deck of Japanese Submarine I-19 with his hands clasped over his straw stetson. Despite the fact that several guns were trained on him, Wood refused to show any sign of fear – after all, he was an American, and by God, he was going to act like an American! Wood was being marched to the vessel's hatch by the seven seamen he had mistaken for trees; once inside, he would be interrogated by Captain Mitamura.

Wood had regained consciousness five minutes ago and had found himself in a rubber raft being rowed out to sea by the seven sailors. It had taken him only moments to realize what was happening to him, and this had sobered him up quite quickly. He had started yelling, but was promptly answered by a pistol pointed at his face; he had then asked all of the obvious questions in a more subdued tone of voice, but it rapidly became clear that not one of his captors could understand English. He had desperately watched for an opportunity to escape, but not one had presented itself. And so he had spent the rest of the trip leering at the enemy sailors, especially at the one the others called 'Ito', who was fascinated with Wood's big Cathedral Model radio. 'What'cha think you're gonna do with my radio, Shorty?' Wood had asked him. 'Ain't you smart enough to know you gotta plug her in to get Amos 'n Andy?'

Wood had been shocked to discover the presence of a

79

Japanese submarine so close to home. He had also decided it was a remarkable stroke of luck that he, of all people would be taken prisoner. Remarkable because Wood imagined himself to be a man of great courage, strong moral fibre, and intense loyalty to the red, white and blue. He had made up his mind that not only would these Japs get nothing out of him, but that he would escape and bring back the Army, the Navy and the Marines. And then the Japs would be sorry they ever bombed Pearl Harbor!

Wood's pot-belly and heavy coat made it difficult for him to squeeze through the hatch. He howled in pain as two Japanese sailors pushed down his head to force him through! Finally, he made it inside, and practically fell down the ladder! The rest of the Japanese followed, with Ito bringing up the rear. Ito discovered much to his dismay that Wood's radio was too big to fit through. Try as he might, he was unable to make it fit – it was that damned cabinet! Well, he'd just have to unscrew the chassis, and to hell with the cabinet.

Wood was taken into the submarine's control-room and shoved into a chair under a light bulb – the standard interrogation set-up. He looked up with disdain at the Japanese faces that surrounded him, and especially noticed Captain Mitamura whom Wood easily identified as the leader. 'You little sneaks ain't gettin' shit from me,' Wood stated with cocky irreverence, 'except my name, rank and Social Security number!'

Ashimoto quickly related the circumstances of Wood's capture to Mitamura, and stressed the lucky coincidence of the word 'Hollywood' on the American's pick-up truck.

Wood answered their Japanese with his defiant English. 'Wood, Hollis P. Lumberjack. Social Security number 106-43-2185.'

Mitamura stepped forward and addressed Wood in

broken English. 'Where Hollywood?' asked the Commander.

Wood could recognize his name even if it was spoken with a heavy Japanese accent. 'Right here,' he said.

Mitamura did not understand. 'Where?' he asked again.

'You're talkin' to him,' replied Wood.

'Who?' asked Mitamura, understanding even less.

'Holly Wood!'

Mitamura was beginning to get irked. Why wasn't this man making any sense? 'Where?' he asked again. 'Where Hollywood?'

'I'm right here, you dumb Jap!' Wood told him. 'Can't you understand plain English?'

'Hollywood!' demanded the Commander.

'What?' answered the American.

'Where?'

'Here!'

Exasperated, Mitamura grabbed the nautical map of California and shoved it in Wood's face. 'Where Hollywood?' he demanded. 'North? South?'

Wood finally understood what the Japanese Captain was asking him. 'Oh, you want me to tell you where Hollywood is! Well, why didn't you say so in the first place? That's easy! Hollywood is –' Suddenly, Wood caught himself. 'Oh, no, you don't!' he exclaimed. 'You thought you were gonna get me to tell you where Hollywood is, huh? Tryin' to sneak up on me, just like you did at Pearl Harbor, huh? Plannin' to bomb John Wayne's house, ain't ya?'

Ashimoto picked up on the one word he understood. 'John Wayne!' he repeated.

'I knew it!' shouted Wood. 'Well, I ain't tellin' you nothin'. You can torture me, or do anything you want, but my lips are sealed. Mum's the word!' Now Wood noticed von Kleinschmidt hovering nearby. 'Jesus Palomino!' he cried. 'A Nat-zee! You're all in cahoots! Well, I'll tell you somethin', Mister Heinie, I fought your kind in the Great War, and we kicked the livin' hell outta youse!' Wood jumped to his feet and began singing, loudly, proudly, and out of tune. 'Over there! Over there! Send the word, send the word, over there!'

Von Kleinschmidt's command of English was far better than Mitamura's, and he had understood every word. He was extremely angered at being insulted by a common American peasant, so he stepped over to him and slapped him hard across the face. Then he shoved Wood back into the chair.

Wood kept singing through it all. 'That the Yanks are comin', the Huns are runnin' . . .'

Now Ito walked in with the chassis and guts of Wood's radio. He had finally removed the cabinet, which he had discarded on deck. Wood was outraged upon seeing this – that radio had been a birthday present from his sister in Oxnard. Again Wood jumped to his feet in protest. 'Hey! What'd you bust up my radio for? What's the big idea?' He was about to attack Ito, but he was immediately subdued by several Japanese and shoved back into his chair. Three sailors held him down.

'Search him!' Mitamura ordered in Japanese.

The three sailors began going through Wood's pockets. Wood started to resist, then thought better of it. He was heavily outnumbered. 'Aw, go ahead and search me if you want,' he told them. 'I ain't got nothin' of any use to you.'

Ashimoto took charge of the search and began removing items from Wood's pockets. First he produced a rabbit's foot.

'One genuine American jackrabbit's foot,' explained

Wood. Ashimoto examined it, totally bewildered by its purpose, then handed it to Mitamura. Mitamura was likewise bewildered. He handed to to another crew member, who similarly examined it and passed it around.

Ashimoto found the keys to Wood's pick-up truck.

Again Wood explained. 'One set of genuine United States steel truck keys to one General Motors pick-up truck made in Detroit City, USA!' Again the Japanese examined them and passed them around.

Ashimoto pulled out Wood's pocket-knife and opened one of the blades.

'One authentic early American Harry Carey knife,' Wood told them. 'Go ahead and pass it around. Maybe some of you'd like to use it.' However, none of them took his advice.

Ashimoto discovered Wood's hip-flask.

'One bottle of Grade A American moonshine!' said Wood proudly.

Mitamura took the bottle, opened it, smelled it, then tasted it. He immediately spat it out with revulsion! The other Japanese sampled it, and they too reacted the same way.

'Now that's what I call a waste of fine liquor!' said Wood.

Now Ashimoto found an opened box of Crackerjacks in Wood's coat pocket. He examined it curiously – he had never seen anything like this.

Once again, Wood explained. 'One ten-cent box of delicious, nutritious caramel-coated Crackerjacks!'

The Japanese crowded around to have a look. It was a mystery to all of them, and the picture of the young sailor on the wrapper confounded them even more. Mitamura stepped forward and took the box to see for himself. He stared at the words printed on the package, but his English was not good enough to make sense out of it. He shook the box, but was unable to identify the contents by the sound.

He handed it back to Ashimoto. 'Open it,' he ordered.

Ashimoto carefully peeled off part of the wrapper and delicately opened one end. He poured some of the Crackerjacks out on the table. The Japanese chattered excitedly and moved in for a closer examination. They picked at the caramel corn and peanuts, sniffed them, and even ventured a taste. Then Ito came over to see what was going on. He examined the box, then poured out the rest of the contents. In the midst of the remainder of the caramel corn was a small white envelope: the surprise package. Ito had no idea what it was. He held it up with an exclamation of surprise, and then, after everyone had seen it, proceeded to open it. He exercised extreme caution, tearing the paper open with deft co-ordination, not knowing what to expect. The other Japanese watched with hushed curiosity. Wood, of course, knew exactly what to expect, and shook his head, laughing to himself at how ridiculous it was to see a group of grown men getting all worked up over a box of Crackerjacks.

Ito pulled back the white paper package and discovered a tiny toy compass, the size of a nickel. His eyes lit up and he shouted with glee. A compass! Yes, it was small; obviously, it was a toy; but it was still a compass, and even if it wasn't accurate enough to reckon their position, he could certainly use it to calculate the error on the ship's own instrument. He showed it to Mitamura and excitedly explained this tremendous stroke of luck. Mitamura examined the compass himself and nodded with delight. The excitement quickly spread to the rest of the crew, and a joyous cheer of salvation went up!

Wood looked around at the ecstatic Japanese, unable to understand what they were all so happy about ... and then it suddenly dawned on him. They had been asking him where Hollywood was, so obviously they were lost. And now they were shouting Japanese hallelujahs over an itty-bitty compass! In an instant, Wood realized his duty as an American. He leaped to his feet, ripped the compass out of Mitamura's hand, and swallowed it! He immediately started choking – it hadn't gone down right – so he grabbed his flask of moonshine off the table and took a long, long swig to wash the compass down. And down it went! Wood belched.

The Japanese were horrified, to say the least. They stared at Wood with obvious anger, but Wood answered their stares with a cocky grin. 'Let's see you find Hollywood now!' he laughed.

Wood watched and listened as the Japanese conferred amongst themselves. The talk was sharp, quick and angered, and Wood couldn't understand a damned thing. Finally, Mitamura barked an order to Ashimoto, who ran quickly off through a doorway. Mitamura faced Wood once again, his anger replaced by smug assurance. Wood could tell that the Japanese leader had something up his sleeve, but whatever it was, Wood was sure he could handle it. He returned Mitamura's gaze with a sneer.

Now Ashimoto returned, carrying a bottle full of a brown liquid. Mitamura smiled upon seeing it, and Ashimoto unscrewed the cap. Wood watched with growing uneasiness. 'What's that?' he asked suspiciously.

Ashimoto said something in Japanese, and four sailors grabbed Wood to hold him tightly down in his chair. Ashimoto shoved the bottle against Wood's mouth and tried to get him to drink. Wood took one sniff of the brown stuff and immediately knew what it was. 'Prune juice!' he shouted with horror. 'Oh, no, you don't! Oh, no, you don't!' Wood jerked his head away, but it was a lost cause: the sailors grabbed his head, pushed it back, and one of them held his nose. The only way Wood was going to breathe was through his mouth, and as soon as he opened it, Ashimoto poured prune juice down his throat!

9

Santa Monica, California
2.09 p.m.

The Douglas family lived in a two-storey ocean-front home in Santa Monica. In fact, the cliff-side house commanded one of the finest views of the Pacific in the area, and it had been for that reason that Ward Douglas had over-extended his credit twelve years ago so that he could own it. However, in another hour or two, that fine ocean view would exist no longer. Ward Douglas was painting all of his windows black.

Ward Douglas was forty-one years old, an average-looking man with thinning brown hair. He was the vice-president of a real-estate company, and it had been his connections in the real-estate business that had enabled him to get his hands on the house he now owned. He was financially solvent, and tremendously dedicated to the American way of life. He had a wife, Joan; a daughter, Betty; and three young sons: Macey, twelve, Stevie, nine, and Gus seven. In short, Ward Douglas was the personification of the suburban American dream.

Like most Americans, Ward Douglas had been outraged at the attack on Pearl Harbor the previous week. He had been so outraged that on Monday morning, 8 December, he had gone to the recruiting office to volunteer for Army service. Unfortunately, Ward was forty-one years old, too old for duty. This fact outraged Ward almost as much as Pearl Harbor, because it meant he was going to miss out on another war due to his age. In 1917, Ward had attempted to join the Army so that he could fight in the Great War in Europe. At that time he was rejected because he was too young.

So Ward Douglas made up his mind that he was going to do everything he could to protect his family and his home. Unknown to his wife, he had purchased a shotgun and a pistol several days ago and had hidden them in the house. Ward hadn't told her about this because he knew that Joan hated guns with a passion, and that if she found out about it, it would lead to an argument. Ward lost more arguments than he won with his wife, so he decided that what she didn't know wouldn't hurt her.

Surprisingly, Joan had not offered much resistance to the idea of blacking-out the windows. She had assumed that this was as far as her husband was going to go with his ideas of home defence, so why not let him play at war for a few weeks? After all, painting the windows black was harmless enough, and it was certainly more practical than keeping all of the lights turned out at night. Ward was so certain that the Japanese were going to try to bomb the house, that all week he had forbidden the use of electric lights at night for fear the enemy 'planes would spot the house from the air. Now that it was Saturday, he had time to black out the windows. Joan figured she'd let him have his way, and after a few weeks, the hysteria would wear off and everything would return to normal. She couldn't have been more wrong.

Joan Douglas was forty, with blonde hair and blue eyes, and quite attractive. Her daughter had inherited her good looks. Joan Douglas could be very headstrong at times; that is to say, she was a nag. She was very good at it, so she got her way most of the time. But Joan was aware that things were beginning to change, and that her views and opinions were starting to carry less weight than usual. It was because of the war. For example, Betty had joined the USO without even consulting her. She had asked her father, and when he heartily approved the idea, she gave him the permission paper to sign. Joan's opinion had not been solicited because, as Betty put it, 'it was my patriotic duty and the right thing to do, and there was nothing to discuss'. Similarly, the boys had insisted on wearing their scout uniforms continuously because they 'had to stay in uniform during the war', and became extremely obstinate when she demanded they change their clothes. Ward supported them, so Joan had been forced to back down. She didn't like it, but there was really nothing she could do about it.

But when Joan discovered the double-barrelled shotgun under the bed, that was the last straw. She ran downstairs in a rage, carrying it awkwardly and confronted her husband in the living-room.

'Ward Douglas, where did this come from?!?' she wanted to know.

Ward slopped another brushful of paint across the windows before turning around. He was going to stand his ground this time, he decided, and to hell with what Joan wanted or didn't want. 'I picked it up on my way home Thursday,' he told her. 'Good thing, too – it was the last one they had in the store.'

'And just what did you think you were going to do with this?' she demanded.

'Defend my home!' answered Ward defiantly.

'You know how much I hate guns!' she shouted. 'I forbid you to keep this gun in the house!'

Ward put down his paintbrush, walked over to her and ripped the shotgun out of her hand. 'I don't really care what you want!' he said firmly. 'This country's at war, and I intend to defend our home!'

'Ward Douglas, if I've told you once, I've told you a thousand times, I will not allow guns in this house!'

While the family discussion continued to explore the various aspects of home defence in even more descriptive language, outside, a sedan full of USO girls pulled up to the Douglas home to drop off Betty and Maxine. Maxine waved good-bye exuberantly; Betty's wave was very half-hearted. Betty opened the gate and they walked along the side of the garage towards the house. Maxine was singing. Betty had a lot on her mind.

'I just can't do this to Wally,' Betty was saying. 'He's been waiting a long time for tonight.'

'Do you mean to tell me that you're going to turn your back on our men in uniform just so that you can go out with a criminal?' Maxine asked indignantly.

'Wally's not a criminal!' protested Betty. 'He's just . . .' well, he's just. . . .' She groped for a word. 'He's original!' she said proudly.

'You mean, he's a car thief!'

But before Betty could come to Wally's defence, an arm reached out of the back door of the garage and yanked Betty inside. Betty was shocked and startled, and it was a moment before she realized who the black-garbed figure was. 'Wally!' she exclaimed.

Wally grinned. Betty smiled too, but her relief quickly turned to worry. 'What are you doing here? If my father finds you here, he'll kill you!'

Now Maxine entered, realizing that this was the only place that Betty could have gone. She scowled with disgust upon seeing Wally.

But Wally ignored Maxine and proceeded to model his zoot-suit for Betty. 'I had to show you these new drapes I picked up for tonight. Pretty snazzy, huh? And watch these new steps I've been practising!' Wally did a few steps and a spin-out, slipped on an oil spot and fell right into a rack of garden tools! 'Well,' he explained, picking himself up, 'it works better on a wooden floor.'

Betty took a deep breath and prepared to drop the bomb. 'Wally, about tonight,' she started. But she could go no further. She couldn't find the words. She just didn't know how to break the news.

Maxine however had no such problem. 'What she's trying to say is that you can forget about the dance tonight,' Maxine said snidely. 'They won't even let you near the place dressed like that! It's a USO club now, for servicemen only, and we're Hostesses!' Maxine proudly pointed to her USO name-tag.

Wally turned to Betty and noticed that she too was wearing a name-tag. He didn't understand what this meant. 'What do you mean, *hostess*?' he asked. 'Is that like a waitress or something?'

Betty dropped her head, ashamed to look Wally in the eye. 'It means we're supposed to dance with men in uniform.'

'*Real* men,' added Maxine.

Wally still wasn't sure he understood. 'What do you mean? You enlisted in some screwy organization that tells you who you can or can't dance with?'

'I wanted to do something for our country,' Betty explained. 'After all, there is a war on, you know.'

Wally was hurt. 'What about us, Betty? I mean, what am I supposed to do?'

As usual, Maxine had all the answers. 'Get a uniform,' she told him.

Wally glared at her. '*This* is my uniform!' he said proudly, pointing to his zoot-suit.

Betty was all twisted up inside. Why couldn't she make Wally understand? 'Wally, you've got to believe me!' she said. 'I didn't know what I was getting myself into! I didn't know they weren't going to let you in!'

Wally could see that she was completely sincere.

'Betty, do you want to go out with me tonight?' he asked calmly.

'I don't know!' She was practically in tears. She honestly didn't know what the right thing to do was.

But Wally knew that he wanted to be with Betty tonight more than anything else in the world. He also knew he couldn't make her go out with him, and that this was certainly not the time to try to force her into a decision. All he could do was to put the odds in his favour. 'I'll tell you what,' he said with complete understanding. 'I'll meet you in front of the dance hall at eight. If they won't let me in, we'll do something else. We'll go to a movie or something. How does that sound?'

It sounded easier than saying no, thought Betty, but before she could reply, Maxine started in on her. 'Why, you dirty traitor!' Betty turned her head away from both of them.

She glanced through the window in the back door and saw her father approaching the garage with the shotgun. She was mortified. 'Oh my God! Here comes my father – and he's got a gun!' She turned anxiously to Wally. 'Quick, go out the other door,' she told him, pointing to the main sliding garage door. 'I'll stall him!'

'Do we have a date?' asked Wally in a loud whisper.

'I don't know!'

'Will you think about it?' he asked.

'Yes! Now go! Hurry!'

Wally started for the car-port door, then realizing he had forgotten something, ran back and kissed Betty. 'I'll see you tonight!' he grinned, then ran back towards the sliding door.

Betty went out the back door, pulling Maxine with her. 'If you say one word about this, Maxine, I'll brain you!' she warned. Then she waved happily to her father. 'Hi, Daddy! How are things around the house?'

'Just fine,' said Ward, suspecting nothing. 'Hello, Maxine. How was your meeting?'

While Betty continued to make small talk with her

92

father, Wally tried the sliding door – but it wouldn't budge! He tried it again, jerking harder, but to no avail. Wally had no way of knowing that Ward had locked the door from the outside with a padlocked hasp! After one more vain try, he looked around for another way out: there wasn't any. He couldn't go through a window without being seen from the front yard, and there were no other doors. Then Wally figured he could hide in the car. He tried the doors, but the car was locked too. There was no other hiding place in the garage, just a workbench, some tools and some gardening equipment. Then Wally glanced up: there was a storage area that had been made by throwing several wooden planks across two beams. It wasn't the sturdiest-looking place in the world, but it had to be one hell of a lot better than being discovered by an irate father with a shotgun! Wally jumped on the workbench and proceeded to climb up there.

Outside, Betty was stalling her father as best as she could, telling him the most boring details of the USO meeting. Ward was sick of hearing about it already. 'You know, Betty,' he interrupted, 'it really makes me proud to know you'll be spending your time with our boys in uniform instead of that car thief you were running around with. Now why don't you go in the house and tell your mother all about it?' He turned away from her and walked through the garage door. Betty gulped, expecting the worst. Maxine smiled, expecting the best! Ward entered, expecting only to get some more black paint to finish the job he had started.

Ward had lost the argument with Joan, at least for the time being, and that was why he was carrying the shotgun. He had agreed to keep it in the garage. Joan had been more adamant than usual, insisting on 'no guns in this house!' But Ward knew he would have the last laugh: there was still the ·44 revolver he had hidden under a cushion on the couch.

And so Wally Douglas entered the garage without having the slightest reason to expect to find Wally in there. And Wally certainly wasn't about to give him any such reason. He had scrambled into the storage loft just in time, and now watched as Ward obliviously sauntered over to the workbench, yanked a tarpaulin off a large assortment of paint cans, and proceeded to stir up a can of black. It looked like Ward was taking his time, so Wally figured he might as well get comfortable. He leaned back on a 100-pound bag of fertilizer. The beam creaked! It wasn't sturdy at all! Wally held his breath – luckily, Ward was too wrapped up in his thoughts to notice. Now if the damned thing would just hold for a few more minutes until Ward left. . . .

Out in the yard, Betty and Maxine had been listening for some sound from the garage. Betty sighed with relief. Her father had been in there long enough to have discovered if Wally was still in there. Maxine reacted with disappointment, overdoing it a little for Betty. 'Damn!' she said, 'I didn't hear any gunshots! I guess he got away.'

As Betty turned towards the house, she noticed that a large old, worn-out European-style rug had been laid out over a section of the front lawn, with a large stone on each of the four corners. 'What's that rug doing out here?' she wondered out loud. And then she noticed that her brand-new blue hat was sitting right in the middle of the rug, the hat she was going to wear to the dance tonight. 'My hat!' she exclaimed. 'That's my brand-new hat!' This smacked of the work of her brother Macey. She ran over to get it, pulling Maxine along with her. But as they stepped on to the rug, the entire carpet gave out from under them, and Betty and Maxine dropped into a huge hole in the earth. They screamed. It was all a booby trap!

94

Macey, Stevie and Gus all howled with delight! They had seen the whole thing from their hiding-place behind the white picket fence which ran around the Douglas property. Now they gleefully galloped out into the yard and ran around the eight-foot-deep pit shouting 'Surrender! Surrender!' Macey wore his boy-scout uniform and carried a baseball bat in the end of which he had driven a dozen five-inch nails – quite a formidable weapon. His younger brothers wore their Cub Scout uniforms along with pots on their heads: home-made helmets. They were armed with their own toy guns. They looked down at their sister and her friend in the pit, all tangled up in each other, and laughed.

Betty was livid, to say the least. 'Macey Douglas, what is the meaning of this?' she screamed.

'You fell in our Jap Trap!' laughed Macey. 'We're gonna cover it over with sticks and junk and when the Japs sneak up, they'll fall in!'

'Yeah!' agreed Gus. 'Then it's curtains!' He drew an imaginary knife across his own throat.

'The Japs are real short, so they won't be able to climb out,' added Stevie.

'We're gonna put 'em all over the neighbourhood,' exclaimed Macey.

'Does your father know about this?' screamed Betty.

'Sure!' replied Macey. 'He thunked it up!'

Indeed, in a manner of speaking, it had been Ward's idea. The kids had been pestering him all week because they wanted to do something to help out in the war effort. The perfect opportunity had developed yesterday when Ward had some workmen come to remove an old septic tank that had been rotting below the front yard for years. This morning, instead of having them come back to fill up the open pit, he had them cart the dirt away. Ward told the kids they could make it into a booby trap for enemy saboteurs. So far, the kids were doing an admirable job.

'Macey Douglas,' yelled Betty, 'when I get my hands on you, I'm gonna kill you!'

'See you around, sis!' shouted Macey, who then ran off with his brothers. Betty and Maxine were left in the pit to climb out on their own. And they soon discovered that getting out was not going to be easy. Maxine gave Betty a boost, and Betty promptly tumbled back down. Betty attempted to give Maxine a boost, but Maxine was too heavy for her. While they struggled, they heard a rumble of what sounded like approaching trucks. The rumble steadily increased, and it was soon accompanied by the voices of men. Whatever it was sounded like it was moving into the yard. If only Betty and Maxine could see out of the hole.

In the house, Joan had decided to vacuum the living-room. It was quite a mess, especially with her sons constantly tracking dirt all over the place. As she cleaned under the sofa, she noticed how filthy the couch was. Why not clean it too, she figured. So, she pulled back the cushions and promptly jumped back with a start. From under a cushion protruded the barrel of Ward's hidden revolver. Joan was enraged. She picked it up like a dead fish, carrying it by the tip of the barrel and holding it away from herself at arm's length. She marched towards the front door, preparing to toss it outside as if it were rubbish. 'I will not have guns in this house!' she muttered under her breath. But before she could reach to open the door, it was pushed open by the gigantic barrel of a Bofors 40 mm anti-aircraft gun! Joan screamed and dropped the pistol. The 40 mm barrel was pointing directly at her head!

Sergeant Frank Tree ran to the door, taking charge of the situation. 'Move that thing forward, Reese!' he ordered. The cannon on wheels was still hitched to the back of their truck, which Reese was driving. Reese had backed it into the Douglas yard, but had backed it in a little too far! Reese shoved the truck into first gear and edged forward, while Sitarski, Quince and Foley walked along with the cannon to guide it. Tree turned to Joan apologetically. 'Excuse us, ma'am,' he said. 'The gun sort of got away from us there.' He walked away from Joan, leaving her standing there, white with shock.

Now Ward came running out of the garage to see what the commotion was all about. Macey, Stevie and Gus came running out too. Ward immediately recognized Tree as a Sergeant. 'What's going on here, Sergeant?' Ward wanted to know.

Tree glanced at some papers on the clipboard he was carrying. 'Are you Mister Ward Douglas?' he asked.

'That's right,' replied Ward.

'Mr Douglas,' said Tree, 'I'm Sergeant Frank Tree, United States Army Tenth Armored Division. Sir, the Coast Artillery Command has determined your property to be strategically advantageous for the installation of an aircraft defence battery.'

'A what?' asked Ward.

'This forty millimetre anti-aircraft gun, sir,' explained Tree, pointing to the cannon. 'We'd like to put it in your yard.'

Ward's amazed expression slowly became a smile. At last he was getting his chance to really do something in the war! Imagine, the Army needing *his* property to defend the shores of California! It was almost too good to be true.

Macey, Stevie and Gus were extremely excited. They jumped up and down all around Ward. 'Can we keep it, Dad?' they asked eagerly. 'Please, can we keep it?'

Ward turned to Tree with stars and stripes in his eyes.

'Son, I'll be proud to have this gun in my yard!' he said.

'That's the spirit that's going to win this war, sir!' said Tree, delighted. 'Now, if I could just ask you to sign these forms.' Tree handed Ward the clipboard and a pen.

'Oh, boy! Look what we got!' shouted the kids.

As Ward glanced over the forms, Joan stormed out of the house, completely shocked and irate about what was happening here. 'No!' she screamed. 'Absolutely not! I will not have this – this *thing* in my yard!'

'Nobody asked you!' Ward told her.

'Nobody has to ask me!' she shot back. 'This is my house too and I will not have that giant gun sitting outside my bedroom!'

'Well, you'd just better get used to it, Joan, because the gun stays!' And with that, Ward put his signature on the forms.

'Ward Douglas,' said Joan firmly, 'either that gun goes, or I go!'

'Then go!' Ward told her. 'Anything's better than being married to a Jap-lover!'

Joan was outraged. Ward had never talked to her like that before, and to say that in front of strangers! She clenched her hands into fists and prepared to belt him, but Tree interceded.

'Please, ma'am – sir! Let's not fight. If there's one thing I can't stand, it's Americans fighting Americans. I can't stand that.' Tree separated the two and turned to Joan. 'Now, ma'am, I understand your concern, but I want you to understand just one thing: that gun is built for only one purpose, and that's to protect American lives.'

'You hear that, Joan?' shouted Ward. 'American lives! You should be ashamed of yourself!'

'But why does it have to be in our yard, Ward?' asked Joan.

'Because the Army says so. For Chrissakes, Joan, we're at war! The whole goddamn world's at war! American boys are dead. Do you think I'm gonna sit idly by with my thumb up my ass? Hell, no! I'm gonna do my part.'

'Then why not join the Civilian Defense like Mr Scioli suggested?' countered Joan. 'You could become a block warden!'

'I'm not gonna run around with a whistle and a torch yelling "Lights Out!"' said Ward. 'That's not defence. You look at that,' he told her, pointing to the cannon. '*That's* defence!'

Tree turned to his men who had now moved the cannon a safe distance away from the house. 'Sitarski! Quince! Reese! Foley! Unhitch that ordnance and push it over into the centre of the yard!' Reese shut off the truck, and assisted the others in doing as Tree ordered.

In the garage, Wally had climbed down from the upper storage area, thinking he would finally be able to slip out unnoticed. But as he looked out the window in the back door, he discovered that that would be impossible. These were the same soldiers from the cafe, he realized, and if Betty's father didn't take a poke at him, he knew that Sitarski certainly would. So Wally just stood quietly at the window, watching and waiting.

Joan was rapidly running out of arguments to dissuade her husband from what was beginning to appear to be an irrevocable decision. She attempted one last strategy. 'Ward Douglas, the least you could do is to think about your children. After all, if we have this cannon in our yard, it'll make our home a target!'

'We're all targets in this war,' Ward told her. 'At least I'll be able to shoot back!'

'You?' Joan reacted with alarm. 'You're going to shoot this gun?' She turned to Tree. 'Sergeant, is my husband going to shoot this gun?'

'You're goddamn right I am!' proclaimed Ward.

Tree answered Joan's question as well. 'No, ma'am,' he said, 'that's against regulations. The Army will be sending some men over on Monday. They'll actually install the gun and will be assigned to it, to maintain it, and fire it if that ever becomes necessary.'

But Joan's alarm increased. 'You mean a whole group of soldiers will be living in my yard?'

Tree was getting exasperated with all this domestic squabbling. Why couldn't he be in Europe right now, beating down the Huns? 'Ma'am, I really don't know,' he told Joan. 'I'm a Tank Commander. My men are a tank crew. Today we're just—'

Now Ward interrupted him. 'Monday?' Ward asked with extreme paranoia. 'Did you say Monday, Sergeant? You mean I've got to wait till Monday before a gun crew is sent over? Jesus! Maybe you'd better check me out on this thing, just in case.'

'I'm afraid I can't do that, sir,' said Tree. 'It's against regulations.'

'Sergeant, don't you realize how serious this situation is? Monday is two days away. We may all be dead by Monday! Don't you know that two squadrons of Jap 'planes tried to bomb San Francisco last night? What if they try something like that down here?'

'Well, Mr Douglas, I'm afraid you'll just have to take your chances with everybody else.'

Joan still had a lot on her mind too. 'Where are they going to go to the bathroom?' she asked the Sergeant.

Tree hadn't the slightest idea what she was talking about. 'Who?'

'These soldiers who are going to be living in our yard!' said Joan. 'Where are they going to go to the bathroom?'

'Ma'am I really don't know. I don't know anything about any of this. We just deliver the guns. We don't know what the Army's going to do with them, or anything else. All I can do is suggest to you that you go back in your house and do whatever it is a housewife is supposed to do.'

Sitarski, Quince, Reese and Foley were moving the gun up a slight incline into the middle of the yard. Sitarski was on the coupling, pulling backwards, while the others were around the front, pushing. Sitarski was straining like hell; Reese, Foley and Quince were taking it easy, letting Sitarski do all the work. Sitarski didn't realize it, but he was heading backwards towards the Jap Trap!

And in the Jap Trap, Betty had managed to climb on to Maxine's shoulders. This time it looked like she was finally going to be able to make it out.

Sitarski continued backward, his feet moving ever closer to the edge of the pit. When he was mere inches away, he stopped. Suddenly, Betty's hand reached out of the hole and grabbed on to Sitarski's ankle. Startled, Sitarski lost his grip on the gun. The sudden release on his end was too much for the other three and the cannon began rolling towards the house! Quince, Reese and Foley chased it and managed to stop it about five feet away from the front door.

Sitarski turned to see who the hand on his ankle belonged to. He gazed into the Jap Trap and saw Betty Douglas. Even covered with dirt she was a knock-out, and for Sitarski, it was lust at first sight. He smiled at her, then reached down and gently lifted her out of the hole, into the sunlight. She seemed to weigh nothing in his arms.

Betty wasn't sure what to think. This soldier was certainly a lot more attractive than the ones she had seen at the USO club. And he did have a rather nice smile.

'I always imagined an angel like you coming from up there,' quipped Sitarski, nodding towards heaven. At the same time, he put a hand on her arse and gave her a good firm squeeze!

Wally, watching from the garage door window, saw Sitarski's move and was outraged. 'You bastard!' he muttered under his breath.

Betty was just as outraged. She now knew exactly what to think of this soldier. 'What do you think you're doing?' she asked him, totally irate. 'Practising the *Manual of Arms*? Let go of me this instant!'

She was referring to his hand on her arse, and of course, Sitarski knew that, but he couldn't allow such an obvious moment to go by without taking full advantage of it. 'Whatever you say, doll,' he grinned. He promptly let go of her and dropped her back into the hole. He chuckled.

Betty did not think this was very funny. It was a good thing the carpet was in the bottom of the pit to cushion her fall. Maxine on the other hand was not at all concerned about the humour of the situation. She had needed only one look at Sitarski's handsome features to fall hopelessly, desperately in love with him. 'Remember,' she told Betty, 'I saw him first! He's mine!'

At the same time, Ward had turned to Tree, addressing himself to the problem of the rolling anti-aircraft gun. 'Sergeant, I've got some cement blocks in the garage. Maybe we could shove 'em under those wheels.'

Tree nodded, then called to Sitarski. 'Sitarski! Quit goldbrickin'! Get a cement block out of the garage and stabilize that ordinance!'

Sitarski grumbled and headed for the garage.

Earlier, Wally had come to the conclusion that today just wasn't his day. Now he was sure of it. He saw Sitarski approaching the garage and quickly scrambled back up onto the loft storage shelf. Again the beam creaked loudly under Wally's added weight. It seemed less sturdy than before. He prayed that it would continue to hold him.

Wally watched as Sitarski entered and began to rummage around for a cement block.

Outside, a very strange-looking vehicle pulled up at the Douglas residence. It was once a 1939 Plymouth, but it was now hard to tell, since most of the body was covered with half-inch steel plate. The headlights were painted blue and masked into slits, the inside was lined with sandbags, and there was a gun rack with a Springfield rifle and fixed bayonet in the back! The entire body was painted with hand-written slogans, such as 'Remember Pearl Harbor', and 'Let's Slap the Jap Right off the Map!'

Tree stared at the vehicle in utter disbelief. He turned to Macey who was standing nearby. 'What in the name of the Declaration of Independence is that?' he asked the boy.

'Oh, that's our neighbour, Mr Scioli,' explained Macey. 'He turned his car into a tank!'

Dominic Scioli stepped out from his 'tank' and walked into the Douglas yard. Scioli was about fifty, and his large black handlebar moustache gave him the appearance of an organ-grinder. He wore a Civilian Defence helmet and armband, and carried a baton. Accompanying him was Claude Crump, also about fifty. Crump had grey hair, and his habit of chain-smoking indicated his nervous nature.

Joan immediately ran over to Scioli. 'Dominic, am I glad to see you!' she said. 'Maybe you can talk some sense into Ward – I think he's gone crazy!'

Scioli raised his hands in a gesture of helplessness. 'Joan, I'm not here to take sides in any arguments. The only reason I came by was to try once more to convince Ward to do some airplane spotting.'

'Are you the Precinct Captain around here?' Tree asked.

'No, I'm just in charge of airplane spotters,' answered

Scioli. 'They're using my Ferris wheel down at Ocean Park. You can see it from here.' Scioli pointed south down the coast. Sure enough, Tree could see the amusement park, Santa Monica Pier, and the Ferris wheel all about a mile away. 'Terrific vantage point,' continued Scioli. 'Overlooks the ocean and you can see everything. On a clear day you can see Catalina Island.'

Ward had spotted Scioli and came over, beaming with pride. 'Hey, Scioli, see that?' he asked, pointing to the 40 mm cannon. 'Those Japs ain't gonna drop any bombs on this soil!'

'Look, Ward,' Scioli said, 'I'm still short on aircraft spotters. I need two more men to put up on the Ferris wheel. Unfortunately, Claude here is afraid of heights.'

'Oh, no! Not me!' Ward declared vehemently. 'I'm not gonna sit up in some Ferris wheel and freeze my ass off all night. I'm in artillery now!'

Scioli pleaded with him. 'Ward, it's only for a few hours a week. And it's an important job. Somebody's gotta watch for enemy 'planes!'

'He's right, honey,' added Joan. 'Spotting the 'planes is a very important job.'

'I don't want to just spot Japs! I want to shoot 'em down! I want to blast those bastards right outta the sky! Like this!' And with that, Ward ran over to the gun, jumped on to the seat, and started cranking the barrel around.

Scioli looked at Joan and shook his head. 'See you later, Joan. Come on, Claude.' Scioli and Claude went back to Scioli's armoured vehicle and drove off.

Quince turned to Tree and whispered confidentially. 'That crackpot better hope that thing never is fired. The report'll break every window in his house.'

Tree shrugged. 'That's his problem.'

Again, Ward cranked the gun barrel around. This

time, his sudden movement caused the cannon to start rolling towards the house again. All of the soldiers ran over to stop it.

In the Jap Trap, Betty had once again climbed on to Maxine's shoulders and this time she was going to get out. She had made up her mind that she was going to give that soldier a piece of her mind.

While in the garage, Wally watched as Sitarski lifted a very heavy cement block up off the floor. Sitarski fumbled it, crunching his little finger, which triggered a psychotic rage. 'Goddamn son-of-a-bitch!' he screamed. 'Goddamn this Army shit!' He picked up a fishing rod and snapped it in two. Then he picked up a rake and broke it in half over his knee. Then he started kicking the family car. 'Do this! Do that! Stabilize that ordnance! The hell with you, Sarge!' he cursed. 'You can stabilize your goddamn ordnance yourself!' With that, Sitarski picked up the cement block and slammed it down on the bonnet of the car. He made a huge dent in it. He raised the block again, but then saw Betty approaching the back door. She hadn't seen his outburst. Sitarski managed to get an immediate grip on himself.

Betty entered. Her dress was stained with dirt, and she was good and mad! Wally grinned, he could tell that Betty was really going to let him have it, and he couldn't wait. Betty confronted Sitarski, fuming. 'Don't they teach you manners in the Army?' she asked sarcastically. 'You know, there are proper ways of introducing yourself!'

Sitarski turned on his most practised, result-getting, lady-killing charm. 'You're right,' he smiled, putting down the block. 'I'm Corporal Chuck Sitarski, United States Army. My friends call me "Stretch".' He extended his hand warmly. But Betty didn't make the slightest effort to shake it. She just glared at him.

'Well, I can see you're still sore,' Sitarski continued.

'And you have every right to be. I acted like a real louse, and I apologize. If it'll make you feel better, you can haul off and slug me.' Sitarski turned his jaw towards her and pointed out an appropriate place for a fist. 'Go ahead, plant one right on the kisser. I deserve it.'

Betty was totally disarmed. How could she argue with someone who was agreeing with her? And besides, he really didn't seem *that* bad. In moments, her anger vanished, and she became her usual sweet self. 'Don't be ridiculous,' she said. 'I'm not going to hit you.'

Sitarski smiled. 'I'm glad to hear that. I didn't figure you for that kinda girl.'

She couldn't resist the opportunity to flirt with him. 'What kind of girl did you figure me for?' she asked coyly.

Wally was shocked that Betty could be playing along with this rat. He leaned forward attentively to make sure he didn't miss a word of this. The beam creaked again. There was no doubt about it, it was getting progressively weaker.

Sitarski pretended to think it over a moment, and then launched into a patter he had used on a hundred other women, with excellent results. 'I figure you're the kind of girl who's decent. . . .' He paused for exactly the right amount of time; ' . . . clean . . . sincere . . . good-looking . . . good cook, good housekeeper. . . . You're the kind of girl a guy could get serious about. You're the kind of girl we're fighting this war for.'

Wally rolled his eyes and shook his head. Sitarski had to be a real sap if he thought Betty would fall for a load of crap like that!

Wally, however, was quite mistaken. Betty was falling for it hook, line and sinker. She blinked her lovely inno-cent eyes at Sitarski, overwhelmed at the idea that the war was in fact being fought for her. 'I am?' she asked sweetly.

'Absolutely,' replied Sitarski, with as much sincerity as he could muster. He noticed her USO badge and realized how easy this was going to be. He was practically inside of this broad's pants already! 'And I'd say you're the kind of girl who's interested in doing her part. You know that a lonely guy who's away from his home, his family and his friends, would give anything to spend a little time with a girl like you before he ships out. And I'll bet that's why you joined the USO, isn't it, Betty?'

Betty was astonished that this young man could know so much about her so quickly. 'How'd you know that?' she asked. 'How'd you know my name?' Then she remembered her badge, and turned red. 'Oh . . . !' She dropped her head with embarrassment.

Wally's heart was pounding. The blood was rushing to his head. If only he could do something, something to show her what Sitarski was really like. But he was helpless. He shifted his weight slightly, and the beam creaked very loudly. Sitarski glanced up, but Wally managed to hide his head behind the sack of manure before he could be spotted. If Wally had been able to see the spot where the beam joined the wall, he'd be even more worried: the entire shelf was holding on by mere splinters!

Sitarski looked back at Betty. It was time to get to the point. 'Betty, could I ask you something?'

She looked up at him and nodded.

'Well, you see, I'm kind of unfamiliar with these USO clubs and how they work, and all, but if an ordinary Joe like me sort of wandered into one and came up to a girl like you, and he asked her to dance. . . .' Again he paused for just the right moment. ' . . . Do you think she'd say yes?'

She smiled. 'It's possible.'

He smiled back. 'What USO club do you work at?'

But before she could answer, the few remaining

splinters that had been holding the beam gave way, and the entire upper shelf collapsed. Wally fell to the floor, followed by the 100-pound bag of fertilizer which covered him in manure. Betty and Sitarski were both startled, stunned and shocked.

Wally began to pick himself up. It took Betty only a moment to recognize him. 'Wally!' she said, appalled. And then Sitarski recognized him. 'You!' he shouted.

Wally brushed off some of the fertilizer and turned urgently to Betty. 'Betty, you can't listen to this joker! He's no good, believe me! He's just a smooth talker! All he wants is—'

Betty interrupted him, not interested at all in anything Wally was saying. She was too outraged for that. 'Wally Stephans, what in the world were you doing up there?!? You were spying on me, weren't you?'

'No, Betty!' Wally protested. 'You don't understand!'

'Oh, I understand fine, Wally,' she told him. 'This is the most disgusting, disgraceful thing you've ever done! I never want to see you again!' She headed for the back door.

'Betty, wait!' begged Wally. 'I can explain!'

Betty turned around – but not to Wally. She turned to Sitarski, and smiled sweetly. 'Stretch, I'll be at the Hollywood USO club tonight.'

'Swell!' said Sitarski enthusiastically. 'I'll see you there!'

Betty exited. Sitarski looked at Wally with a victorious grin. 'This isn't your day, is it, kid? Say, that suit of yours looks real nice with all that shit on it!' Sitarski laughed loudly.

Wally had had it with this arsehole. Because of Sitarski he had lost his job and his girl, and now he was going to do something about it. Wally clenched his hands into fists and started to move in on Sitarski. Sitarski was ready.

He would be more than happy to beat the shit out of Wally.

But just as Wally was about to lay into him, Ward ran in, followed by Tree and the other soldiers. They had heard the crash of the beam and storage shelf, and had come to investigate. Ward was outraged to see Wally.

'You!' he screamed, pointing an accusing finger at Wally. 'You lousy punk hoodlum, I told you I never wanted to see you around here again!' Then Ward noticed the shambles of the garage. 'What the hell did you do to my garage? And my car!' screamed Ward, noticing the dents Sitarski had put into the bonnet. 'Look what you did to my car!'

'What's going on in here, Sitarski?' Tree wanted to know.

'Sarge, this is that jerk waiter from that cafe. He followed us over here,' Sitarski lied. 'I think he's a spy – a fifth columnist!'

'You've got no proof of that,' responded Tree.

'Look at these clothes he's wearing!' shouted Sitarski. 'Anybody runnin' around in a get-up like that has gotta be a lousy Jap-lover!'

Tree took a good look at Wally's zoot-suit and shook his head. 'You do have a serious wardrobe problem, kid,' Tree told him.

Ward picked up a piece of two-by-four and shook it threateningly at Wally. 'That'll be the least of your problems when I get through with you!'

Once again, Tree interceded. 'No need for that, sir,' he told Ward. 'My men are trained for this sort of thing.' He turned to his men. 'Reese! Foley! Extract this transgressor!'

'With pleasure, Sarge,' grinned Reese. He and Foley grabbed Wally – Reese by the arms, Foley by the feet – and carried him out into the yard. 'Betty!' Wally shouted as they carried him along. 'You gotta listen to me! I can explain! Betty, please! Betty!'

Reese and Foley carried him to the street where a refuse truck just happened to be passing by. The two soldiers exchanged a grin, swung Wally back and forth to get some momentum going, and finally threw him into the rear of the moving truck! Wally landed in a pile of reeking rubbish, and was still shouting as the truck drove off. 'Betty! You've gotta believe me! I love you!'

In a few moments, the truck disappeared around a bend, and Wally's voice could no longer be heard. Ward turned to Tree. 'Thank you, Sergeant,' he said.

'You're welcome, sir,' said Tree.

10

Commander Akiro Mitamura once again stood on the bridge of his submarine and gazed at the foggy California coastline. He had let the vessel drift southward in the hope of sighting an identifiable landmark by which he could pinpoint their position, thereby making further attempts to obtain Hollis Wood's toy compass unnecessary. Unfortunately, he could see nothing that was of any help; furthermore, Mitamura knew that the longer the sub stayed surfaced, the greater their chance of being detected. Ito's continued attempts to repair the vessel's instruments had been futile, so Mitamura realized their best chance was still the compass which was somewhere in the American's digestive system. He could only hope they could retrieve it.

Mitamura handed the navigational charts back to Ito, who stood on the bridge beside him. 'We must submerge,' he told Ito. 'It is far too dangerous for us to remain surfaced for so long.' Ito nodded. Mitamura called the order into the intercom. 'Prepare to dive!' The Captain proceeded down the hatch; Ito followed.

Mitamura's destination was the ship's head, where the prisoner had been taken. Hollis Wood had been sitting on the toilet with his trousers and underwear around his shoes. Despite the two bottles of prune juice that had been forced down his gullet, he had not been co-operating with his captors. Wood leered at the two sentries who had their bayonets pointed at his bare chest, and sneered at

Ashimoto, von Kleinschmidt and the Japanese crew who were watching through the doorway.

'You devils ain't gettin' shit from me!' Wood told them for the umpteenth time. 'I been constipated all week, and there ain't nothin' you can do about it!'

Von Kleinschmidt stepped forward and confronted him. He had had quite enough of this ridiculous circus, and decided it was time to use the German method of persuasion. He addressed Wood in English. 'If it is problems of ze digestion, zere are other ways to make quickly your relief.' With that, he drew out his Nazi dagger and picked a fingernail with it. Von Kleinschmidt smiled sadistically at Wood.

Wood gulped. He didn't like the Kraut, and the idea of being cut open by his knife was not particularly appealing. It appeared he was going to have to co-operate, at least for the time being. Wood raised his arms in surrender. 'All right, all right, I'll give it my best shot,' he said, 'but you guys are askin' for an awful lot! I mean, Christ, look at the conditions here! You call this thing a toilet? Back home we call this a potty. A little baby's potty!'

Now Mitamura arrived to see what progress, if any, had been made. Wood watched as Mitamura conferred with Ashimoto and von Kleinschmidt. The German pointed to Wood and gestured with his dagger, this time speaking Japanese to the Commander. It appeared to Wood that Mitamura was considering what the Nazi was saying, so Wood decided he'd better speak up on his own behalf.

'Now, wait a minute, there, General,' Wood called out to Mitamura. 'I'm trying the best I can, but tell 'em I'm gonna have to have some privacy. I mean, how's a fella supposed to have a bowel movement with a buncha buffalo rifles pointin' at him? Sheee-oooot! I got enough trouble pissin' in the public rest-rooms!'

Mitamura understood the request, explained it to the others, and they discussed it. Even if Wood had been able to understand Japanese he wouldn't have been able to pick up much of the conversation because it was obscured by the sound of the warning buzzer, which let the crew know that the submarine was about to submerge. Wood didn't know the exact meaning of the warning buzzer, but when he saw the hurried activity of the Japanese sailors behind Mitamura, he was able to guess. He knew that if the ship submerged, he was going to have a helluva time trying to escape. He prayed that the Japs would give him a few minutes of privacy so that he could try something. Finally, he saw his captors nodding in agreement. Whatever was going to happen was going to happen now.

Ashimoto entered the head, and said something to the two sentries. They lowered their rifles and exited. Wood sighed with relief. Then Ashimoto removed the flush chain from the toilet, broke the lock on the door, and left, closing the door behind him.

The Japanese had decided to honour the American's request for privacy. After all, what could they lose? There was certainly no possibility of escape – there was only one door, and no windows. And they preferred not to kill him until all other possibilities of retrieving the compass had been exhausted. Ashimoto had removed the flush chain for obvious reasons: they could not risk having the compass flushed into the sea. In fact, had the flush chain not been removable, they would not have left Wood alone.

Now, Ashimoto, Mitamura and the sentries quietly gathered around the door to listen. They could plainly hear Wood groaning from inside. 'Uuuuuhhhh! Ooooo-uhhhh! Uhhh-eeeee-uuuhhh!'

Listening to this was a little more than Commander Mitamura could handle. After all, he was the Captain of this ship, and a gentleman. 'I feel that this is not honourable,' he told the others, and quietly left the area.

Wood continued to groan. 'Uhhhhh-ooooo-uhhhh! I'm pushin' as hard as I can!' However, had the Japanese opened the door at that moment, they would have discovered that Wood was not 'pushing' at all. In fact, he wasn't even sitting on the toilet. He had pulled his trousers up and was standing with his ear to the door, listening for any suspicious activity outside. He heard nothing besides some idle chatter, so he began to remove one of his shoes. Again he 'groaned' for his audience. 'Eeeee-uhhhhh! Uuuuuhhhhh!'

On the other side of the door, the Japanese continued to listen expectantly as the groans got louder. 'Eeeeaaayy-oouuhhh!' This was followed by the sound of a 'Splash – Ker-plunk!' The eyes of Ashimoto and the sentries lit up – they knew that could only mean one thing! Again they heard Wood groan loudly. 'Oooohhhhh! Uhhh-oh-eeehh! Better out than in!' This was followed by another 'Splash – Ker-plunk!' Then Wood sighed with great relief. 'Aaaahhhhhhh!'

Ashimoto nodded to the sentries. They immediately charged into the head, weapons drawn – only to discover that it was empty! Wood had vanished! They rushed over to the toilet, looked in and were astonished to find only a pair of shoes therein – Wood's shoes. Suddenly, they were frightened out of their wits by the sound of a rebel yell. 'WAH-HOOOOOOO!' Wood pounced upon them from above. He had been hanging by the pipes along the ceiling, waiting for this moment. Now Wood had the element of surprise on his side, and he made the most of it. He slammed the heads of the two sentries together, shoved them into the toilet, and slammed the toilet seat down on them.

Wood bolted out of there, like a bat out of hell and kicked Ashimoto in the gut, then ran through the sub's corridors like a maniac, hollering like an animal, pushing sailors out of his way, slamming their heads into walls. He retraced his route to the control-room where he scared the hell out of everyone with his screaming, and then headed for the ladder which led to the hatch.

The sailors that he had already run down regained their senses and dashed down the corridors in pursuit, yelling in Japanese 'Stop him!' One trigger-happy sailor took the advice too seriously, pulled out his automatic pistol and fired several shots at the escaping prisoner. The shots missed Wood and hit into the walls around him, puncturing them. Water began to pour into the submerging vessel, adding to the pandemonium Wood had already created. The Japanese didn't know whether to plug up the leaks first or to attempt to restrain the American, and the resulting confusion allowed Wood to reach the hatch ladder without incident.

At the top of the ladder, Ito was in the process of sealing the hatch shut. Wood scrambled up the ladder, grabbed Ito, threw him down, and began unscrewing the hatch. By the time Ito had regained his senses, Wood had thrown it open and was climbing out. But once again, Wood's belly got him stuck halfway through. Wood could see that the sub was rapidly submerging. Water was already pouring across the deck and began splashing around him, and Wood could see that unless he could free himself quickly, he'd be dragged down with the sub and would surely drown.

Ito quickly ascended the ladder and grabbed Wood's dangling legs. He yanked as hard as he could in an effort to pull the American back down, and promptly received a kick in the face for his trouble!

Wood continued to strain like hell, but try as he might, he still couldn't free himself. The water was up to his shoulders now, and below, he could feel someone tugging at his trousers.

Inside, one of the rifle-bearing sentries climbed up the ladder to assist Ito, but in so doing, accidentally jabbed the point of his bayonet into Wood's arse. Wood howled in pain, and leaped out of the hatch. The jab was all he needed! Ito fell backward down the ladder, left with Wood's empty trousers. Thousands of gallons of the Pacific poured through the open hatch, but in a super-human effort, the sentry who was still on the ladder managed to get it shut.

Above, Wood swam away as fast as he could, clad only in his white boxer shorts. He found the wooden shell of his Cathedral Model radio, which Ito had earlier discarded on deck, drifting nearby, so he grabbed on to it and used it as a float. Wood headed for shore. Behind him, the submarine had completely disappeared.

11

Ocean Amusement Park, Santa Monica
Dusk

Dominic Scioli drove his home-made tank through Ocean
Amusement Park, towards the giant Ferris wheel which
overlooked Santa Monica Pier and the ocean. He was
accompanied by the two volunteers for tonight's aircraft
spotting shift, Claude Crump and the new man, Herbie
Kaziminsky. Well, 'man' wasn't exactly the right word
for Herbie. Herbie was eighteen, tall, skinny and wiry,
with too much energy. To call him obnoxious would be
an understatement. Scioli would have preferred to put
someone else up there with Claude, but Herbie was the
only volunteer he could find. At least Scioli didn't have
to spend five hours with the kid; Scioli could only hope
that Claude would get used to him. Unfortunately, from
the way things were going, the likelihood of that seemed
highly remote. Claude hadn't uttered one word to Herbie
during the entire trip over there. Well, Scioli thought, it's
wartime, and we all have to make sacrifices.

Scioli pulled up at the Ferris wheel and climbed out
of his vehicle. Claude and Herbie followed. Both of them
wore Civilian Defense helmets and armbands, and had a
lot of gear with them, including torches, lunchboxes with
thermoses, and binoculars. Claude carried a ·30 – ·06
Winchester lever-action rifle; Herbie had a ·44 Magnum
pistol shoved in his belt. Herbie also carried a large gunny
sack. Scioli and Claude had both been afraid to ask him
what was in it, and they were in no hurry to find out.

Herbie excitedly ran over to the Ferris wheel. 'Oh, boy!

A Ferris wheel!' he shouted with glee. 'I love Ferris wheels! We get to stay up there all night, huh?' Then he turned to Scioli with sudden indignation. 'Hey – wait a minute! We're not gonna have to pay, are we? I mean we're workin' for the government now!'

Scioli sighed with exasperation. This was only the eighth time he'd had to answer this same question. 'No, Herbie, you do not have to pay.' Scioli unhooked the padlock on the master control box which was mounted on the nearby electric control shed. All electric power for the amusement park was channelled through this shed.

Herbie came running over as Scioli opened the control box, and gazed with amazement at the three dozen knife switches within. 'Hey, how do you turn this thing on, anyway?' Herbie asked. 'I always wanted to run one of these babies!'

Herbie reached for a switch, but Scioli slapped his hand out of the way. 'Don't touch that!' he scolded. 'These are the master control switches! You start fooling around with these and you'll turn on the whole park!'

Scioli threw a switch and a motor whirred to life. He led Herbie and Claude over to the Ferris wheel, opened the safety bar on the bottom gondola, and gestured for the two of them to take their places. Herbie was in the seat before Scioli had even got the safety bar all the way open! Claude was a lot more hesitant. He reluctantly took his place in the car. Scioli picked up a telephone that was sitting on the platform and handed it to Claude. It had an extremely long cord. 'Now remember what you're supposed to do,' Scioli told them. 'If you see or hear any 'planes, pick up the 'phone and yell 'Army Flash!' That will connect you directly to Interceptor Command. Then you report what you saw, and where.'

'Hey, Mr Scioli, just how high up is this thing, anyway?' asked the kid. 'Is that cord gonna reach all the way up to the top?'

'Yes, Herbie, the 'phone company installed it specially.'

'I guess that means all our calls are gonna be long distance!' Herbie laughed loudly at his own joke, then elbowed Claude who wasn't laughing. 'Get it? Long distance!'

'Dominic, what if we see something?' Claude asked nervously. 'I'm shaky enough in high places as it is – I don't want to be stuck up there in an air raid. . . .' Claude leaned over to Scioli and whispered confidentially ' . . . with this kid! Jesus Christ, Dominic, they gave him a gun!'

'Believe it or not, the kid's a crack shot.' Scioli lowered his voice so Herbie couldn't hear the rest. 'Just do the best you can, Claude. I'll try to find a replacement for you.' With that, Scioli locked the safety bar closed. Herbie reacted with great disappointment.

'Hey, we don't have to use the safety bar, do we? What if we have to jump?' Herbie grinned and elbowed Claude again. Claude however did not find much to appreciate in Herbie's sense of humour. Neither did Scioli.

'The safety bar remains locked at all times!' screamed Scioli. 'And another thing, Herbie,' warned Scioli with an accusing finger. 'I don't want you acting up like you did last summer. No standing, and no rocking!'

Claude's eyes suddenly opened wide in terror. 'You mean, this thing rocks?'

Scioli hit the switch and the Ferris wheel jerked into motion. Indeed it did rock! Claude immediately turned white. 'Don't worry, Claude,' Scioli told him. 'Just don't look down and you'll be fine!'

Claude heeded the advice religiously: he immediately looked upward, and made up his mind not to look down, no matter what!

Scioli called to them once more before they got out of earshot. 'I'll be back for you at the end of your shift – ten o'clock!'

Herbie grinned as the gondola swept upwards towards the top of the fifty-five-foot structure. He looked over at Claude who did not appear to be enjoying himself. 'Believe me, you got nothin' to worry about,' Herbie reassured him. 'Nothin' can happen to you up here. I once rocked one of these cars 180 degrees and I didn't fall out! These things are completely safe – there's no way you can fall out, unless you want to. I was here a couple of years ago when that guy committed suicide from the top of this thing. He just stood up in the car, spread his arms out, and did a swan dive!' To demonstrate, Herbie stood up in the gondola and waved his arms. 'Who knows, maybe he thought he was gonna hit the ocean!'

Claude had closed his eyes and was gripping the safety bar as tightly as he could. 'Just sit down, please!' he whispered to Herbie.

Herbie obliged, adding a further comment that he knew Claude would appreciate: 'He was splattered all over the pier! What a mess!'

When they reached the top of the Ferris wheel, Scioli cut off the motor. A mild sea-breeze blew across their faces, and the vantage point offered a tremendous view of a sumptuous Californian sunset. Unfortunately, neither of them was enjoying this view. Claude was too obsessed with looking straight up to pay any attention to the red orb on the horizon. And Herbie, well, Herbie couldn't appreciate a sunset if it came up and burned him on the arse. Claude stuck a cigarette in his mouth and fumbled with his matches, trying to get it lit. His hands were shaking so much that it proved to be extremely difficult. Herbie looked down and watched as Scioli padlocked the control box and headed back to his 'tank'.

'Say! Look how little Mister Scioli is!' exclaimed Herbie. 'He looks like an ant! How high up do you think we really are? It looks like about a mile! Hey – do you think if I dropped a penny off of here and it hit Mr Scioli on the head, it'd kill him?'

At this point, Claude was willing to say anything to get the kid to shut up. 'Yes!' he answered.

'Really?' asked Herbie with doubt.

'No! I don't know!' The older man was perspiring gallons of sweat, and still trying to light his cigarette with his umpteenth match. In his mind, he cursed Scioli for putting him up here, he cursed himself for volunteering in the first place, and he cursed the Japs for having started this whole mess!

Herbie on the other hand was having a marvellous time! He especially enjoyed making Claude as uncomfortable as possible – that was the kind of kid Herbie was. He rummaged through his lunchbox in search of something to eat. He pulled out a grapefruit, examined it, then looked over at Claude. 'Hey, this grapefruit is rotten. Is it okay if I throw it over the side? You don't mind, do you? I just want to see how long it takes to hit the ground!'

Claude never looked over at him, nor made any effort whatsoever to answer. He simply closed his eyes tightly.

Herbie smiled, then held the grapefruit over the side, keeping his eyes on Claude. 'Well, here goes!' But Herbie didn't let go of it – he just kept watching his partner. 'Wow! Look at that! Look at it go! Going ... going ... going. ...' Finally Herbie let it go. The fruit plummeted towards the pier, ' ... going ... gone!' The grapefruit resounded with a SPLAT on impact. It was loud enough for Claude to hear. The older man's eyes bulged completely out, and his complexion turned several shades of bright green: it had been a full ten seconds until impact!

Herbie was delighted at this reaction. 'Wow!' he exclaimed, 'I didn't think we were *this* high up! Aw, I forgot to time it! I shoulda timed it – then I coulda figured out exactly how high we are, because objects fall at thirty-two feet per second! Then I'd have known for sure!'

Claude had had all he could take of this! He exploded, and screamed at the top of his lungs. 'Would you just shut up about heights?!? I don't want to hear another word about heights!'

There was a long, long moment of total silence. Then Herbie licked his finger and checked the wind.

'I sure hope the wind picks up.'

'Just shut up!' Claude screamed. 'Don't say another word to me!'

Herbie shut up. Completely. There was not a sound from the top of the Ferris wheel for a full minute. Claude heaved a sigh of relief. He was proud of himself – he had shown the kid who was boss around here, and the kid had understood. He just might make it through the night after all. Then Claude noticed out of the corner of his eye that Herbie was rummaging around in that gunny sack of his. What the hell is in there, Claude wondered. He didn't have to wait long to find out. In a few moments, another head appeared between the two of them. Claude's mouth dropped open and his cigarette fell out: it was a ventriloquist's dummy! The wooden dummy was clad in a sailor's suit, and looked exactly like Herbie! Claude could not believe what he was seeing, nor could he believe that he was actually going to have to spend four or five hours of his life here!

The dummy, controlled by Herbie, turned its head around and stared at Claude, clicking its eyes back and forth. Claude stared back, dumbfounded. There was a long silence; then the dummy 'spoke'.

'Afraid of heights, huh? Me too!'

Claude turned his head away and attempted to light another cigarette.

The dummy turned around and stared at Herbie, an irate expression on its face. 'What'd you drag me up here for?' the dummy asked Herbie. 'You know I'm afraid of heights! I've got better things to do than to spend all night on a stupid Ferris wheel with you! What have you got, sawdust for brains?'

Claude fumbled another lighted match. The dummy turned around angrily. 'Hey! Watch where you're throwin' those matches, bud!'

Claude closed his eyes. It was going to be a long night.

Part Two

NIGHT

12

The periscope and radio antenna of Imperial Japanese Submarine I-19 cut through the moonlit waters of the Pacific, heading south. In the control-room, Ito was jury-rigging the guts of Hollis Wood's Cathedral Model radio into the instrument panel. He made one final connection to the power circuits – a spark exploded, and then the voice of an American radio announcer came on.

'... and this is KMPC, tonight broadcasting live from the Crystal Ballroom in downtown Hollywood! It's seven o'clock!'

Ito recognized one word: 'Hollywood!' He reacted instantly. 'Hollywood!' he cried. 'Captain,' Ito shouted in Japanese, 'listen! Hollywood!'

Mitamura hurried over and listened as swing music began: Sal Stewart's rendition of Count Basie's 'One O'Clock Jump'. Mitamura nodded, very pleased. 'Lock in on that signal, Ito,' he ordered. 'We'll follow it to Hollywood!'

'Yes, sir!' Ito replied, quite proud of himself.

The Douglas Home
7.01 p.m.

For the first time in a week, the Douglas family were sitting down to a civilized dinner, under electric lights. That is, the Douglas family, minus Betty – she had eaten earlier, because she was expected at the Crystal Ballroom USO Club no later than eight o'clock. Betty, dressed in her patriotic new outfit – a white dress, and a blue jacket with red trim, was in the porch now, waiting for the taxi she had called to arrive. Ward had insisted she take a taxi rather than drive herself, because he didn't want her driving around in the family car during an air raid.

Betty had been having second thoughts about Wally, 'Stretch' Sitarski and the USO all afternoon. Perhaps she had been a little rough on Wally ... but then again, he had had no business spying on her in the garage like that. No, Betty decided, she had her duty to perform at the USO club, and if she and Wally were going to make up, then he should be the one to apologize. Besides, she was genuinely looking forward to the dance and seeing 'Stretch' again ... he certainly was a handsome young man.

Judging from the radio, the dance was already in progress. Like the Japanese, the Douglases were listening to the KMPC broadcast from the Crystal Ballroom. The console radio in the dining-room played while the family began their first course: lima bean soup.

Macey Douglas hated lima beans. But thanks to the war, he had devised a way to make the soup palatable. Macey Douglas was slurping his soup through a gas-mask! He wore the gas-mask completely over his face, with the filtered snout end dangling in his thick green soup. By inhaling, soup came up through the hose, but the lima beans got stuck in the filter!

Joan Douglas looked up from her soup at her eldest son. She didn't know whether she was more disgusted by the sight of him, or the slurping and suctioning noises he was making. 'Macey Douglas, take that gas-mask off!' she shouted. 'That's no way to eat your soup!'

Macey replied with something unintelligible to his

parents. Gus translated. 'But Mom, he likes it that way. No lima beans can get through!'

Joan looked to her husband for support. 'Ward . . .' she beseeched.

Ward looked at Macey. 'Son, you heard your mother.' But Macey continued to slurp. Joan gave Ward a 'do something' look, so Ward simply reached over and yanked Macey's gas-mask off. A half-pint of thick gooey green soup poured out all over Macey's face and the table-cloth!

Joan was ready to raise hell, but before she could, Betty stuck her head in the doorway. 'Mom, Dad, I'm leaving now!'

'Have a good time, dear,' Joan told her.

Just as Betty started for the door, Ward rose from the table and called to her. 'Just a minute, Betty,' he said. He walked her into the living-room after flashing the porch light to the taxi waiting outside.

'Sit down, Betty,' he told her, indicating a chair. He pulled another chair up close to her. Ward had been putting off this talk with Betty all day, but now he could put it off no longer. He spoke in a low tone, confidentially. Betty realized that this was going to be important.

'Betty, you and I have never had much of a chance to talk . . . you know, a real father – daughter kind of a talk.'

Betty nodded, expecting the same sort of 'birds and the bees' talk that she had had from her mother three years ago. But it wasn't going to be quite like that.

'You see, Betty,' Ward continued, 'I'm too old to get into this war. Macey and the kids, well, they're too young. You're the only one . . . the only one I've got left. So it's up to you. Now, I don't know what they told you over at the USO club about how you're supposed to act to-night. But you're going to be meeting a lot of strange men, men in uniform, far away from their homes, lonely men, desperate men ... men with one thing on their minds. ...' Ward turned his head away a moment, took a deep breath and looked her straight in the eye. 'Show 'em a good time.'

Betty gulped. And outside, the taxi honked once again. It was time. ...

Chavez Ravine Army Barracks
7.03 p.m.

The radio in an Army barracks at Chavez Ravine, a few miles east of Hollywood, was also tuned to KMPC. This barracks was the current home of Sergeant Frank Tree and his men. At the moment, its three inhabitants were Privates Reese, Foley and Quince, who were all getting ready to go to the dance they were listening to on the radio. 'Stretch' Sitarski was conspicuous by his absence: he had already left for the USO club without permission, a good thirty minutes ago. Sitarski had promised to maim any man who blabbed his whereabouts to the Sergeant, and so Reese, Foley and Quince were all keeping their mouths shut. It was no big deal, they figured, since they all had leave tonight anyway. Sitarski had simply decided to start his a little earlier.

Sergeant Frank Tree now entered the barracks, all business-like. 'All right, you lovers!' he shouted. 'You can quit getting dolled up! We're not going to any dance tonight! We've gotta play wet-nurse to "Lulubelle"!'

'Aw, Sarge,' moaned Quince, 'we got plans!'

'The only thing you Joes are doing tonight is overhauling and lubricating one M-3 General Grant Tank! Those are orders from Lieutenant Cusimano!' Now Tree noticed that Sitarski was nowhere in sight. 'Hey! Where's Sitarski?'

129

Quince, Reese and Foley exchanged worried looks, wondering what would be worse – the wrath of their Sergeant or the psychotic rage of their Corporal.

'Well, you see, Sarge,' Quince stuttered, 'he had to, uh—'

'What he means, Sarge,' interrupted Reese, 'is that Sitarski said he was gonna have to, uh—'

'Actually, Sarge,' interjected Foley, 'he's going to be, uh—'

'Goddammit!' shouted Tree, 'if that goldbrick went AWOL, I'll ream his arse!'

Reese, Foley and Quince simply shrugged.

The Crystal Ballroom USO Club, Hollywood
7.04 p.m.

Corporal 'Stretch' Sitarski wandered around the USO club in search of Betty Douglas. He'd been there for fifteen minutes and had seen no sign of her yet. It was too much for him to believe that she might not show up – he had met girls like Betty Douglas before, and he knew that they always showed up, just like they always did their school homework.

On stage, Sal Stewart was conducting his big band in a rendition of 'Begin the Beguine'. Servicemen and USO Hostesses crowded the dance floor. Those that could did the 'Lindy Hop'. Those that couldn't, well, it was enough for some of these guys just to have their hands on a girl ... much to the disgust of those girls! In one corner of the dance floor, an artistically-minded fellow had chalked caricatures of Hitler and Tojo so that servicemen and their partners could take turns dancing on their heads.

Around the perimeter, and at the various tables, the Army, Navy and Marines all kept to themselves in tight cliques. It was an unwritten law that you could not mingle with a member of another service branch. When such mingling did occur, it inevitably led to fisticuffs, at which time some burly member of the Shore Patrol would rush over to break it up ... and perhaps break some heads as well.

At the refreshment tables, Hostesses and chaperones served punch, pie, cake, and hot dogs to the young men. Nearby, another group of Hostesses sat patiently in chairs, waiting for military men to ask them to dance. Among them was Maxine Dexheimer, in her new magenta print dress. Maxine had been the first of the Hostesses here tonight, not wanting to miss out dancing with any young man. Unfortunately, from the way things were going, it looked like she would also be the last one to leave. So far she had been doing a lot of sitting and a lot of eating, but very little dancing. It was then that she noticed 'Stretch' Sitarski walking around, without a partner! Maxine prayed that he would see her – then, could it be? Yes! He did see her! And he was coming this way! Her heart skipped a beat. Sitarski came right over to her and smiled a most charming smile. 'Hi,' he said.

Her heart soared. 'Hi!' she replied.

'So, where's your friend Betty tonight?' Sitarski wanted to know.

Maxine's heart came back down to earth. 'Oh, she'll be here pretty soon.' Then, she asked hopefully, 'Wanna dance?'

Again Sitarski smiled. 'Sure. . . .'

Maxine was on cloud nine! She stood up, ready, waiting . . . Take me, take me! she was thinking.

Sitarski continued, ' . . . as soon as she gets here.' He walked away, leaving Maxine, heartbroken, crestfallen, completely destroyed.

Maxine sat down again and watched as several of the really lovely Hostesses seated next to her were asked one by one to dance by some very homely servicemen – in fact, each man seemed uglier than the next. Of course, the girls had to dance, those were the rules. Then a shadow fell across Maxine. She was afraid to look up, expecting to see a buck-toothed, pimple-faced, runny-nosed jerk. She took a deep breath, then turned her eyes upwards. Her face lit up: he was a very good-looking young sailor, tall and lean – not as handsome as Sitarski, but certainly attractive. Maxine stood up and smiled. The sailor glanced at her name-tag and proceeded to introduce himself – but as soon as he spoke, he began to spit huge globs of saliva! 'Max-theen Dex-theimer! Pleathed ta meetcha! I'm Thee-man Fir-thst Clasth—' He sounded just like Daffy Duck!

Maxine interrupted him. 'Save it, sailor!' She pulled a handkerchief from her purse, dried her face, then accompanied him to the dance floor. Maxine was thankful that she liked the silent type.

Downtown Los Angeles
7.06 p.m.

Even a General in the United States Army had to relax sometimes, and that was exactly what General Joseph W. Stilwell had decided to do tonight. He had decided to get his mind off the insanity of defending southern California by going to the movies. So it was that Stilwell's motorcade, which included his entire staff and his dozen bodyguards pulled up to the Los Angeles Theater in the heart of downtown LA, where a brand new motion picture had opened the day before: Walt Disney's *Dumbo*.

Stilwell smiled as he stepped out of his car and looked up at the big letters on the theatre marquee. 'Dumbo!' he exclaimed. 'I'm going to enjoy this!' Stilwell liked movies, and especially enjoyed cartoons – they were among the few things that could make him laugh. He stepped into line behind several eleven-year-old kids, who stared with wide eyes and gaping mouths at the dozen MPs armed with machine-guns who accompanied the General.

Captain Birkhead helped Donna out of the car, even though she made it quite clear that she didn't need his help. Nevertheless, he gave her a big smile. She gave him a big cold shoulder.

Stilwell purchased tickets for himself and his entourage, then let out a sigh of relief, thinking that at least for the next two hours he would have a little peace of mind. But Stilwell had thought too soon. Before he was two steps away from the ticket booth, an Army motorcycle roared up to the front of the theatre and hopped the kerb. Pedestrians scattered off the pavement and the Harley zoomed up to Stilwell and his group. Both the cycle and the driver were covered with dust, dirt and muck. The driver wore a helmet and goggles and had a machine-gun slung over his back. There was something insane about this man. He turned to Stilwell and saluted half a pound of dust all over him! 'General Stilwell, sir!' he shouted. 'I'm Corporal Mike Mizerany with an urgent message from the 501st Bomb Disbursement Unit, in Barstow, sir!' Mizerany held out an envelope for him.

Stilwell did not want to take the envelope. He looked at Mizerany for a long moment, then asked him quietly, 'Is that from Colonel Maddox, son?'

'Yes, sir!' shouted Mizerany.

Stilwell shook his head. 'I thought I told Maddox to hold his position,' he muttered. He turned to his aide. 'Birkhead, see what he wants.'

Birkhead reached to take the envelope, but Mizerany withdrew it. 'I'm sorry, General,' he shouted, 'my orders are to give this message directly to you!'

Stilwell sighed, took the envelope, opened it and read the message aloud. ' "Request relief column. Invasion imminent. Murderers are parachuting from the skies." ' Stilwell looked at Corporal Mizerany. 'Son, are these Jap murderers or Kraut murderers?' he asked facetiously.

'The Colonel didn't specify, sir! However, he believes they're coming from hidden air strips in the Pomona alfalfa fields!'

'You've seen these murderers, son?' asked Stilwell.

'No, sir!'

'But Colonel Maddox has, is that it?'

'No, sir! Colonel Maddox has seen flashlight activity in the hills after dark! This leads Colonel Maddox to believe they're dropping them in at night!'

'You know, son,' said Stilwell very soberly, 'Colonel Maddox is mad.'

'If you say so, sir!' replied Mizerany without batting an eye.

Stilwell shook his head. He was getting that old sinking feeling. He had a problem here and he didn't know quite what to do about it. Certainly Maddox had to be relieved, but if his entire company had become as insane as this Mizerany fellow, then he'd have to relieve the entire company.

Captain Birkhead had been listening to all of this with increasing interest, and had been formulating a plan of his own. Birkhead's plan did not really deal with Maddox or Stilwell's problem; no, it rather dealt with his own problem concerning Miss Donna Stratton. Birkhead checked to be sure that Donna was in earshot before he stepped forward and spoke. 'Uh, excuse me, sir, but doesn't Colonel Maddox have some *'planes* out there, sir? I mean, after all, it is a bombing range.'

Donna's eyes lit up on hearing this. It was precisely the reaction Birkhead had hoped for.

'Well, he might have some 'planes out there,' replied Stilwell. 'So what?'

'Well, sir, I seem to recall that Maddox has a huge stockpile of bombs. Now, given the man's state of mind, there's no telling what he might do. Perhaps it would be wise for me to take a jaunt out there and see if I can appease the Colonel – with your permission, of course, sir.'

Stilwell stroked his chin. Something seemed a little peculiar here: it wasn't like Loomis Birkhead to volunteer for anything. On the other hand, he was going to have to send someone out to Barstow anyway, and Birkhead would be the logical choice. Stilwell looked at Birkhead with a slight tinge of suspicion, trying to fathom a possible ulterior motive. Unable to come up with one, he nodded. 'All right, Loomis. Take my car, get out there as fast as you can, and keep that maniac at bay. Above all, don't let him get his hands on an airplane!'

'Yes, sir!' answered Birkhead with a curt salute. He did an about face and walked towards Stilwell's car, slowing down as he passed Donna, muttering, ' . . . probably has at least two B-17's, either a P-38 or a P-40 . . . maybe both . . .'

And yes, Donna heard. She heard, and she desired, and she quivered with excitement. She looked back at Birkhead who stood coolly at the General's car, holding the door open . . . for her, of course. Then she turned back and followed Stilwell to the theatre doors. 'Uh, excuse me, sir,' she said, catching up to him, 'but I'm going to have to take a rain-check on the movie. I've got a splitting headache, and I'd really rather go home.'

'Why, that's a shame, Donna,' replied Stilwell sympathetically. 'Would you like me to call a cab for you?'

'No, sir, that won't be necessary,' she told him. 'I think I can persuade Captain Birkhead to give me a lift.'

Birkhead grinned triumphantly. In two seconds she was in the car. He closed the door, zipped around into the driver's seat, revved-up the engine and peeled out at eighty!

Stilwell was, of course, suspicious. However, it was too late to do anything about it now. And besides, he wanted to watch *Dumbo*. So, he entered the theatre. And Corporal Mike Mizerany decided that as long as he was here, he might as well watch the show himself.

13

A city bus drove past the brightly illuminated exterior of the Crystal Ballroom, and Wally Stephans leaped off the rear bumper and into the Hollywood Boulevard. Riding on the back of buses was a little more dangerous than riding inside them, but it was also more economical, and right now that was pretty important to Wally: he was flat broke. Wally had had to scrounge every penny he had in order to get the refuse stains removed from his new zoot-suit in time for tonight. He had wanted to look his best when he met Betty here. He had practised what he was going to say to her a thousand times in his mind, and now he only hoped that he wasn't too late, that Betty hadn't run off with that creep Sitarski.

Wally ran across the street to the entrance of the dance hall where a group of zoot-suited Chicanos – *pachucos* as they were known – were milling around with their girlfriends. They seemed pretty angry about something. Wally knew some of these guys from the neighbourhood – Luis Martinez, Johnny Lopez, Pete Juarez – and they knew him. This was, of course, the first time they had seen Wally in a zoot-suit and they were quite impressed. They complimented him on his taste, shaking his hand and slapping him on the back. 'So what's going on here?' Wally wanted to know.

'They took over our dance hall!' shouted Martinez. 'The *pincha* Army! They won't let nobody in without a uniform!'

'Is Betty here yet?' Wally asked urgently.

Martinez shrugged. 'I don't know, Wally. We've only been here about ten minutes.'

Uniform or no uniform, Wally knew he was going to have to find out whether Betty was inside. So, he took a deep breath, adjusted his wide-brimmed hat, pushed his way through the crowd of servicemen hanging around at the entrance, and marched right up to the door. He found his way blocked by a rough-and-tumble Shore Patrolman named Vito. Vito carried a baton, wore a helmet and an SP armband over his Navy uniform. Although he was two inches shorter than Wally, he weighed about eighty pounds more. All in all, he was one mean-looking son-of-a-bitch! Vito stood next to a big sign which said, in big red letters, 'Servicemen Only. No Civilians.' As Wally attempted to walk past Vito and through the door, he was met by the Shore Patrolman's baton in his gut. 'What army you think you belong to, kid?' Vito asked. 'The Salvation Army?' Vito laughed loudly at his own joke. So did some of the servicemen gathered around.

'I'm just looking for somebody,' Wally told him, and again tried to get past him.

Vito poked the baton harder into his ribs. 'You're lookin' for a fat lip! Now, beat it!'

Wally stared at him for a moment, then turned as if he was going to walk away – suddenly he whirled around and charged through the door! But Vito's arm was just as quick, and yanked Wally back outside, roughly shoving him out into the street. 'I said, beat it, jackass!' he yelled.

Vito was promptly serenaded by a chorus of hooting and catcalling from the *pachucos*. He glared at them and waved his baton threateningly. 'Why don't you Mexican jumping beans go back to the *barrio* where you belong?' he taunted.

This comment was met by cheers and applause from the group of soldiers and sailors. There was clearly the makings of a brawl here, but for some remarkable reason, it didn't erupt.

Wally picked himself up and manoeuvred himself so that he could peer through the door, hoping to catch some sign of Betty. In a few moments, a sailor came out. Wally ran over to him. 'Excuse me, but did you notice a girl in there, blonde hair, about five foot six—'

But the sailor interrupted him before he could finish. 'Say, kid, I like that suit you're wearing! How far did you have to chase a nigger to get it?' He laughed. Vito laughed even louder. And so did the servicemen.

Wally ignored the insult, but Vito was having too good a time to continue to ignore Wally. The Shore Patrolman came over and gave Wally a good swift kick in the arse. Wally went flying into the arms of his fellow zoot-suiters. Outraged at such treatment of their friend, the zooters threw Wally back at Vito. Wally fell backwards, past Vito and into the arms of a soldier who had just stepped out of the dance hall: 'Stretch' Sitarski! Wally realized that now things could only get worse.

Sitarski grinned upon seeing what Santa Claus had brought him. 'You got a lotta balls coming here tonight,' he told Wally. 'You know why?'

'Why?'

'Because when I get through with you, you ain't gonna have any left!'

Wally knew that Sitarski would probably beat the shit out of him, but he planned on getting at least a few good licks in during the process. Sitarski pulled him towards the street, tightening his grasp on Wally's shirt. But as Sitarski raised his fist, he noticed that he was encircled by a dozen angry-looking zooters. Not even Sitarski was interested in risking those kind of odds, so his manner abruptly changed: he unclenched his fist and smiled brightly at the *pachucos*. 'Hey, *hola, amigos! Buenos noches!*' he exclaimed in rather poor Spanish. '*Como estan ustedes?*'

But they weren't buying it. The *pachucos* stared coldly at Sitarski, just daring him to start something.

Sitarski decided to 'explain' what he had been doing with Wally. 'This is your friend, huh? Well, he's my friend, too – me and him are old pals! We were just having a friendly little talk here, that's all!' As Sitarski was saying this, he surreptitiously withdrew his cigarette lighter from his trouser pocket, then put his arm around Wally. 'But, I can see I'm interrupting something,' he continued, 'so I guess I'll let you have him back.' Unseen by anyone except Vito, Sitarski had set the tail of Wally's zoot-jacket on fire! Sitarski walked back to the dance hall doorway to watch the fun. It was all Vito could do to keep himself from laughing.

Wally brushed the front of himself off, unaware that his arse was about to catch fire! Then Martinez sniffed the air curiously. 'I smell something burning. . . .'

Wally sniffed – now he smelled it, too. 'Yeah,' he agreed. 'Smells like garbage. . . .'

As Wally turned, looking for the source of the peculiar odour, Martinez and the others suddenly noticed the flames and black smoke coming from the back of Wally's suit. 'Wally!' Martinez exclaimed, 'it's your zoot!'

Wally howled in pain as the fire reached his skin. Martinez and the others pushed Wally into the gutter, and he rolled around in the slime and sewer water to extinguish the flames! Sitarski and Vito were laughing so hard they had tears in their eyes!

The fire extinguished, Wally climbed to his feet. The rear of his suit was a mess, with his underwear showing through the charred hole in his trousers! But that wasn't

what was on his mind now. Blood was on his mind –
Sitarski's blood! Wally took a deep breath and prepared
to engage his enemy. This time, he wasn't going to let
anything stop him. He wasn't, that is, until a taxi
pulled up at the Crystal Ballroom and Betty Douglas
stepped out. Wally's heart skipped a beat when he saw
her: she looked like an angel in her white dress.

Sitarski had seen her too, and in a moment, he was
beside her, helping her out of the taxi. She had a bright
warm smile for him, which made Wally hate Sitarski
even more.

'Betty, please, I want to talk to you,' said Wally running over to her.

Sitarski gave him a shove. 'Well, she doesn't want to
talk to you, bud, so amscray!'

'Please, Betty,' Wally beseeched, 'I want to apologize
for this afternoon – I can explain the whole thing!'

Betty was willing to listen, but Sitarski never gave
her the chance. 'I said, get lost, and I meant it!' he said,
and kicked him right in the balls! Wally staggered backward in excruciating pain and fell into the gutter again.

Sitarski turned back to Betty, putting on a most
charming smile. 'Shall we?' he invited, taking her arm.
But Betty was horrified at what had just happened to
Wally. She looked at him crawling around in the street,
and it began to occur to her that she just might be with the
wrong guy. She wanted to go to him, to help him, to
listen to him. Sitarski, however, had other ideas, and his
vice-like grip pulled her towards the Crystal Ballroom
and her duty as a USO Hostess.

Wally's anger was greater than his pain, and that was
what enabled him to climb to his feet despite his excruciating agony. He picked a broken bottle out of the
gutter and was ready to assault Sitarski with it when
suddenly he was restrained by a marine. Wally whirled

around, ready to give it to the guy. 'Look, you, this is none of your goddamn bus—' He stopped short upon recognizing him. 'Dennis!' he exclaimed, completely dumbfounded by the sight of his best friend in a Marine uniform. Dennis was accompanied by two of the most beautiful girls Wally had ever seen.

'Take it easy, Wally,' Dennis told him. 'That guy'll put your lights out for good!'

'Dennis, what the hell are you wearing?'

Dennis grinned. 'I'm tellin' you, Wally, these uniforms work like a son-of-a-bitch!' He put an arm around each girl.

'I – I can't believe it,' Wally stammered. 'You – you joined up . . . ?'

'Who said anything about joining up? I just got me a uniform!' He then showed Wally his Sergeant's stripes, and whispered confidentially, 'Western Costume Rentals – only two bucks!'

Wally nodded. He looked back at the USO Club, then again at Dennis. 'Well . . . have a good time.'

Dennis was about to head for the dance, but then thought better of it. After all, this was his best friend here, and he was very obviously in trouble. 'Look, Wally, you want this uniform? I'll give it to you – you can owe me the two bucks.'

Wally considered this. If he had seen the horrified expression on Betty's face after Sitarski had kicked him below the belt, he might have taken Dennis up on the offer. But he hadn't, so all he knew was that Betty had gone into the dance without having said a single word to him. 'Forget it, Dennis,' Wally told him. 'It's all over.' And with that Wally sat down on the kerb, his life a shambles, a broken, defeated, empty shell of a young man.

14

Highway 66, California
8.15 p.m.

Under normal conditions, the drive from Los Angeles to Barstow took somewhere between two-and-a-half to three hours. However, Captain Loomis Birkhead was not driving under normal conditions. He had Donna Stratton in the car with him. Therefore, he was determined to arrive at his destination in approximately half the usual time. And, it looked like he was going to make it. Birkhead certainly didn't have to worry about being pulled over by any police. After all, he was driving the car of a United States Army General on a vital mission during time of war. In fact, the only thing Birkhead was worried about was exactly what he would find when he arrived at the 501st Bomb Disbursement Unit Headquarters in the desert. There was really no guarantee that Maddox actually would have any 'planes at his base, and if there weren't any, well, having to deal with Donna in that case was going to be less than pleasant, to put it mildly. As it was, she hadn't said a word for the past sixty miles, and those words that she had said previously all had to do with aeroplanes. There was, of course, the other possibility, which was that Maddox *did* have aeroplanes at the base. That would mean that Birkhead would have to take Donna up, that is, if he wanted to get anywhere with her – and he didn't know if he remembered how to fly! Well, all he could do was to cross that bridge when he came to it – unless ... yes! A terrific idea was coming to him that just might solve his problem! He looked over at her, sitting there quietly, gazing out her window, a radiant vision of loveliness, a goddess – he wanted her so badly that – well, no, after all, rape was a pretty serious crime … he wasn't ready to cross that line – not yet! He glanced out of the window at the darkness outside. This stretch of Highway 66 between San Bernadino and Barstow ran through the desert, and even on a moonlit night like tonight, it was pretty dark. He cleared his throat.

'Sure is dark out here.'

Donna did not react at all.

He continued. 'You look out the windows and you can't see a thing – not a thing. Just like flying at night, isn't it?'

He looked at her, waiting for some sort of response. There was none.

'Well, I'll tell you this: it's sure a whole heckuva lot safer than flying at night. In fact, if I didn't know better, I'd swear we were airborne right now. This car feels just like an airplane, doesn't it? Say, what does this feel like?' He popped the clutch several times, and the car jerked and accelerated alternately. 'Forward thrust, right? It feels just like forward thrust, doesn't it, Donna?'

Finally Donna looked at him. 'You just get me up in an airplane, Loomis. Then maybe I'll feel some forward thrust!'

Birkhead gulped. There were no half-way measures with a woman like this! He pushed the accelerator all the way to the floor and prayed to God that Maddox would have something he could fly.

15

Betty Douglas was not feeling very well. She was feeling pain inside, because of what Sitarski had done to Wally and because of what he might do to her, and she was feeling pain outside because Sitarski hadn't loosened his grip on her arm for the past ten minutes. They were waiting in line at a refreshment table, and had been for several minutes. Finally, Sitarski decided he was tired of waiting. He brutally shoved six people out of his way, and pulled Betty up to the front. 'You do want some punch and cookies before we dance, don't you, Betty?' he asked, too politely.

Betty didn't want any. 'Yes, thank you,' she answered fearfully, after Sitarski gave her a cup of punch and a handful of chocolate-chip cookie crumbs.

The gangly, bespectacled sailor standing next to Betty leaned over to make sure she was wearing a USO Hostess badge. He smiled upon seeing it. 'Betty, would you care to dance?' he offered.

'You don't know her well enough to call her by her first name!' thundered Sitarski.

'Uh – excuse me?' replied the seaman.

'You don't even know her!' shouted Sitarski. 'You don't have the right to call her by her first name! You don't dance with her, you don't even talk to her, you don't even look at her! Now ship out, swabbie!'

The sailor got the hell out of there!

'A napkin for you, Betty?' asked Sitarski, not waiting

for a reply, as he handed one to her. Her hand was shaking – she took it, and dropped it. Sitarski the gentleman bent over to pick it up.

Thus, the young marine who looked over at Betty thought she was alone. He stepped up to her with a big bright grin. 'Hi, babe! Wanna cut a rug?'

Exactly one second later, the young marine found himself face to face with Sitarski. And Sitarski was not glad to see him. Luckily for his own physical well-being, the young marine was able to read Sitarski's expression quite clearly: he too got the hell out of there!

'You dropped this, Betty,' said Sitarski, handing her what used to be a napkin. It was now a crumbled ball of refuse, dripping with the sweat from Sitarski's hand.

'Thank you,' responded Betty without much spirit. She could take solace in only one thing: this was a public place, with chaperones, and if Sitarski got too far out of line, he'd be kicked out. Maybe.

Outside, Wally dejectedly ambled along the side of the dance hall. He had no money, no job, no girl friend, no life. He looked at the traffic rushing past on Hollywood Boulevard and considered how easy it would be to do the honourable thing. Why not? After all, who would miss him? He glanced the other way and found himself facing the big plate-glass window of the Crystal Ballroom. Something drew him closer to gaze at the dance inside – a morbid fascination, perhaps ... or perhaps he wanted to truly convince himself that Betty was having a good time before seriously considering the alternative. And then he saw her, from behind, dancing with Sitarski – that is, if you could call it dancing. Actually, it was more like Sitarski was dragging her around on the dance floor, his hands all over her, trying to feel her up. Wally was sickened. He wanted to turn away, but he couldn't –

146

not until he saw her face. He didn't have long to wait. Sitarski spun her around and Wally could see on Betty's face what he had missed a little while ago: tortured pain. Wally didn't know how to react – he was both delighted and nauseated that she was so miserable. Wally watched as a sailor attempted to cut in. Sitarski's answer was a slug in the groin! The sailor staggered back, and Betty tried to use the opportunity to get away. Sitarski however was too fast: he grabbed her, pulled her back and continued his disgusting conduct. Wally pressed his face against the glass and banged on it. 'Betty!' he screamed. 'Betty!'

Whether she could have actually heard him through the window was doubtful; nevertheless, call it coincidence or telepathy or true love, Betty turned that way as if she did hear. Their eyes met, and Betty's face lit up. There was no mistaking what her expression meant. Again, Betty tried to escape Sitarski; again he wouldn't let her go. She looked back at Wally with those pleading, tearful blue eyes, her tortured expression saying, 'Please, help me, Wally, I love you'.

Wally was reborn! Maybe he didn't have a job, or any money, but he had his life back, and he wasn't about to throw it away. No, sir, Wally was going to go in there and save that girl! He ran back towards the corner, back towards the entrance. He rounded the corner, then suddenly stopped short: Vito the Shore Patrolman was coming towards him, dragging an innocent-looking sailor along by the scruff of the neck. And Vito looked even meaner than usual. He had a bottle of booze with him, which he had apparently wrestled from the slightly red-nosed seaman. 'You little son-of-a-bitch!' Vito was telling the sailor. 'I'll teach you to drink in here! I'm gonna beat your brains out, that's what I'm gonna do!'

Wally dodged back around the corner with two

thoughts in his mind: first, to keep away from Vito at all costs; second that with Vito away from the front door, he just might be able to slip into the dance. Wally could hear Vito's voice approaching – he was coming around the corner. Wally ran a little further along the side of the building and darted into the alley that ran behind it. Vito's voice continued to get louder. Then Wally realized that if the Shore Patrolman was actually going to beat the young sailor's brains out, a dark alley like this one would be the best place to do it. It was then that Wally discovered he was in a blind alley – he had no place to run, no place to hide ... and in a few more seconds, Vito would be there! He looked around frantically for some place to take refuge, and then he spotted the fire-escape. Wally jumped up on a dustbin and scrambled up the ladder, just as Vito rounded the corner. He ran up three flights of stairs in record time, hopped over a ledge and made it to the roof before Vito had gone another fifteen feet. He was safe!

Wally backed away a few feet from the edge and suddenly tripped over a heavy, solid crate. 'Owww!' he yelped as he fell backwards – then stifled his cry, realizing that he might be heard below. Investigating, he saw that the crate was loaded with 40 mm shells. He looked around and found several of these crates lying about ... and then discovered there was a 40 mm anti-aircraft gun emplacement up here with him, manned by two artillery men! Luckily, the two soldiers, named Willy and Joe, were so absorbed in the cannon that they weren't paying attention to anything else. They were cranking it around, aiming it at the moon.

'Boy, I could knock that moon right out of the sky!' Willy was saying, squinting through the sight.

'Aw, leave it alone,' Joe told him. 'I've got leave to-morrow night. I'm gonna need that moon.'

Now Wally heard voices coming from the alley. He peered over the edge of the roof. Vito was holding the young sailor by the hair and poking him in the gut with his baton. The words 'No Parking' were stencilled on the nearby wall in white paint.

'There's no drinkin' allowed inside, kid!' Vito was telling him. 'That's why they put up this sign here, see that?' Vito twisted the kid's head around so that he could see the sign. 'See what it says there? "No Drinking"! Can't you read?'

'But it says, "No Parking",' protested the youth.

Vito slammed his head into the wall. 'You're drunk! Read it again!'

' "No Parking"! "No Parking" !'

Again Vito threw the lad's head into the wall. The poor kid howled in pain.

Wally shook his head. He was certainly glad he was up on the roof and not down there. At the same time, he wished he could do something to that son-of-a-bitch in the alley. And then an idea occurred to him, an idea that would solve all of his problems! He quietly removed the lid from one of the crates, pulled out a metal ammunition canister, opened it, and withdrew two 40 mm shells. Again he peered over the edge of the roof: Vito was continuing to brutalize the young sailor.

'Go on, read it again!' ordered Vito as he shoved the kid's face into the wall once more.

'Okay, you're right! You're right!' the kid told him. 'It says, "No Drinking" !'

'Don't crack wise with me, you little runt!' screamed Vito. 'It says, "No Parking" !' He threw him against the wall, then raised his baton for a 'lights out' blow.

But Wally was ready; he was holding a 40 mm shell out over the edge of the roof, aiming at Vito's head. He let it drop – the shell whistled straight down and narrowly missed the Shore Patrolman, whooshing right past his face! Vito immediately looked up, not knowing what had happened. He spotted Wally and recognized him. 'Hey!' he shouted. He was promptly answered by another shell – this time right between the eyes! Vito went down for the count! The young sailor thanked Providence for the heavenly intervention, then got his arse out of there as fast as he could!

Wally zipped down the three flights of stairs, and seconds later began stripping the uniform from the unconscious Shore Patrolman. Wally knew he needed a uniform to get into the USO Club and now he was going to have one!

Inside, the big jitterbug contest was about to get under way. Sal Stewart, the bandleader, was moderating. 'Ladies and gentlemen, we're about to start our jitterbug contest, so I'd like to introduce our judge, Meyer Mishkin, a talent scout for RKO Motion Picture Studios!'

Meyer Mishkin, a flamboyant, cigar-chomping Hollywood character, was greeted by a round of applause as he stepped up on stage.

'As you know,' continued Sal Stewart, 'our first prize is a chance to appear in an RKO movie musical and an option for a seven-year movie contract with RKO! Of course, from the looks of things, we may have to wait a few months until after the war to award the prize, but in the meantime, we're sure that the lucky winner will be able to stay in practice by dancing around Jap bullets!' There was laughter, and a lot more applause. 'Okay, now, if you haven't got a partner yet, you'd better find one fast!'

Sitarski had his partner, but he wasn't interested in participating in any dance contest. Sitarski had something else in mind, something he'd been looking forward to all afternoon and all evening. And now he was ready, ready to give Betty an experience she would never forget. Sure, Betty was unwilling at the moment, but all that would change; Sitarski was sure of that. And if it didn't, well, Sitarski planned on enjoying himself regardless. He knew how to deal with stroppy women, and he figured she'd probably thank him for it by the end of the night. He dragged her towards the door. 'Listen, it's getting too crowded in here,' he was telling her. 'I'll call us a cab and we can go someplace where these slobs won't be around to bother you.'

But Betty wanted to stay right there, thank you. She grabbed at every serviceman she could get her hands on. 'You wanna dance with me, sailor? Hey, soldier, dance with me, please! Somebody dance with me!'

But the young man who really wanted to dance with Betty hadn't arrived yet. Wally was still out in the alley, putting on Vito's uniform. It wasn't the best fit in the world, and it certainly wasn't a zoot-suit – but it would do.

Sitarski dragged Betty closer to the exit. Had there been anyone there who'd had doubts about whether mankind had in fact descended from the apes, one look at Sitarski would have put those doubts to rest. Through the open door, Betty could see several taxis waiting. She was afraid that one of them was waiting for her. 'Help!' she screamed. 'Help me!!' She could barely be heard above the din of the crowd. However, Maxine Dexheimer heard . . . and saw. She was horrified to see her best friend being dragged away by the man she loved. She ran over, grabbed Betty's free hand, and pulled, only to find herself being pulled along with Betty. Sitarski was too strong! Maxine grabbed on to a table for anchorage, but the table was pulled right along with them!

In the alley, Vito groaned: he was slowly regaining consciousness. But Wally had foreseen this possibility, which was why he was tying the burly Navy man to a telegraph pole with his zoot-suit braces. That finished, Wally picked up the discarded bottle Vito had taken from the young sailor and broke it over the Shore Patrolman's head! Vito went out again.

'Okay, folks,' Sal Stewart was saying inside. 'let's count down this tremendous, stupendous, momentous, absolutely incredibly remarkably wonderful ... uh ... er ... oh, let's get on with it, already! Ten! Nine! Eight! Seven!' The crowd counted along with Sal.

Sitarski was almost to the door, along with Betty, Maxine and the table. 'Six! Five! Four!' A pimple-faced marine who needed a partner spotted Maxine. He quickly ran over and pulled her away from Betty. 'Three! Two! One!' Betty was out the door with Sitarski – but a split second later, she was inside again with Wally! Wally had yanked her away from Sitarski so quickly that neither of them was quite aware of what had happened.

Sal Stewart immediately whirled around and began leading his band in their own version of Louis Prima's classic 'Sing, Sing, Sing', one of the swinging-est tunes ever written. The contest was under way. And jitterbuggers mobbed the floor.

Wally spun Betty out on to the dance floor. She still hadn't recognized him in the Shore Patrolman's uniform, but it didn't take her much longer ... and total joy illuminated her face! 'Wally!' She threw her arms around him and began to hug and kiss him. Then Wally spotted Sitarski coming after them.

'Not now, Betty,' he said, breaking the hug. 'We've gotta dance!' And dance they did. Wally's behind-the-theatre-screen sessions with Fred Astaire now paid off handsomely as he and Betty jitterbugged the jitterbug the way it was meant to be jitterbugged.

However, Sitarski was not about to stand idly by and

152

watch. With clenched fists, he was after Wally, and out for blood! Wally decided he couldn't turn tail and run – nor did he want to stop dancing to slug it out with the soldier. Wally had waited a long time for this dance, and he wasn't going to let Sitarski spoil it, not when he could simply keep dancing. So, that's what he did. Sitarski came at him, winding him up for a Sunday punch. Wally whirled and ducked under another dancer's arm just as the soldier threw his punch; and his fist slammed right into a support post! Sitarski bellowed in pain. In moments, the Corporal was after Wally again, screaming at the top of his lungs, 'Stop him! He's a fake! He's a civilian!'

But nobody heard. Or if they did, they didn't care. Wally continued dancing with Betty and continued eluding Sitarski, executing spectacular moves to keep out of his way. Wally weaved in and out of other dancers, flinging other partners into Sitarski's path to slow his maniacal advance. When Sitarski got too close, Wally spun Betty out of her blue jacket, and shoved the garment over the Corporal's head. Sitarski stumbled blindly and was knocked down by other jitterbuggers.

Betty, meanwhile, was having a wonderful time. Besides the total euphoria she was feeling by being with Wally, she was spending more time in the air than on the ground as Wally continually lifted her over tables, chairs and other dancers. And everything was in perfect time to the music!

Wally and Betty were rapidly becoming the centre of attention. Meyer Mishkin couldn't take his eyes off them, and spectators on the sidelines began clapping in time to the music, cheering them on. Dennis, his arm around his two lovely ladies, was especially proud of his friend. 'That's my pal!' he yelled happily. 'That's Wally!'

Sitarski, back on his feet, moved across the floor like a

locomotive, not stopping for anybody or anything! Wally was completely unaware of the soldier's rapid advance on him from behind. That's when Maxine saw him: she broke away from her own partner and ran after him, sliding into his legs like a baseball player sliding into home plate! She grabbed those legs and held on as tight as she could. Sitarski looked down, shook his head, picked her up and dropped her on a nearby table. He continued after Wally.

Outside in the alley, Vito had regained consciousness. He was astonished to find himself tied to a telegraph pole, and completely naked except for his red striped underpants! It didn't take him long to wriggle out of the zoot-suit braces that bound him. In a flash he was on his way back to the dance hall – then he stopped short, realizing that he was nearly stark naked! He ran back into the alley, and looked around for something to wear. There was nothing except Wally's discarded zoot-suit. Vito had no choice but to put it on.

Inside, Wally and Betty were really cooking on the dance floor, and Meyer Mishkin looked like he was ready to sign both of them. Wally sent Betty between his legs, and then into a spin-out. He executed a spectacular 'round-the-back'; that is, he threw Betty across his own back, back to back. The crowd loved it! From there, they moved into a wild variation on the 'Shorty George' step, after which Wally performed an incredible back flip. He whirled across the dance floor, spinning faster and faster, moving away from Betty, and WHAM! He had spun right into Sitarski's fist! Wally reeled backwards, not sure what had hit him, and staggered right into the arms of his own zoot-suit: Vito!

'You son-of-a-bitch!' screamed Vito. He whacked Wally in the jaw, sending him tumbling across the dance floor. Betty rushed to his crumpled form. Sitarski rushed for Betty, but just as he got to her, he felt a tap on his shoulder. He turned, and was greeted by Dennis's fist in his face!

All of this had happened extraordinarily quickly, but not so quickly as to go unnoticed by a good number of servicemen. And what they had seen looked like this: a soldier had hit a Navy Shore Patrolman, a zoot-suiter had also hit the Navy man, and a marine had hit the soldier! The powder keg ignited! The Army rushed to avenge their fellow soldier by assaulting the marines! The Navy went after the Army! And several Shore Patrolmen went after that goddamned zoot-suiter!

'Hey, fellas, it's me! Vito! It's me!' protested Vito, but his fellow Shore Patrolmen didn't recognize him. They raised their batons, bashed him on the head, and threw him right out the door, into the gathering of *pachucos* outside! The Mexican youths saw the zoot-suit, but not Vito's face, and assumed the Navy had beaten up one of their own. Outraged, they charged into the USO Club for vengeance!

In moments, what had been a USO dance became a slugging match. Everyone was fighting everyone else – Army, Navy, Marines, zooters, even the band! It didn't matter who was who, or what was what! Some girls and women ran for cover; others started throwing food. Chairs began flying, tables began breaking, bodies began falling. It was pandemonium of the highest order – a full-scale riot! And so it began: The Great Los Angeles Riot of 13 December.

16

The 501st Bomb Disbursement Unit was not actually in the Barstow city limits, but rather several miles outside of town.

Captain Loomis Birkhead turned on to the dirt road that led to the base. Freshly painted signs along the road warned, 'No Trespassing, Violators Will Be Captured, Questioned and Shot.' There were no lights visible anywhere, although by now both Birkhead's and Donna's eyes had adjusted to the moonlit darkness, and they were able to see piles of bombs on either side of the road. There seemed to be every type of bomb ever made here, from the little two-pounders to incendiary bombs to the gigantic five-hundred-pound variety. A lone runway and a spotter's tower could be seen off to one side, although there were no 'planes visible anywhere. Everything was strangely still, and there was nothing that even hinted at the presence of life. Birkhead slowed the car to a stop, rolled down his window, and listened. He heard nothing.

Donna continued to stare in the direction of the airfield. 'I don't see any 'planes, Loomis,' she said threateningly.

'I think I'd better have a look around,' he told her. Birkhead climbed out of the car and walked forward into the beam of his own headlights, looking for anything that might indicate the presence of a human being. He saw nothing but piles of bombs and stores of ammunition. 'Hello?' he called out. 'Anybody home?'

Suddenly the darkness lit up with a burst of automatic

weapons fire and thousands of bullets ripped into the ground around Birkhead's feet! Birkhead raised his arms and waved frantically. 'Don't shoot! Don't shoot!'

The shooting stopped, and Birkhead was promptly hit by a spotlight beam which blinded him. A voice called out from in front of him. 'Identify yourself!'

Birkhead answered, his hands raised, 'Captain Loomis Birkhead, United States Army! General Stilwell sent me!' Birkhead's eyes slowly adjusted to the light, and he saw in front of him, not bombs, but sandbags piled up, and hundreds of soldiers armed with machine-guns and automatic pistols peering over them, staring at him. In the centre was a man in a Colonel's uniform. Birkhead knew who this was: Colonel 'Madman' Maddox.

It has been said that insane men have a peculiar look in their eyes which is extremely unnerving to normal human beings. Colonel Maddox's eyes fitted that description. He was approaching fifty, and his closely-cropped brown hair was flecked with grey. The right lens of his wire-rimmed glasses was shattered, which heightened the unnerving effect of his wild grey eyes. Maddox was an intimidating man, not because of his physical stature, which was of medium build, but because of how he carried himself: like an axe-murderer! Maddox forever seemed to be on the edge of committing extreme physical violence to whomever he was looking at. He inspired fear, rather than respect, and it was this quality that had allowed Maddox to maintain an iron grip on his men. No one dared question him. Maddox squinted and eyed Birkhead with suspicion. 'Birkhead, huh? What the hell kinda name is that?' he asked.

Birkhead started to lower his arms and step forward, but Maddox waved his ·45 automatic at him. 'Just hold it right there, Birkhead!' he barked.

Birkhead held it right there.

Maddox turned to his aide, a fierce young Lieutenant named Winowski. 'Whaddaya think, Winowski?' asked the Colonel. 'Is he legit?'

'I wouldn't trust him, sir,' advised Winowski.

Maddox took another look at Birkhead. He could see that Birkhead was easily six foot tall. 'Kinda tall for a Jap, though, wouldn't you say, Winowski?' wondered Maddox.

'Yeah, but those Japs are sneaky little bastards. You just never know.'

Maddox considered the advice of his aide, then nodded. 'You're right. Check him for stilts.'

'Yes, sir!' replied the Lieutenant enthusiastically. Winowski approached Birkhead with extreme caution. The Lieutenant was only five foot two, and Birkhead watched the shorter man with uncertainty, realizing he was up to something. The two men stared at one another for a moment, then Winowski kicked Birkhead in the shin! Birkhead howled in pain, and hopped around on one foot. He was obviously not walking on stilts.

'He's on the level, sir!' shouted Winowski as he hurried back to Maddox's side.

The Colonel lowered his weapon, greatly relieved. His men followed suit. Maddox walked over to Birkhead with outstretched arms and a big smile, as if he was greeting a long-lost son. He hugged Birkhead, proud of this young man. 'Thank God, Captain!' exclaimed Maddox. 'Thank God you were able to get through!' Suddenly Maddox's eyes darted back and forth nervously as he stared into the darkness behind Birkhead. He stepped away from Birkhead and reacted with alarm. 'But my troops, man! Where are my troops? I asked Stilwell for troops!'

'Uh – well, we're a little short-handed,' explained Birkhead. 'Stilwell's trying to hold LA!'

'My God, doesn't he realize how desperate my situation

is? Murderers! They're parachuting into the hills. We've got reports of a secret Jap air strip hidden in the alfalfa fields of Pomona!'

Birkhead looked back at Donna who was watching eagerly from the car window. Birkhead knew what her expression meant, and decided he'd better pop the important question. 'Colonel,' he asked, 'have you got any bombers out here?'

'Bombers? Have I got any bombers?' Maddox laughed as if it was a great joke. 'If I had bombers, I'd be bombing the hell out of 'em right now! I don't have any bombers out here!'

Birkhead's heart sank. He was trying to figure out how he would break the news to Donna when Maddox turned a spotlight into the darkness to their right. 'All I've got is that trainer over there!' Maddox told him, pointing. The spotlight illuminated a twin-engined Beechcraft that had been covered with nets and camouflage. Birkhead's eyes lit up! He looked at Donna in the car, and saw that she was practically drooling!

The Captain cleared his throat. 'Colonel, I just happen to have a reconnaissance expert from out Intelligence Office in Washington in the car with me. With your permission, sir, we'd like to take that trainer up and see if we can spot that enemy airfield.'

'My God, man! That 'plane hasn't got any guns! You're talking suicide!'

'Colonel,' replied Birkhead bravely, 'I haven't any other choice.'

Maddox was overwhelmed by this tremendous show of courage, so overwhelmed that he did something extremely rare: he saluted Captain Birkhead. The Captain returned the salute.

Inside of five minutes, the Beechcraft was on the runway, ready for take-off. Birkhead and Donna sat in the cockpit, each with vastly different things in mind. Birkhead was trying to recall take-off procedure, scared shitless that he might not remember how to fly. And Donna was snuggling up to him, getting more and more aroused.

So far, so good: Birkhead managed to start both engines without any problem. But the vibrations served to make Donna even more excited, and she couldn't keep her hands off him. 'Let's see,' Birkhead muttered. 'The landing gears are locked, the stabilizers are—' He raised his voice at Donna, distracted by her behaviour. 'Donna, please! I'm trying to remember what I'm supposed to do!'

'Don't worry, Loomis,' she cooed. 'I know my way around a cockpit.' She grabbed at the joystick. Birkhead pushed her away.

'Don't touch that!' he shouted. Then, as Birkhead studied the instrument panel he came to a shocking realization. He opened the side window and yelled at Colonel Maddox who was standing at the edge of the runway. 'Colonel! This 'plane hasn't got a radio! You've got to let Interceptor Command know I'm up there! I don't want to get shot down!'

'Don't worry!' Maddox yelled back. 'I've got a phone! I'll call 'em for you!'

Then Birkhead remembered one other bit of information that might be useful to know. 'Colonel!' he shouted. 'Which way is Pomona?'

Maddox pointed a few degrees south of due west. 'That way! Towards LA!!'

Now the runway lights came on. The soldier in the spotter's tower waved to Maddox; Maddox waved back. The Colonel called to Birkhead for the last time. 'You're cleared for take-off! God bless you, son! The whole country's counting on you!' Maddox gave Birkhead a 'thumbs up'. Birkhead returned the gesture and closed his side window. Maddox watched as the Beechcraft jerked forward into motion and taxied erratically down the runway. Any sane man would have realized that Birkhead didn't know what the hell he was doing. But Maddox wasn't a sane man. He turned to Winowski and said, 'That boy's got guts. Real old-fashioned red-blooded good old American guts!'

The Beechcraft jerked first one way, then the other, nearly crashing into a pile of 500-pound bombs! Birkhead swerved away, only to find himself heading directly for the spotter's tower! 'You're gonna hit that tower, Loomis!' screamed Donna. Again Birkhead swerved, whipping the nose away just in the nick of time. 'I made it with room to spare,' he told her proudly.

Wrong! The right wing-tip had sheared through one of the tower's wooden supports. The tower buckled, tipped and crashed to the ground, taking with it the telephone line that ran through the roof. This wire in turn brought down an entire telegraph pole, to which was connected all of the 501st's telephone and radio equipment!

The on-duty operator at his post behind a wall of sandbags was completely dumbfounded as all of his equipment – transmitter, microphone and headset – suddenly disappeared from his table, only to be dashed to pieces on the ground. He was left holding a telephone handset with a dangling wire.

Now Maddox rushed to the operator's post, ready to make his call to Interceptor Command. He grabbed the handset away from the operator. 'Hello! Hello!' Maddox cried, only to realize he was holding a receiver with nothing attached to it. 'Oh my God – we've been cut off!' His eyes filled with paranoia as he ran out to his troops, blowing his whistle, drawing his automatic. 'Men! They've cut us off! They must be ready to launch their attack. Get ready! Get to your positions! Make every shot count! And don't fire until you see the slant of their eyes!'

Maddox's men took their positions, weapons cocked, ready and waiting for the enemy that wasn't there.

And meanwhile, Birkhead and Donna flew westwards, towards Los Angeles, completely ignorant that no responsible authority was aware of their existence.

17

The riot continued, even further out of control, and the Crystal Ballroom was rapidly becoming a shambles. The Christmas decorations had for the most part been ripped down and destroyed. A good number of unconscious rioters were lying on the floor, surrounded by broken chairs and other debris. They were frequently stepped on by others who kept on fighting.

On stage, a big fight had developed around the orchestra. Servicemen and zooters grabbed musical instruments and swung them at one another. Some of Sal Stewart's band members fought for their instruments, but were rewarded with knuckles in their jaws. A sailor broke a clarinet over the head of a *pachuco*. A marine choked a sailor with a trombone slide. Fifteen soldiers picked up the piano and threw it on top of ten marines.

Sal Stewart, miraculously untouched by the fisticuffs, was broadcasting a play-by-play description of the riot to the entire city over KMPC. 'Ladies and gentlemen,' he was saying, 'the incredible scene before me can only be described as pure pandemonium. Everywhere, people are fighting or running for cover. To my right, there's a sailor strangling a soldier. To my left, there's a zoot-suiter beating up a member of my own orchestra. Directly in front of me, I see innocent young females cowering with fear under refreshment tables. I don't know how else to put this, ladies and gentlemen, but this is a full-scale riot!'

Among those listening to this broadcast were Sergeant Frank Tree's men, on duty in the Motor Pool Garage at the Chavez Ravine base. Quince, Reese and Foley were busily scrubbing down the exterior of 'Lulubelle', while Tree himself was inside the tank, checking the ammunition supplies.

Quince stuck his head through the turret hatch. 'Hey, Sarge, did you hear that? There's a riot at the USO club in Hollywood! We'd better get over there!'

Tree, who could barely hear the radio, had been paying no attention to the broadcast. 'Knock it off, Quince,' Tree told him. 'You're not going to that dance!'

'But Sarge, this is on the level!' protested Quince. He called out to Foley. 'Turn that up, would you?'

Foley turned the volume up as loud as it would go. Tree couldn't help but hear it now. 'I just can't believe what I'm seeing here, ladies and gentlemen,' Sal Stewart was saying. 'Our own boys ... Americans ... fighting other Americans, at a time when our nation is facing her darkest hour. ...'

Tree heard it all right: Americans fighting Americans! These words struck a deep chord within the Sergeant. His head appeared from out of the turret with a most serious expression on his face. His brow tightened, his chin and cheeks quivered with rage, and his eyes burned with the intensity of a thousand fires from hell. Tree cocked the ·50 calibre machine-gun which was mounted on the turret, then glared at his men. 'Mount up!' he ordered.

Quince, Reese and Foley grinned. Action! They were going to see action! They grabbed their gear and climbed into 'Lulubelle'.

Meanwhile, back at the USO Club, a sailor noticed that Sal Stewart was still broadcasting. The seaman ran up behind him, yanked him away from the microphone, and laid him out with a solid punch in the nose. The sailor grabbed the microphone and yelled into it. 'Calling all seamen! Calling all seamen! We got ourselves a buncha greasy-haired queers runnin' around in zoot-suits! Get your asses down here and help us kick hell out of 'em!'

A soldier ran to the microphone and broke a chair over the sailor's head! He began broadcasting. 'Any of you dogfaces out there listening to me, we got a riot going on at the Hollywood USO club and the Army needs reinforcements! Get over here as fast as you—'

WHAM! He was taken down by two marines. A third marine grabbed the mike and went out live over KMPC. 'Calling all marines! From the Halls of Montezuma, to the shores of Tripoli! Let's show 'em all we're the first to fight! Come on, let's—'

BAM! A huge double-bass, wielded by three *pachucos*, was smashed into his skull! One of the zooters took over the microphone, screaming into it at the top of his lungs. '*Attención mis amigos! Necisitamos su ayuda muy prontismo!*' He continued his call for *pachuco* reinforcements in Spanish.

All over Los Angeles the distress calls were heard ... and met with immediate response. The entire crew of a Navy vessel docked in Los Angeles harbour deserted their ship, hailed taxis in San Pedro and caravaned for Hollywood. In nearby Long Beach, this scene was repeated. Other sailors in waterfront bars deserted their booze and floozies in hopes of a really good brawl. If there were no taxis available, the sailors halted traffic and commandeered civilian vehicles, tossing the hapless drivers out into the street. Soldiers and marines, on or off duty, responded the same way. After all, if they couldn't fight the Japs or the Krauts right now, why not fight the Navy or Mexicans or each other? And in the *barrios*, *pachucos* and other Chicano youths hurried out of taverns, pool halls and bowling alleys, or wherever they might be, and into cars and pick-up trucks. Some of them even took the bus to get to the riot. If the riot had been big before, it could only get bigger!

18

Colonel 'Madman' Maddox and his men were still waiting in their positions for the invasion that was never going to come, as Maddox had ordered just after Birkhead and Donna had taken off. Since that moment, almost twenty minutes ago, they had heard nothing at all peculiar, nothing that could possibly indicate the presence of enemy forces nearby. That was all about to change. The dead stillness of the night was gradually interrupted by a low buzz, a buzz that was becoming louder and louder. A motor! An aeroplane motor! Maddox cocked his head: he knew what it was, and he scanned the sky in the hope of sighting it. Abruptly, out of the darkness, the aeroplane appeared – a single-engined fighter plane – and it was going to land on the runway. Was it friend or foe? Maddox squinted, and then spotted the shark's mouth painted on the nose. It was a P-40! 'Hold your fire, men!' he yelled. 'It's one of ours!' Maddox watched as the P-40 dipped down at a seventy-five-degree angle, pulled out of the dive and bounced on to the runway. It was a landing like Maddox had never seen before, and his mouth fell open in amazement as the fighter finally screeched to a maniacal halt. 'What the hell kinda lunatic is that?' Maddox wondered aloud.

It was a lunatic of the hightest order: Wild Bill Kelso! Kelso threw open his canopy and stood up on his seat, his engine still running. Kelso seemed to be even more wild-eyed than he had been at noon. It was a credit to the

Captain's eyesight that he had spotted the runway in the moonlight, and he looked over the seemingly deserted air strip, curious as to why there were no lights. 'What the hell kinda lunatic runs this place?' he wondered aloud. Then he spotted the fallen tower. It occurred to him that the Japanese might have already taken this base, so he reached for his automatic. But he didn't have time to draw it, because Maddox ran on to the runway, levelling twin automatics at Kelso.

'Identify yourself!' shouted Maddox.

Kelso climbed out on to the wing and jumped on to solid ground. 'I'm Captain Wild Bill Kelso, United States Army Air Corps!'

'You just hold it right there!' Maddox told him. 'Winowski!' he called. The short Lieutenant ran over to his Commanding Officer. 'Check him!' ordered Maddox.

Winowski ran over to Kelso and circled him, eyeing him with some trepidation. Unlike Captain Birkhead, Kelso showed no sign of fear or even suspicion. He merely looked at Winowski with disgust, blowing cigar smoke at him. As before, Winowski kicked Kelso in the shin. But unlike before, Kelso responded by slamming his fist into Winowski's face!

Maddox lowered his weapons. That was an American punch – no foreigner could possibly deliver a punch like that! Kelso was 'legit'.

'Where the hell am I?' Kelso wanted to know.

'501st Bomb Disbursement Unit, Barstow, California!' Maddox replied. 'Where you comin' from?'

'San Francisco! I been trackin' a Jap squadron for a day and a half, but I lost 'em somewhere over Fresno!' As Kelso spoke, he headed over to the 'headquarters' area behind a wall of sandbags. He had sniffed the aroma of hot coffee, and was drawn to it like a bloodhound. He picked up the battered coffee-pot from its bed of hot coals and poured the boiling black liquid all over his face! 'Ahhhhhh!' he sighed, invigorated by the coffee's stimulating effect. He turned to Maddox who had followed him there. 'You seen any Japs around here?'

'Hell, boy, they're all over the place! They've got a secret airfield in Pomona – that's where they're all comin' from!'

Wild Bill Kelso's eyes lit up with fanatical passion. 'How do I get to Pomona?' he demanded urgently.

Maddox pointed a few degrees south of due west. 'That way! Towards LA!'

Kelso ran back to his P-40 and jumped up on to the wing. He addressed Maddox and the troops, screaming at the top of his lungs. 'Now you men listen to me, and listen good! My name is Wild Bill Kelso and you remember it! You remember it just like you remember Pearl Harbor! I ain't had no sleep in two days, but I intend to be the first American to shoot one of those little yellow monkeys down!'

This was the kind of talk that got Maddox's adrenalin flowing. 'You tell 'em boy!' he yelled. 'That's the kinda talk I like to hear! Now, lemme hear your guns!!'

'My guns?'

'Yeah, lemme hear 'em, boy! I just want to hear 'em!'

Wild Bill Kelso grinned a maniacal grin, climbed into his cockpit and fired a short blast on his wing-mounted ·50 calibre machine-guns. The kick of the guns actually lifted the front of the 'plane a foot off the ground, and the bright tracer bullets quickly faded out into the desert horizon.

'That's music to my ears, boy!' screamed Maddox. 'Let's hear 'em again!'

Kelso was only too happy to oblige. He laughed an insane laugh and fired another burst. Maddox hooted and hollered like a cowboy! He pulled his twin ·45 automatics – one from his holster, and his emergency spare from the back of his trousers – and fired both of them into the sky, still whooping it up! His behaviour was contagious: in moments, his men ran to the edge of the runway and began firing their machine-guns and pistols into the sky, hooting and hollering just like their Colonel!

Wild Bill Kelso laughed loudly, fired one last burst on his wing-mounts, then closed his canopy and took off amidst the thunder of automatic weapons fire. No American pilot ever had a more glorious send-off!

19

Birkhead was flying west. It had taken him a while to get the hang of flying again, and although he wasn't functioning with the assuredness of a truly competent pilot, he was all right as long as he kept his mind on what he was doing. That, however, was not what Donna wanted at all. The flight was really getting her hot, wet, and stimulated, her firm breasts begged for a man's strong hands, and her erect nipples cried out for a wet male tongue. She wanted satisfaction, good God, how she wanted it! And yet, Birkhead continually ignored her, keeping his eyes perpetually on the controls. She would have him, though – she made up her mind she was going to have him, no matter what she had to do, no matter how much initiative she had to take. She blew in his ear, and cooed softly. 'This is as good as a B-17.'

'Yeah – it handles pretty well!' he replied.

'But does it have as much . . . range?'

'Huh?' asked Birkhead, not recognizing his own earlier innuendo.

'Will it stay . . . up . . . for a long time?' she whispered suggestively.

'Oh, sure!' answered Birkhead cheerfully. 'We've used less than an eighth of a tank, and we're already over the Riverside County Reservoir! If you look out the window, you can see it!'

Donna didn't look out the window. Instead she began nibbling on his ear.

Some 15,000 feet below Birkhead and Donna, two Civilian Defence aeroplane-spotters were on duty at the Riverside County Reservoir. Their names were Joey Koos and Frank Manos and they were seventy-two and seventy-three years old respectively. They were, of course, volunteers. Because the qualifications for aircraft-spotters were virtually non-existent, Koos and Manos had been readily accepted for duty by their local organization despite the fact that Koos was hard of hearing and Manos was nearly blind. That they had been put on the same shift at the same post was further testament to the brilliant efficiency and foresight of the government officials in charge of the defence of southern California. Manos was the first to hear the drone of the Beechcraft overhead.

'I hear something up there!' exclaimed Manos.

'What?' asked Koos.

'I said I hear something up there!' Manos repeated loudly, into his ear.

'I heard you the first time! What does it sound like?'

'What?' asked Manos.

'I don't know!' answered Koos. 'I can't hear it!'

'I don't know what you're talking about,' Manos told him, but I can hear a 'plane up there – maybe two 'planes! I can't tell if it's one 'plane with two motors, or two 'planes with one motor! Can you see anything?'

Koos scanned the sky. The Beechcraft had three lights: one on each wingtip, and one on the tail. 'I see 'em!' exclaimed Koos. 'But there's three of 'em! Flying in formation! Two of 'em are flying together, and the other one's right behind 'em!'

Manos immediately picked up the 'phone, dialled the operator, and yelled, 'Army Flash! Army Flash!'

In moments, Manos was connected to Interceptor Command Headquarters in Los Angeles. Interceptor Command was the brain centre for southern California's

172

defence and was actually functioning with a good degree of competence. It was staffed by some fifty volunteers, including telephone operators and messengers, and a number of military personnel who kept track of troop movements and supplies in the area. On every wall and table in Interceptor Command Headquarters was a series of four coloured light bulbs to indicate the alert condition: yellow, blue, red, or white for clear. At present, the white lights were illuminated. A huge map of southern California had been painted on the floor, with a grid to divide the area into numbered sectors. Various markers were placed on the map to indicate the location of troops, supplies, and aircraft activity. The movement of 'planes was the main order of business, and as reports were received from aircraft-spotters, they were checked against flight plans and airport information. Then the aeroplane markers were moved across the map accordingly. So far, the only sightings of aircraft with no clearances had turned out to be birds. Nevertheless, such sightings were treated seriously and had caused several yellow, or precautionary, alerts in the past few days.

Manos identified himself to the answering Interceptor Command operator according to the expected procedure. 'Post: Riverside County Reservoir, code name Strawberry,' he told her. The code names of every post in the southern California area were fruits or vegetables because the officer who had been responsible for naming them had been a grocer in civilian life.

The operator took down Manos' information and repeated it aloud for all to hear. 'Strawberry!' called the operator. 'Three single-engined, high, heard! North-east of five, west! It was a verbal shorthand, confusing to the uninitiated, but quite understandable to the Interceptor Command personnel. What she was actually saying was that three single-engined aircraft at a high altitude had been heard, rather than seen, five miles north-east of the Strawberry post, heading west.

A woman clarified the code name for the man at the map: 'Strawberry is in Sector Fourteen.'

A man at the map placed a marker at the correct position, putting the number '3' on it, and 'H' for high altitude, and pointing it west.

Lieutenant O'Shaughnessy, in charge of confirmation of flight information, immediately responded. 'No clearance for aircraft in Fourteen! Repeat, no clearance! Request visual information!'

The operator who had taken the report responded. 'Apparently three single-engined aircraft are flying in formation. Further visual information is not available.'

Lieutenant O'Shaughnessy turned to his assistant. 'Attempt to establish radio contact with aircraft in Fourteen,' he ordered. The assistant picked up his own 'phone and called the airport in Ontario, California, so that this could be done.

Then another operator called out a bulletin. 'Tangerine confirms Strawberry! Aircraft proceeding west!'

Army Colonel Elward Neevil, a gruff, cigar-chomping rascal, was the supervisor on this shift. From his desk, Neevil could see everything that was going on. He immediately realized the seriousness of the situation and without hesitation, picked up the red 'phone on his desk. 'Attention all units!' he growled. 'Condition yellow! I repeat, yellow alert! A condition yellow exists until further notification from me!'

At once, the white lights went out and yellow lights came on. Southern California was under a yellow alert!

Despite the yellow alert now in effect, life outside of Interceptor Command Headquarters went on as usual. The public was not notified of yellow or blue alerts, for fear that such alerts might cause unwarranted panic. Thus, the unwarranted panic going on at the Crystal Ballroom continued full steam ahead, without needing the rationale of a yellow alert.

Usually, when there is a riot and there are cream pies in the vicinity, the pies get thrown. This was exactly what was happening in the Crystal Ballroom right now. Not only were pies being thrown, but every morsel of food that was throwable was being thrown! At one of the refreshment tables, two sailors were working the punch-bowl: one of them filled the glasses, and the other threw them. It was one of these poorly-thrown glasses of punch that finally revived Wally. Wally had been lying unconscious in the middle of the dance floor, but as the riot had proceeded, he had been gradually kicked under a table by thousands of pairs of constantly moving feet. The glass of punch that had been thrown at a marine shattered instead on the floor near Wally, and cold red punch splashed on the lad's face. In moments, he regained consciousness. Wally staggered to his feet, only to find he was the target for a zooter with a banana-cream pie! Wally saw the flying pie just in time: he ducked, and the pie hit an Army Sergeant behind him, right in the face! The Sergeant had seen Wally duck: he walked over to him and tapped him on the shoulder. Wally turned and the Sergeant ripped off his Navy top and used it to wipe the pie off his face. Wally didn't like people ripping the clothes off his back, even if the clothes belonged to somebody else. So, he picked up a music stand and cracked the Sergeant on the head with it! The Sergeant went down, and Wally proceeded to remove his tunic. After all, it was chilly outside, and Wally wasn't about to run around the street with no shirt on. Had Wally been paying more attention to the brawl around him instead of what he was wearing, he might have noticed the fighting going on by the huge Christmas tree nearby. Unfortunately, he didn't. A *pachuco* floored a marine who fell right into the Christmas tree. This marine was about the fifty-third person that night to have fallen into the tree, and the tree had had enough: it tipped over, and fell right on Wally. Once again, Wally fell to the floor, unconscious!

Outside, on Hollywood Boulevard, the reinforcements finally began arriving. Twenty taxis each carrying six or seven sailors pulled up at the Crystal Ballroom, but before any of the Navy men had a chance to go into the dance hall, an army of *pachucos* arrived in their beat-up cars and pick-up trucks.

'Let's get the chilli-eating bastards!' shouted one sailor, and his fellows proceeded to take the advice. After all, a riot was a riot, whether it was taking place inside or outside. As long as everybody was outside, why not slug it out right there?

More cars began to arrive, but with sailors and zooters rioting in the streets, there was no place to park. Vehicles crashed into one another, and a massive traffic jam developed immediately. Newly arriving soldiers and marines quickly got into the fray. Civilians deserted their cars in droves, especially when rioters began climbing on top of them to beat each other up!

It didn't take long for the noise level outside to become louder than the noise level inside the Crystal Ballroom. Some of the rioters inside, afraid that they might be missing something, ran out to investigate. When they discovered they *were* missing something, the news quickly spread into the USO Club. Three seconds later, the crazed mob inside poured into Hollywood Boulevard. What had been a contained full-scale riot was now an uncontained full-scale riot!

Servicemen began throwing one another through shop windows on the Boulevard. Several zooters were hurled

176

through the display windows of the Broadway Department Store. Thinking quickly, they grabbed the window
mannequins, tore off their arms and legs, and leapt back
into the fracas using these limbs as clubs!

Now three squad cars arrived. Whatever the six police
officers inside thought they were going to do to quell the
riot would never be known: the men were immediately
yanked out of their vehicles by soldiers, marines and
zooters and promptly beaten before they knew what hit
them!

There were now close to five thousand participants in
the Hollywood riot, and there was no end in sight!

20

Somewhere over Riverside County, California
9.17 p.m.

As the Beechcraft trainer approached the eastern edge
of Los Angeles County, Donna Stratton became more
and more like a wild animal. She was practically attacking
Birkhead now, attempting to get her hand in his trousers.
He continued to squirm, trying to fight off her advances
so that he could steer the aircraft.

'Donna, lay off, would you? I'm trying to steer!'

She planted a hand firmly on his crotch . . . but she
was not pleased by what she felt. 'Loomis, what's wrong?'
she whispered in a low, sexy tone. 'You're not airborne
yet!'

'What are you talking about? Look out the window!
Of course we're airborne!'

'We are . . . but *you're* not!' She climbed on top of him
and smothered him with a deliciously wicked kiss, still
keeping her hand in place. And finally, it happened: she
began to feel the throbbing between his legs . . . Loomis
was becoming 'airborne'! At last her passion had become
contagious!

He began kissing her back now, first with his lips, then
with his tongue. He no longer cared about the aeroplane
or where it was heading . . . he cared only where *they*
were heading!

Interceptor Command, however, cared a great deal about
where the aircraft was heading . . . or the 'three' aircraft
as they continued to believe. Headquarters was a flurry

of activity as civilians and military men made frantic 'phone calls, desperately trying to identify the unknown ''planes'. Boy scouts, wearing roller skates, carried messages to and fro, bits of information that might be useful to someone on the other side of the huge room.

Another telephone operator called out a new sighting. 'Post: code name Lima Bean reporting! Aircraft engines heard east, proceeding west! Altitude, high!'

'Request visual information,' shouted Colonel Neevil.

'Negative visual information,' replied the operator.

'Sir, the weather service reports a low cloud bank east of Los Angeles,' explained a volunteer at a telephone. 'Visibility ceiling: 3000 feet.'

'Lima Bean is in Sector Thirteen!' called the code lady.

'No clearance in Sector Thirteen!' replied Lieutenant O'Shaughnessy. 'Repeat, no clearance!'

'Request status on radio contact!' demanded Colonel Neevil.

O'Shaughnessy's assistant responded. 'Sir! Negative radio contact! Bandit aircraft refuse to respond!'

'Tell 'em to keep trying!' Neevil told him. Then the Colonel grimly picked up his red 'phone once again. 'Go to blue,' he ordered. 'Condition blue! Blue alert!'

The yellow lights in Interceptor Command Headquarters immediately turned to blue.

Just off the coast north of Santa Monica, the radio antenna of Imperial Japanese Submarine I-19 cut through the dark choppy Pacific. Inside, Ito had determined that the radio signal from KMPC was at its strongest. He had previously fiddled with the tuner and discovered he could pick up a number of Los Angeles radio stations. There could be no question about it: the Japanese were in the vicinity of Hollywood! Thus, Mitamura gave the order to surface.

The ballast tanks blew water into the ocean and in moments the conning tower of the I-19 rose out of the churning sea. The deck and part of the hull followed like a dark behemoth rising from the deep; then the ocean became calm again.

Fog had rolled in an hour ago, and it was thick enough to hide the submarine from the view of anyone on shore, unless they knew exactly where to look. Luckily for the Japanese, there was no one around who knew where to look.

Ward Douglas had been in his front yard, admiring the 40 mm Bofors Gun when he had heard the disturbance in the sea. Ward had never heard a submarine surface before, and could not identify the sound; he only knew that it was unlike anything he'd ever heard, and thus might warrant investigating. So, Ward ran to the garage and got his shotgun. With a war on, he figured that even the slightest suspicion of anything was reason enough to carry a weapon. He walked around to the back of his house and on to his overhanging porch which commanded a fine view of the ocean. Ward looked out. He could see nothing, nothing but fog.

Macey Douglas had seen his father returning from the garage with the Winchester from an unpainted section of window in his upstairs bedroom. He immediately ran downstairs to find out what was going on. He didn't bother to inform his brothers; they were with Mom, getting ready for bed, and Macey knew that his mother would spoil the fun.

'What is it, Dad?' asked Macey as he ran on to the porch.

Ward just stood there, staring out to sea. 'Thought I heard something out there.'

'What?' asked Macey excitedly. 'Japs?'

'No, just ... something.'

They both listened for a moment, but the only sound that could be heard was the clanging of a buoy not far away.

'Macey, bring me my field glasses. They're in my room.'

Macey eagerly ran back into the house to comply.

The two other people in the Los Angeles area who might have seen the Japanese sub if they had known where to look were sitting on top of the Ferris wheel at Ocean Amusement Park, eating. Well, not quite: Herbie Kaziminsky was eating, while Claude Crump was trying not to throw up. Herbie's manners did not make things any easier on Claude – the youth was wolfing down food like there was no tomorrow, chewing with his mouth open, and getting as much food on him as in him. He held his precious dummy with one hand while he ate with the other. Herbie was making so much noise that neither of them had heard the submarine surface, although being nearly half a mile further south of it than Ward was, they might not have heard it anyway. Claude dumped a packet of Alka-Seltzer into his canteen. Herbie heard the fizz and, realizing that Claude was feeling pretty queasy, pulled out his own thermos.

'If your stomach's upset, you should drink some of this,' Herbie told him, offering him the thermos. 'It'll make you feel a lot better!'

'What is it?' Claude asked, taking the flask.

'Buttermilk.'

Claude's face contorted and he immediately gave it back to Herbie. Claude quickly downed his Alka-Seltzer!

Then the dummy's head turned to Herbie. 'Well, if he's not gonna drink it, give it to me! My stomach's upset too!'

Herbie did as his dummy requested, and poured buttermilk into its mouth. None of the buttermilk went down – instead, it dribbled down the dummy's mouth, and then came squirting out its nose and ears! A strange character, this dummy!

Herbie proceeded to put the thermos away, but the dummy's mouth stayed wide open, as far open as it could go. Its head turned first one way, then the other, the mouth perpetually agape. The dummy was groaning – it sounded like it was in pain. Herbie looked at it, then realization lit his face. 'So you got lockjaw again, huh?'

Herbie grabbed the dummy's head and began banging its jaw against the gondola's safety bar. The mouth continued to remain open, so Herbie banged it still harder! Buttermilk sloshed out of it!

Claude watched this bizarre scene and was appalled: after all, he and the dummy had been getting along pretty well. 'Hey,' Claude told Herbie, 'you're being kinda rough on the little fella, aren't you?'

'Naw,' replied Herbie. 'He likes it!'

Commander Mitamura stood on the deck of his submarine, scanning the horizon for a suitable objective. The bright lights of the Los Angeles metropolitan area were diffused by the fog, thus making identification of anything more than a quarter of a mile inland virtually impossible. Ashimoto, Ito, von Kleinschmidt and several other crew members were also on deck, all of them scanning the horizon with binoculars except the Nazi, who had no binoculars.

Mitamura had decided to let the vessel drift southward. This would allow them to scan every inch of the Los Angeles coast. With the heavy fog, their chances of being spotted were miniscule, and Mitamura decided that this small risk was well worth taking for the chance of inflicting heavy psychological damage upon the American people.

Suddenly Ashimoto let out a yell and pointed towards

a house on the coast. He had seen something. The other Japanese officers turned in that direction and looked through their binoculars. They began chuckling: a well-built young woman was undressing! The Japanese marvelled at her sensational 40-inch bust!

Mitamura handed his binoculars to von Kleinschmidt. 'Lieutenant, take a look at the size of these American torpedoes.'

The German's face lit up as he took the glasses. Von Kleinschmidt had expressed his particular interest in weapons and torpedoes to Mitamura on several occasions, and the Commander knew he was especially interested in American armaments. Now von Kleinschmidt eagerly took a look for himself. One look was all he needed: he immediately turned away and handed Mitamura back his binoculars with a hateful scowl. The Japanese laughed. Obviously, the Lieutenant did not appreciate the Captain's sense of humour.

Hollywood Boulevard was a disaster area, and getting worse. By now, there was not a single window intact in a two-block radius! Several minutes ago, someone had broken into a Fire Alarm box on the street. Now the Fire Department arrived. Two 'hook-and-ladders' swerved wildly into the mob-infested intersection near the Crystal Ballroom, and rioters dived out of the way! Vito was not so lucky, however: now clad in only his red striped underwear, Vito did not notice that one of the fire truck's ladders had broken away from its restraining hook. The ladder whipped wildly into the thick of the crowd, caught Vito in the gut, and threw him through the window of an Italian restaurant!

In moments, the fire trucks were overrun by rioters. *Pachucos* uncoiled hoses and swung them at servicemen. Four sailors grabbed a ladder, and with two men on ea end, they ran down the street with it, bowling people over!

Then, a new sound began to arise from the din: a low rumble, which became steadily louder and louder, and finally became so loud that it could not be ignored. Heads turned to see what it was, and astonishment immediately lit the faces of the onlookers: it was 'Lulubelle', the M-3 tank, barrelling into the intersection! It didn't matter that abandoned cars snarled the streets and made it imposs-ible for lesser vehicles to pass, the M-3 tank drove right over them, crushing them like insects! As soon as the tank pulled to a stop in front of the Crystal Ballroom, rioters attempted to climb on to it. But they hadn't counted upon the wrath of Sergeant Frank Tree! Tree threw open the cupola hatch, jumped up on the turret, and knocked out a marine and a sailor! He grabbed the turret-mounted ·50 calibre machine-gun, yanked it off its mount and fired a tremendous blast into the night sky. The combined effect of the gunfire along with the image of the tank itself was immediately sobering to the rioters: the pandemonium quickly died down. All eyes turned to the tank. Tree looked upon the sea of faces with total outrage.

'What the hell do you people think you're doing?' he thundered. 'You're acting like a bunch of Tojo stooges! What are you trying to do? Put Yamamoto in the White House? Wise up! This is no time to be fighting among yourselves! We've got the lousy Nips to fight!'

These were strong words, delivered by a strong man. And the people listened.

While all of this was going on in the street, Betty Douglas had finally worked up enough courage to peek out of the Ladies' Room in the Crystal Ballroom. She had hidden there early in the riot, along with a number of other

Hostesses; it had been a good idea, because they had all come through it virtually unscathed. Betty had a scratch on her face, and her new white dress was stained and soiled, but other than that, she was fine. Besides the Hostesses and members of the orchestra, the only people left in the dance hall were unconscious. It was quite safe for Betty to emerge from the lounge. She had one thing on her mind right now, and that was to find Wally.

'Wally?' she called, looking around for some sign of him. Wally, however, was still unconscious under the Christmas tree, and completely hidden from her view. She moved towards the front door, thinking he might be out on the street. As she did so, the heel of her shoe hooked on to a piece of fallen Christmas garland. She jerked her leg and pulled the garland which had got wrapped around the leg of a folding refreshment table. The table leg gave way, causing a half-filled bowl of punch to slide off the table and spill right on to the face of the unconscious 'Stretch' Sitarski! Exactly how Sitarski came to be under the table was unimportant; what was important was that he revived just in time to see Betty walk out the door. Sitarski staggered to his feet and followed her. He too had only one thing on his mind.

The same thing was on the minds of Birkhead and Donna, but the fact that they shared the same lustful thoughts made it much easier for them to do something about it. The Beechcraft continued to fly due west without much attention from Birkhead, although he occasionally found himself glancing over his shoulder to check the controls. Donna had removed his tunic and shirt, and now he was once again opening her jacket.

'Is the target in sight yet?' she asked suggestively -- playing the scenario of the afternoon.

'Target in sight,' he whispered, hungrily gazing at

185

purple lace bra. 'But I think I'd better go in for a closer look!' He reached around her back and unfastened the bra, then removed it, exposing her gorgeous breasts. Then, Birkhead went down for an extremely close look.

Interceptor Command had been getting progressively more frantic as every attempt to identify the mysterious aircraft failed. The actual number of 'planes seemed to vary with succeeding reports, ranging between one and twelve, but the location and direction of the aircraft was confirmed and re-confirmed by every spotter. Something was up there, and that something was heading west.

'Post: Cauliflower!' shouted an operator. 'Aircraft twelve o'clock, proceeding west!'

'That's Sector Twelve,' reported the code lady. 'Los Angeles County!'

The man at the map pushed the marker further west into Sector Twelve. 'Sir, they're heading straight for LA!'

Colonel Edward Neevil was down at the map in the thick of the activity, chewing nervously on the end of his stogie. This was an extremely serious situation. 'What's the status on radio contact?' he asked once again.

'Sir, still negative radio contact!' replied the assistant. 'Aircraft refuse response on every available frequency! Behaviour presumed hostile!'

'Sir, we still have no confirmed visual information,' reported Lieutenant O'Shaughnessy.

'The hell with visual information!' shouted Neevil. 'They're Japs! Let's go to red! Red alert for Los Angeles! We've got a goddamn air raid here!'

Immediately, every volunteer picked up every available 'phone and began spreading the alarm. The lights on the walls went from blue to red. In a few minutes, the sirens would sound and the city of Los Angeles would brace itself for a full-scale air raid!

21

Corporal 'Stretch' Sitarski followed Betty Douglas out of the USO Club only to lose her in the crowd gathered around 'Lulubelle'. When Sitarski saw Tree atop the tank, he decided he'd better make himself scarce. He was in trouble enough as it was for being AWOL, but if Tree spotted him now, he knew he'd never have a chance to find Betty. Tree, totally wrapped up in his speech, did not spot Sitarski. But Maxine Dexheimer did! Maxine had participated fully in the riot, both inside and outside. She had knocked out as many servicemen as anybody, and had come through it all without a scratch. And, she had enjoyed herself immensely. Upon seeing Sitarski, she quickly lost all interest in Tree's speech, and pushed through the crowd to catch him. Unfortunately, by the time she got where she had seen him, he too had vanished into the multitude.

Sergeant Frank Tree, meantime, was spouting Americanism as Americanism was meant to be spouted. Had the presidential election been held right then and there, Tree would have been swept into the White House unanimously. 'Make no mistake about it,' he was telling the crowd, 'the Japs have only one idea: to kill! To kill you and to kill your families, and to keep on killing until they conquer the world! If they win, you won't be able to speak your free mind, or worship God in your own way!' He paused for a moment, then pointed to a large, brightly lit Santa Claus decoration which adorned a nearby lamp-

187

post. 'Look at Santa Claus! Isn't Santa Claus cute? Do you think the Japs believe in Santa Claus?'

Tree was answered by a chorus of No's from the crowd.

'Instead of turkey for your Christmas dinner, how'd you like to have raw fish-heads and rice?'

The crowd booed loudly.

'That's why we've gotta stick together! This isn't any ordinary war! The Japs aren't just people with the wrong idea – they're trained slaughterers of democracy! This time, we get no second chance! This time, we free the world, or lose it! This time we win, or we die trying! We didn't start this war, but, by God, we're going to finish it!'

Tree was immediately answered by the wail of air-raid sirens, loud, long and clear. The gravity of the situation was not lost on a single soul: all heads turned skywards, with expressions of fear, shock and terror. Tree's eyes burned with raging intensity – this was the moment he'd waited his whole life for!

'This is it!' he screamed. 'Now let's show those lousy Nip bastards what we can do!'

What the crowd did was panic. Once again, Hollywood Boulevard turned into a mad rush of insanity as people scattered in every direction to look for shelter. Betty Douglas ran almost a full block, then took cover under a panel truck parked on the street. Again, 'Stretch' Sitarski missed seeing her. He began running into buildings in hopes of finding her. Maxine took shelter in the Broadway Department Store, climbing in through a broken window, and hiding under a counter. And Wally remained unconscious under the fallen Christmas tree in the Crystal Ballroom.

General Joseph W. Stilwell had enjoyed *Dumbo* so much that he was sitting through it a second time. Unfortun-

188

ately, he was not going to make it all the way to the end. Outside the air-raid sirens were sounding, and they could be heard even inside the theatre. People in the audience began to fidget nervously, not sure what they were hearing or what it meant. Lieutenant Bressler leaned over to Stilwell. 'Sir, it sounds like an air raid!'

The words 'air raid' sparked an explosion: cries of 'Air raid!' and 'Jap attack!' were immediately taken up by the audience. Frightened people jumped out of their seats and charged for the exit doors, trampling children in the process! It was a complete mob reaction!

Stilwell alone kept a level head as he barked orders to his men. 'Keep everybody inside, off the street! Get 'em downstairs, into the lounges! And tell the manager to put his lights out!'

Stilwell's MPs rushed to the theatre lobby to maintain order, and Stilwell himself followed in order to telephone Interceptor Command. In moments, the theatre auditorium was clear . . . with the exception of Corporal Mike Mizerany who preferred to simply watch the movie.

With the sirens sounding throughout the city, Civilian Defense volunteers sprang into action. All over town, a similar scene was repeated as ordinary men with wives and families donned their Civilian Defense helmets and armbands, grabbed their whistles and torches, and turned into power-mad lunatics responsible for enforcing the black-out of all lights! These crazed block wardens ran down the streets of their neighbourhoods screaming, 'Lights out!' at the top of their lungs. When Warden Phillip Strossman came to a house with its porch light on, rather than ring the doorbell and ask the owner to comply with the law, he smashed the offending light-fixture with the butt of his torch! Warden Richard Marshall went even further in his neighbourhood : when he came upon a house with the lights on inside, he broke a window, climbed in and busted up all of the lamps, whether they were on or not! And he did all of this under the disbelieving eyes of the family who resided there!

Luckily, most people knew what to do in an air raid and they extinguished their lights without being told. On business streets drivers pulled over, parked and took cover underneath their cars. Several people who forgot to turn out their headlights had them smashed to bits by other over-zealous CD volunteers!

Electric company workers who had been put on air-raid alert rushed to Department of Water and Power sub-stations in order to throw the switches that would extinguish the street lights of the city. Charles Randolph, responsible for the sub-station which controlled Hollywood Boulevard, had unfortunately forgotten to douse his own headlights as he drove to the sub-station. His automobile was rammed by a fanatical block warden who jumped out of his car, yelling 'Traitor! Saboteur!' and whacked Randolph over the head with a piece of lead pipe! Randolph never reached his destination, and downtown Hollywood remained lit up!

Even as the civilians were blacking out Los Angeles, the Army was moving into action. At various locations throughout the city were the anti-aircraft searchlight units which Stilwell had briefed the press about that afternoon. These 800 million candlepower carbon arc lamps were operated by three-man crews, and used to illuminate the night sky to search for aircraft. An aeroplane caught in the beam of one of these powerful lamps, would become a brightly lit target for anti-aircraft guns. The Army was responsible for these lamps, and the three-man crews rushed to their assigned searchlight units. Many of the searchlights had been placed in the thinly populated hills surrounding Los Angeles; others, hidden away in garages, were moved on to street corners. One by one, the carbon arcs were lit, and soon white ribbons of light sliced through the darkness overhead, searching for enemy aircraft.

Soldiers assigned to the 871 anti-aircraft guns which had been installed throughout the city snapped to their duty. The canvas covers on the guns were torn off, crates of ammunition were ripped open, shells were shoved into breeches, and the gunners cranked their weapons up at the sky. There were three different types of anti-aircraft guns: 20 mm, 40 mm and huge 5-inch cannons. Within three minutes of the sounding of the air-raid sirens, every one of them was manned and ready!

Commander Mitamura and the other Japanese officers stood on the deck of their submarine, watching with great interest as Los Angeles blacked out. To Mitamura, it was both good news and bad news: the bad news was that they would most likely have to remain surfaced for a much longer time in order to find a suitable target to destroy; the good news was that there was now even less chance of their being spotted. To Lieutenant von Kleinschmidt, who had continued to insist they were all in grave danger being this close to a major American city, the blackout was bad news all the way.

'We must have been spotted,' he told Mitamura. 'There is still time to retreat before the Americans destroy us!'

The Japanese Commander was disgusted by the German's cowardly words. 'We shall remain here and fight with honour,' he replied confidently.

'That is absurd!' he protested. 'No officer in our Reich Navy would ever consider jeopardizing his equipment for the sake of some abstract concept!'

'No officer in your Reich Navy even possesses the skill

to pilot a vessel this close to the American mainland without being detected,' answered Mitamura dryly.

After the air-raid sirens had blared for four full minutes, they began to die down. The air-raid and black-out condition would remain in effect until the 'All Clear' sounded: this would be a siren of steady even pitch, quite unlike the undulating wail of the red alert.

As the final siren died out, an eerie stillness pervaded the entire city, like the calm before a storm. Everywhere, gun crews nervously stared at the sky, watching, waiting, worrying.

Sergeant Frank Tree, atop his tank, cocked his ·50 calibre machine-gun and similarly looked skywards. His view was obscured by the lights still lit on Hollywood Boulevard; but he assumed that any moment now, someone would throw the switch that would black out the street.

Betty Douglas, alone under the panel truck that was her refuge, was thinking about her family in Santa Monica. With the Japanese expected to swoop in over the Pacific, she realized they might be in grave danger right now.

Ward Douglas was quite aware of that danger, and for that reason, he had ordered his entire family into the centre of the house. It was here he decided they would be safest. Ward himself stood vigilantly on his near porch, shotgun in hand, searching the sky through his field glasses. He would have felt a lot safer with an Army gun crew manning the cannon in his yard, but as Tree had told him, the gun first needed to be properly installed, and that would not occur until Monday.

Half a mile away, atop the Ocean Park Ferris wheel, Claude, Herbie and the dummy all scanned the sky. Claude couldn't help but steal a glance at the dummy;

the dummy winked back at him!

And downtown, General Stilwell stood in front of the darkened Los Angeles Theater, watching as the last of the lights on Broadway went dark. Stilwell coolly surveyed the scene. The streets of downtown Los Angeles were deserted now, the pedestrians had all found shelter and the traffic had come to a complete halt. Stilwell was here because he had been unable to get through to Interceptor Command: the telephone lines were either jammed or not functioning, mainly because panic-stricken Pacific Telephone Company operators had deserted their switchboards. Those who remained on duty were unable to handle the incredible volume of calls. Theoretically, during an air raid, only military and Civilian Defense personnel were supposed to use the telephone; but obviously the civilian population had either not been informed or were disregarding the directive. Nevertheless, Stilwell could not be too upset by this snag: after all, the war was barely a week old, and only so much could be expected from the citizens of Los Angeles in so short a time. Stilwell was actually quite pleased with what he was seeing – the sirens had worked, the city was complying with the black-out, and the streets had emptied in a fairly orderly fashion. It was an admirable show of spirit and co-operation. As to what, if anything, was actually in the sky, well, that was a matter for conjecture. Stilwell doubted that there could possibly be Japanese bombers in the vicinity; still, it was his duty to expect the worst and hope for the best, and that's what he was doing.

Lieutenant Bressler stepped out of the theatre with a pair of field glasses and handed them to his superior. Stilwell climbed on to the roof of a Studebaker Club Sedan parked nearby and scanned the western sky, standing like a figure of defiance in the night. Had Stilwell known that the ''planes' which Interceptor Command had been tracking were coming from the east, he most likely would have called off the air-raid alert immediately. Any cool-headed man would have laughed at the idea of enemy aircraft approaching Los Angeles from the Mojave Desert. But as the events of the preceding hours had indicated, there were very few cool heads in southern California at this time. And so, General Stilwell watched the western sky while the fingers of thousands of less cooler heads were poised on the triggers of their guns.

22

Somewhere above Los Angeles
9.33 p.m.

So that he wouldn't be distracted from the more important business at hand, Birkhead had devised a rather unique automatic pilot system to keep the Beechcraft trainer on a straight course: he had wrapped Donna's bra around the steering control and had connected it to his seat! It was working very well, too, although Birkhead didn't have time to notice, since he was absorbed in something else. His trousers were down, her skirt was hitched up, and both were in the throes of passion. Their mission was just about to reach its climax!

'More thrust, Loomis, more thrust!' She groaned with pleasure as he gave it to her. 'Oh, yes, yes, yes, yes! You're right on target!'

Fifteen hundred feet above them and half a mile to their north was Wild Bill Kelso. Kelso, in his usual manner of flying, had managed to miss Pomona. However, he was now no longer looking for Pomona. His P-40 was equipped with a radio, and he had been following the reports of the unidentified 'squadron' which Interceptor Command had reported was heading for Los Angeles. Kelso swore that the Japs weren't going to elude him this time! His radio crackled with another report. 'Unidentified aircraft spotted in Sector Twelve, co-ordinates two, zero, niner; tango, ocean, delta.' Kelso banked southward, and he sighted the Beechcraft below him!

'I see the son-of-a-bitch!' he screamed and pulled into

an eighty-five-degree dive! His hand grabbed the machine-gun switch and his eyes sparkled with insane frenzy!

Below, Donna was also in a state of frenzy! 'Give it to me, Loomis!' she cried. 'Give it to me!'

Instead, Wild Bill Kelso gave it to both of them! His ·50 calibre machine-gun bullets ripped through the Beechcraft, knocking loose an aileron which caused the trainer to plummet 1000 feet in altitude! Birkhead and Donna were both thrown into the ceiling of the cabin, and Donna screamed in orgiastic delight! 'Oh my God, Loomis! Oh my God!'

Birkhead screamed in terror, realizing what had happened! 'OH MY GOD!'

Donna had just experienced more ecstasy than she'd ever had in her life! 'I've never felt anything like that before!' she told him, flushed with excitement.

'You're damn right you haven't!' Birkhead replied staring wide-eyed at the bullet holes in the cabin. 'They think we're Japs!'

Again, Wild Bill Kelso swooped down on the helpless Beechcraft, laughing maniacally! 'Take that, Tojo!' he howled, firing another burst on his ·50s.

More bullets ripped into the trainer. Birkhead covered his eyes with fear. 'Oh, God, am I in trouble now!' he moaned. 'Am I in trouble now!'

Donna now realized what was happening. She became forceful and intense. 'Loomis,' she shouted, 'take evasive action!'

But he just sat there, moaning. She pushed him out of the way and took over the controls, ripping her bra off the steering column and pulling back on it.

As the P-40 dived down on the Beechcraft, machine-guns ablaze, the trainer suddenly spun out of its path and zoomed skywards! Kelso's nose-dive was too fast and too steep to stay with the trainer: he cut through the cloud bank beneath him and reappeared over Hollywood, his machine-guns strafing the city below!

These same bullets ripped across the roof of the Crystal Ballroom where Willy and Joe sat behind their 40 mm anti-aircraft gun. Willy and Joe couldn't tell the difference between a P-40 and a Japanese Zero, but they could certainly tell when a 'plane was shooting at them – and this one was! 'JAAAAPPPPSSSS!!!!' screamed Willy. 'JAAAAAAAAAAAAPPPPPPPPPPPPSSSSSSSSSSS!!!!!' They began blasting 40 mm shells back at the invader, not bothering to aim, and not bothering to stop when Kelso streaked upwards, out of range.

Then, herd-instinct and itchy trigger-fingers took over; because Willy and Joe had started firing, another gun crew started firing; then another, and another! The shells exploded in the night sky like fireworks, and ignorant soldiers mistook these explosions for enemy aircraft fire! Fifty more gun crews opened up, shooting at their own flak!

'What the hell are you shooting at?' an incredulous soldier asked his companion.

'Whatever they're shooting at!' he replied.

Inside of another minute, every gun crew in Los Angeles was blasting away at the non-existent invaders!

Kelso climbed rapidly, searching for the 'enemy' Beechcraft. Donna meanwhile was doing an incredible job piloting the trainer. She had picked up quite a bit about flying during her previous experiences in cockpits, and all of it was coming back to her now. But without any guns, she had no idea how long she'd be able to evade their attacker. All she could do was keep on flying.

Far below, on Hollywood Boulevard, Quince stuck his head out of 'Lulubelle's' driver's hatch to see what all of the shooting was about. He was shocked to see that the

197

lights on the street were still burning. Even the marquee of the Crystal Ballroom was illuminated. 'Sarge!' he yelled, trying to be heard over the staccato gunfire, 'why are all these lights on?'

'I don't know,' replied Tree. 'There must be a foul-up somewhere!'

'Well if we don't put 'em out, this whole goddamn street's gonna be a target!'

'You're right! Okay, you take her slowly down the street and I'll knock 'em out! Reese! Foley! Get up here!'

Quince revved-up the tank, and Reese and Foley climbed on top of it.

Meanwhile, inside the Crystal Ballroom, a pair of hands with huge pinky rings pushed the branches of the fallen Christmas tree aside and began slapping the unconscious face of Wally Stephans. Meyer Mishkin had been looking for Wally for the past thirty minutes. He slapped him harder, trying to revive him. Meyer blew a huge puff of cigar smoke into Wally's face; Wally coughed and opened his eyes. Immediately, the talent scout started working on him. 'Kid, you're the greatest trick foot I've ever seen, and I've seen 'em all over the world! You're a natural!' He shoved a contract and pen into Wally's face. 'Just sign right here! A seven-year contract, and we'll start you off at seventy-five bucks a week!'

But Wally wasn't interested in the contract. He wriggled out from under the tree and climbed to his feet. 'Where's Betty?' he asked urgently.

'Betty? You mean that dame you were dancing with? She took a powder! She ran outside somewhere!'

Wally, wearing the Army Sergeant's tunic and the Navy Shore Patrolman's trousers, started for the door. Meyer Mishkin ran after him. 'Wait a minute kid – you can't go now! We've gotta discuss business!' But Meyer Mishkin never caught up with him: the talent scout slipped on a pool of punch and fell right on his arse.

Outside, Sergeant Frank Tree aimed his machine-gun at the street lights next to the Crystal Ballroom and blew them all to hell! Reese and Foley shot out two more street lights with their pistols. Then, Tree took aim at the brightly lit marquee of the Crystal Ballroom, just as Wally came running out!

Wally was stupefied at the sight in front of him. The image of the tank amidst the shambles of Hollywood Boulevard while flak exploded in the sky overhead made the seriousness of the war a grim reality for him. This was not only real, it was here and now!

'Hit the dirt, soldier!' yelled Tree, not recognizing Wally in the half-arsed uniform.

Wally didn't have to be told twice! Seeing the ·50 calibre machine-gun pointing at him was all the motivation he needed to dive the hell out of the way! Tree opened up and sliced the entire dance-hall marquee to ribbons! The lights and wiring exploded brilliantly, and with the supports ripped up, the entire thing collapsed, breaking apart on the pavement with a tremendous crash! Tree spun the machine-gun around and took aim at a Santa Claus decoration on a light standard ... but then his gun jammed. Unable to fire it, Tree yanked off the ammunition canister, figuring that the ammunition belt had got hung up in the feed mechanism. The belt spilled out of the canister, broke off and fell to the ground. Tree yelled at Wally. 'Hey you! Get over here and gimme a hand with this belt!'

Wally protested. 'But I don't know anything about—'

'That's an order, soldier!' barked Tree.

Without thinking, Wally ran over and picked up the fallen ammunition belt. He climbed on to the tank and handed it to Tree. 'Thanks, kid,' replied Tree, still not recognizing him. Wally stared at the tank and the machine-gun with awe, marvelling at its obvious power. As Quince put her into gear, Wally realized that riding a tank was even better than stealing cars! He watched Tree, fascinated, as he quickly put the machine-gun into operating order again. Now Tree fired at the light standard with the Santa Claus, and the bullets cut right through the entire post! The pole toppled, and Santa Claus hit Frank Tree right on the head! Tree fell backwards, his legs in the turret hatch preventing him from falling completely out of the tank. Wally tried to revive him. 'The lights, kid,' muttered the fading Sergeant. 'Knock out . . . the lightsss. . . .' He passed out.

Wally didn't hesitate at all: he took command. 'Back this thing up,' he told Quince. 'We'll start with those lights down there!'

As Quince shifted into reverse, Reese nudged him, speaking so that Wally couldn't hear. 'Quince, isn't he the kid from the cafe this morning?'

Quince took a good look at Wally. 'Yeah, that's him, all right.'

'Well, we can't take orders from him! He's a civilian!'

'He's got Sergeant's stripes, hasn't he?'

'Nobody becomes a Sergeant in one afternoon!' said Reese. 'He stole that uniform!'

'Look, Reese, do you want to take responsibility for this? Stealing the tank, shooting up the street, running over all those cars?'

Reese shook his head.

'Well, I don't either! You don't know where he got that uniform and neither do I. But as far as I'm concerned, he's a Sergeant, so he can give the orders and he can take the rap for whatever happens!'

Reese nodded, Quince backed up the tank, and Wally began blasting out street lights!

Four thousand feet above Los Angeles, Wild Bill Kelso executed a maniacal barrel roll, then pulled into a sharp left bank and came up right behind the trainer. Donna immediately pulled back on her joystick and the Beechcraft climbed out of the way of the P-40's blazing wingmounts.

'Look at that skibbee!' laughed Kelso. 'He's climbing like a homesick angel!' Kelso zoomed after the trainer, hot on its tail.

Despite the fact that Kelso's P-40 was both faster and more manoeuvrable than the Beechcraft, Donna was making moves that would be enviable to any first-rate stunt pilot. That she was at times unsure of what she was doing added an unpredictability to her movements that confused Kelso and helped keep the trainer out of his line of fire. Birkhead, meanwhile, was on the floor, still scared shitless. 'Oh, God, am I in trouble now,' he kept saying.

'Shoot back, Loomis!' Donna ordered. 'Shoot back!'

'But we haven't got any guns!' he protested.

'Use your service pistol!'

Birkhead found his Army-issue ·45 automatic on the floor of the cabin and stared at it, terrified. He had completely forgotten about it, and with good reason. 'This? I've never fired a gun before in my life!'

She shook her head. 'Women always have to do everything! Give me that!' She grabbed the gun away from him and cocked it. Not only had her father taught her how to box, but he'd also taught her how to handle a gun!

'What do you want me to do?' asked Birkhead helplessly.

'Blow him a kiss, why don't you!' She dived earthwards to avoid Kelso's onslaught, passing through a searchlight beam and narrowly missing the flak that was exploding on both sides of her! She suddenly whipped into an unexpected loop-the-loop, right around the P-40!

Kelso was livid! He realized the enemy pilot was trying to make a fool out of him! 'Try this on for size, you yellow monkey!' he bellowed, firing a long, savage burst on his machine-guns! The bullets shattered one of the Beechcraft's cockpit windows. Donna rolled sharply and banked around into a head-on course with Kelso. She thrust the automatic pistol out of her broken window. 'Try some of your own medicine!' she cried as she fired at him. One of her bullets zinged through the P-40's canopy; then she pulled up, out of the collision course.

Kelso was outraged! He had been fired upon, and there was a bullet hole in his canopy to prove it! He stuck a finger in it, just to convince himself it was real. 'All right!' he screamed. 'This is it! This is war!' Kelso reached for his controls only to find that his finger was stuck in the ·45 calibre hole! He couldn't get it out! He steered with his other hand as he struggled to free his finger, grunting and groaning as he pulled harder and harder. But the only thing he managed to do was to drop his lit cigar into his lap! He howled in pain as the burning end seared through his trousers. Kelso had no choice: he took his hand off the controls to grab his cigar, then used his hand to yank his stuck finger out of the bullet hole. Now pilotless, his fighter dived sharply towards central Los Angeles! With a mighty heave, Kelso freed his finger only to find that he was on a collision course with a row of buildings on Wilshire Boulevard! Kelso barrelrolled, his wing-tip missing the edge of a building by mere inches! He pulled back on his steering column and shot upwards once again, in mad pursuit of the Beechcraft!

All of this time, General Joseph W. Stilwell had remained atop the roof of the Studebaker, scanning the heavens.

Despite the constant explosions of flak illuminating the sky, Stilwell was getting very sceptical about this so-called 'air raid'.

Lieutenant Bressler cocked his head. Even with the roar of cannon-fire he was able to discern the drone of the dogfighting aeroplanes. 'Sir, those are 'planes up there,' he told Stilwell.

Stilwell had heard them too, for several minutes in fact. ' 'Planes, maybe, but no bombs. I haven't heard a single bomb. Don't you think they'd bring a few bombs along?' Stilwell lowered his binoculars and climbed down from the car. He had seen enough. 'Bressler, round up the men and the vehicles. We're going to get to the bottom of this "air raid" right now!'

23

Off the Santa Monica Coast
9.38 p.m.

The bewildered crew of Japanese Submarine I-19 watched with complete amazement as flak continued to explode over Los Angeles County. Exactly what the point of all of it was, was totally beyond their comprehension. It seemed to be an air raid, except that one essential ingredient was missing: enemy 'planes! Ashimoto turned around and looked into the western sky. 'Nothing comes from the west,' he observed. 'What can they be shooting at?'

Mitamura and the others shrugged. Von Kleinschmidt looked at them all dryly. 'Messerschmidts, perhaps,' he suggested, chuckling at his own joke. None of the Japanese chuckled. They just glared at him.

Suddenly a buoy started clanging loudly: the sub had drifted into it. Everyone had been so absorbed in the fireworks in the sky that no one had bothered to watch where they were going.

Ward Douglas heard it, too. This was the buoy several hundred yards away from his house, the same buoy he had heard earlier. He immediately turned his attention from the sky to the sea, and adjusted the focus on his binoculars accordingly. He could see virtually nothing – the fog was still too thick. Then he heard the sound of distant voices. It sounded like arguing, but Ward couldn't quite make out the words. 'What the hell is that?' he muttered under his breath, cursing the fog that obscured his view. He wondered if there might be a boat out there.

He strained his ears, trying to pick up the conversation. Was it his imagination, or was he hearing the word 'Dummkopf'?

Several Japanese quickly grabbed poles to push the buoy away from the hull of their vessel. While von Kleinschmidt cursed the incompetence of the crew for allowing such a collision to occur, Mitamura stoically scanned the coastline, watching for any indication that the accident had been heard ashore. Like Ward, Mitamura's vision was thwarted by the fog wafting across the sea.

Then, fate took a hand. A gentle breeze swept across the sea and broke up the fog bank, simultaneously clearing the vision of both men. Ward's eyes bulged at the sight of the submarine, and a cold tingle ran down his spine as he realized that Mitamura was looking right at him! 'J-J-J-J-J-aps ...' he stuttered weakly, trying to summon his courage. Gradually, the courage was summoned. 'Japs!' he stated with a little more strength. And finally, it became a blood-curdling battle cry: 'JAAAAAPPPPPSSSSS!'

'YANKEEEE!' shouted Mitamura, pointing at the American who was looking at them. His crew immediately focused on Ward and watched him, waiting to see what he would do.

Ward Douglas was level-headed enough to realize that his shotgun was useless at a time like this. Clearly the submarine was out of range of his Winchester; but even if it had been in range, his buckshot could do very little damage to the full-sized craft. Ward opened his back door and yelled in to the house. 'Joan! Go across the street and get Scioli! It's an invasion! Japs!'

Joan, dressed in her bathrobe, stormed on to the porch, very piqued. She did not take kindly to her husband ordering her around, no matter what the reason. 'Ward

Douglas,' she scolded, 'I think you're taking this war a little too seriously!'

Macey, Stevie and Gus had followed their mother outside to see what all of the commotion was about. Ward screamed back at Joan. 'Just shut up and do what I tell you! Get Scioli over here, goddammit!'

'I will not permit you to address me in that tone of voice,' she replied, 'and especially not in front of the children!'

'Goddammit, why do I have to do everything around here?' Ward ran around the side of his house, through his front yard, and hollered as loud as he could at the house on the hill across the street. 'Scioli! Come quick! Japs! JAAPPPSSS!'

On the submarine, von Kleinschmidt had taken Ashimoto's binoculars to see the American for himself. To him, the proper course of action was obvious. 'We must shell that house, murder the witnesses and retreat!'

'That would not be honourable,' replied Mitamura. 'He cannot harm us with a useless shotgun, and his home is of no military value.'

'But he can summon the military authorities! They will dispatch an armed force to destroy us!'

'Then let them come. We shall not run from battle. We shall face them like true Samurai, in the name of the Emperor!'

'*Dummkopf!*' replied the Nazi.

Dominic Scioli ran down the hill from his house towards the home of his neighbour. Like Ward, Scioli had been outside watching for 'planes in the western sky, so he had heard Ward's cry immediately.

With Scioli on his way, Ward turned his attention back to the sub. He moved through his yard to find the best vantage point, and stopped right on top of the sticks and leaves which were covering over the Jap Trap! The kids had finished the job just before dinner, and in the darkness, the camouflage was virtually invisible. As Macey, Stevie and Gus ran into the front yard along with their mother, they reacted in horror upon seeing their father standing on top of the booby trap. They traded worried glances. The sticks, however, did not give way.

Scioli dashed into the Douglas yard and ran over to Ward, joining him on top of the camouflaged pit. The kids were even more worried now, but still, the sticks held.

'Ward, are you out of your mind?' Scioli was saying. 'How can there be Japs? There isn't a 'plane in the sky!'

'There's a Jap sub out there, Scioli!' Ward told him, pointing it out. 'Probably planning to torpedo my house!' He handed Scioli the binoculars, and Scioli took a look.

'Jesus H. Christ!' he exclaimed.

Now, a very irate Joan Douglas marched over to her husband. 'Ward Douglas, I demand you cease this idiotic behaviour this instant!'

The kids saw that she too was about to step on to the disguised Jap Trap, and they exchanged extremely fearful looks. Joan walked upon the sticks, and they immediately gave way! Joan, Ward and Scioli plunged into the pit. Macey, Stevie and Gus all sighed with relief. 'It works!' exclaimed Macey with pride.

Further inland and above, Wild Bill Kelso dodged anti-aircraft fire, and remained in hot pursuit of the Beechcraft. The after-images of the constantly exploding flak around him became spots before his eyes, and when Kelso looked at the American 'plane, these spots became the 'big red meatball' insignia of the Imperial Japanese Forces! So far, the 'enemy' aircraft had managed to elude him, but upon seeing a nearby cloud bank, Kelso remembered an old fighter pilot trick. He soared above the clouds, hiding himself from his adversary, then circled, waiting for the twin-engined craft to appear below him. It didn't take long: the Beechcraft came into view below and to the left of Kelso. Kelso banked sharply, then edged into a dive, in perfect position for a kill! Wild Bill roared with crazed laughter as he blasted away on his machine-guns. 'Eat lead, slant!' he hollered. His bullets ripped through the trainer's number two engine and it burst into flames. More bullets cut the wings' ailerons to ribbons. Black smoke poured out of the aircraft and it began to plummet. Kelso pulled upward, laughing maniacally as his kill streaked downward. He slid his canopy back to scream out his parting words. 'Sayonara, sucker!'

Donna had lost control of the 'plane as soon as the engine caught fire, and with the ailerons sheared to nothingness, there was no way she could hope to attempt anything resembling a landing. It looked like this was the end. The cabin began filling with smoke, and she and Birkhead began coughing. The realization of imminent death brought new courage to Birkhead, and he took the controls, hoping to avert disaster. But it was too late. Try as he might, Birkhead could not pull out of the nose-dive. The earth was rushing towards them, the aircraft was in a tail-spin, and all Birkhead could do was hold Donna tightly in hopes of somehow protecting her from the inevitable crash.

About half a mile away, a squad of soldiers at an anti-aircraft battery stared open-mouthed as the burning aircraft hurtled earthwards. Realizing that impact was mere moments away, they braced themselves for a tremendous explosion. But the explosion never came. The blazing Beechcraft disappeared behind a rise in the terrain, and instead of the colossal fireball and the shattering blast which the men were expecting, they saw nothing and heard only a dull thud. They exchanged puzzled looks: something was wrong here. Sergeant Jack Vootie, in charge of the squad, decided it was something worth investigating. He ordered his men into their vehicles and they headed for the site of the downed 'plane.

Birkhead and Donna did not know where they were, but they did know they were alive. Wherever they were, it was dark as pitch. The 'plane was no longer on fire, and it seemed to be intact, although at a rather oblique angle. 'Donna! Are you all right?' Birkhead asked, unable to see her in the darkness.

'I think so,' came her reply. 'Where are we?'

'Let me see if I can find a flashlight,' he said, trying to feel around for the emergency supply kit.

The 'plane seemed to be sinking into something, and they could hear the sound of ominous bubbling all around. Then they became aware of an odour, a familiar odour which neither of them could place. Suddenly Donna screamed. 'Oh my God! What is this stuff? Eeccchhh! It's all over me!'

Birkhead felt it too – some kind of gooey, oozing substance. He found the torch and turned it on: the beam lit up a gigantic monster, hovering just outside the window! It was a Tyrannosaurus Rex, greatest of the prehistoric beasts! On second look, Birkhead saw it was a *statue* of a Tyrannosaurus Rex. Below, a sign proclaimed 'Rancho La Brea Tar Pits, Prehistoric Fossil Site.' So that's where they were – in the world-famous La Brea Tar Pits! These giant pools of thick bubbling tar had yielded some of the century's greatest fossil discoveries. Now Birkhead shone his light on Donna: her nude body was completely covered in sticky black tar! Her two white eyes shining out of the black goo made her look like a refugee from

209

a minstrel show. And he didn't look much better. As the Beechcraft continued to sink in to the tar, they climbed to the cabin door, forced it open and eased themselves out of the aircraft. By carefully stepping across the wing, they made it to solid ground.

In the distance, they could hear approaching sirens and vehicles. More than a few people in the vicinity had come to investigate.

Although Wild Bill Kelso had successfully downed 'the enemy', his real problems were just beginning. The searchlight crews were becoming more adept at handling their carbon arcs, and Kelso was having a hell of a time keeping out of their beams. Everywhere, anti-aircraft fire exploded around him, and a lot of it was coming dangerously close. 'What the hell are they shooting at me for?' Kelso thundered. 'I'm an American!' Of course the gun crews couldn't hear him, but they probably wouldn't have believed him even if they did. Two five-inch shells exploded simultaneously on either side of the P-40, and the resulting concussion convinced Kelso that he probably shouldn't be there. 'Jesus!' he screamed, 'I'd better get my ass out over the ocean!' Exactly what Kelso expected to do over the ocean, how he expected to land or what his long-term plan was, no man could say, not even Wild Bill Kelso. Kelso didn't plan strategies – he simply acted on impulse. Right now, his only impulse was to avoid being shot at! He banked and proceeded on a westward course.

Atop the Ferris wheel at Ocean Park, Herbie Kaziminsky had been desperately trying to 'phone Scioli for the past fifteen minutes. Sizzling shrapnel had been falling from the sky, nearly hitting him and Claude on several occasions, and Herbie had finally agreed that it was time to come down from there. However, with the 'phone company understaffed and the operating circuits taxed to their limit, Herbie was unable to get through to Scioli. It didn't matter, because Scioli was not around to answer his 'phone: he was still struggling with Ward and Joan to climb out of the Jap Trap on the Douglas front lawn. Herbie hung up the 'phone in disgust. 'I can't get through!'

Claude was keeping his eyes closed. The flak terrified him, the noise terrified him, and the height terrified him. At least, he told himself, things couldn't get any worse. But Claude was wrong about that, too.

Herbie's dummy kept 'looking' out to sea, its head turning one way, then the other. Suddenly, its eyes blinked several times. 'Jesus Christ!' exclaimed the dummy. 'There's a sub! Look, you guys, it's a Jap sub! Over there to the north!'

Claude opened his eyes and raised his binoculars. Sure enough, he could make out the outline of I-19 through the moonlit fog! 'Holy shit!' he cried. 'The dummy's right! They're Japs! It must be an invasion!'

Herbie confirmed the sighting, then grabbed the 'phone and dialled the operator. This time he was lucky: he got through. 'Army Flash!' he screamed. 'Army Flash!'

But before he could be connected to Interceptor Command, Wild Bill Kelso swooped down over the amusement park from behind them, flying incredibly low. He buzzed the Ferris wheel, scaring the bejesus out of Herbie and Claude! They both ducked, and Herbie dropped the 'phone!

'You stupid blockhead!' his dummy yelled. 'You dropped the 'phone!'

Herbie looked over the side of the gondola and saw the scattered remnants of the telephone on the ground. 'Yeah, it's long distance now!' he replied.

'That guy tried to kill us!' shouted Claude. 'We've gotta defend ourselves!' He grabbed his lever-action rifle and cocked it. Herbie drew his ·44 Magnum. They both aimed at the fighter 'plane that was whizzing over the ocean, and followed it with their sights.

Kelso had been flying low to stay under the anti-aircraft fire. Upon seeing the ocean in front of him, he figured it was safe at last. Then he looked below to his right and saw the Japanese submarine. 'Hell and red niggers!' he exclaimed. 'Japs! All right, you yellow-skin-ned scum! I'll play you my favourite tune!' Kelso dived at the sub, firing his wing-mounts.

The Japanese saw him coming just in time, and they hit the deck as Kelso strafed them. Most of Kelso's bullets hit the ocean and in two seconds he was out of range. Mitamura watched as the P-40 banked for the coast. Clearly the 'plane was turning around for another attack. He barked orders at the crew. 'Fire at him when he returns!' The gun crew scrambled to their positions and attempted to position the 2·95-inch deck cannon for a shot at the P-40. Other crew members ran below to bring up rifles.

'There isn't time for that!' von Kleinschmidt told the Commander. 'We must submerge, before more 'planes arrive!'

Herbie and Claude were still following the P-40 with their weapons. So far, the 'plane had been moving too fast for them to get a good shot. But now, as it returned from the sub, it was on a straight-line course that would take it right over their heads. They couldn't ask for a better target! As soon as Kelso was in range, Herbie opened up. Claude, however, hesitated: was it his ima-gination, or did that 'plane have US Army markings on it? Herbie fired again and again, the recoil from his ·44 rocking the gondola violently. He kept shooting until the

P-40 buzzed past them, out of his line of fire. 'I hit him!' shouted Herbie. 'I know I hit him!'

Herbie was right. Several of his bullets had sliced right through the P-40's fuselage, and one of them had cut the fuel line. Kelso's engine started to miss. 'Oh my God!' screamed Kelso. 'I'm hit! I'm hit, goddammit!' He attempted to radio for help. 'Mayday! Mayday!' But there was nothing anyone could do to help him now.

Herbie laughed with glee. He had seen the flames coming from the fighter's engine. 'I told you I hit that lousy Jap rat!'

'You sap!' shouted his dummy. 'That was no Jap!'

Claude raised his binoculars and turned around for another look at the plummeting aircraft. 'He's right again, Herbie. That was no Jap . . .'

The real Japanese had seen the whole thing from their submarine. Mitamura gave von Kleinschmidt a smug look. 'Ha!' he laughed. 'They shoot down their own 'planes, and you would run from such fools?'

Von Kleinschmidt simply scowled.

Wild Bill Kelso was in trouble. He was losing power fast, and his cockpit was beginning to fill up with smoke. 'I'm gonna have to ditch it!' he shouted, to no one in particular. At least he could still steer, and if he found a place to land, he might come through it alive. But with the city blacked out, landing was going to be difficult. He would have to drop extremely low in order to see if any buildings were in his way but without power, he'd be unable to avoid hitting them. The shape of the terrain itself was virtually impossible to ascertain, and the constantly exploding flak continued to impair his vision. Kelso might as well have been flying blindfolded. Then, suddenly, he sighted what appeared to be salvation on the horizon: two parallel rows of lights which looked like a runway! Kelso realized it was a lit street a few miles ahead. If he could make it that far, he could land on the street and at least be sure he wouldn't strike any buildings. Kelso made a slight adjustment to his ailerons and headed for his only hope!

24

Hollywood Boulevard
9.46 p.m.

The street for which Kelso was heading was Hollywood
Boulevard where Wally Stephans had been blasting out
street lights for the past few minutes. Wally still had three
blocks of lit lamps to go, and he was also having the time
of his life: shooting lights from a moving tank was a
hell of a lot more fun than hitting ducks at the Ocean
Park shooting galleries It had begun to occur to Wally
that he might have been wrong about the Army. Any
outfit that let you drive around in a tank, and fire a
machine-gun couldn't be all bad!

Less than a block from Wally and the tank was the
panel truck under which Betty Douglas was hiding. She
had barely moved since the shooting had started, and
with good reason: burning shrapnel from exploding shells
had been landing in the street, shrapnel which Betty had
assumed to be Japanese bombs. She trembled with fear
every time a white-hot fragment sizzled into the Boulevard or landed on top of the truck. There was nothing
that could get her out from under her shelter, or so she
thought, until Sitarski stuck his head under the truck!
'Hiya doll!' he grinned.

Sitarski had been looking for Betty all night. He had
searched every building within two blocks of the Crystal
Ballroom, but he hadn't thought of looking under cars
until he had noticed a pair of female legs sticking out
from under a Ford. It had turned out that they belonged
to the bottom half of a department store mannequin;

nevertheless Sitarski had proceeded to check under every car on Hollywood Boulevard. And now that search had paid off.

Betty screamed upon seeing him. 'Oh, God, no! Get away!' Sitarski had no such intentions. He crawled under the truck and began grabbing at her. She tried to crawl away, out into the street, but he was too strong. He kept pulling her back, ripping at her clothes.

'C'mon, baby,' he said firmly, 'there's a war on! Those are Jap bombs falling out there, and it's the end of the line! This is the last chance you'll ever have to experience the greatest thing in the world! Why not enjoy it?'

He tried to kiss her, but Betty bit his nose! The sudden pain caused him to release her just enough for her to stick her head out from under the truck. 'Help!' she screamed. 'HELP! Somebody, please! HELP!'

Wally, recocking the machine-gun, heard the cry and immediately recognized the voice. He turned in the cupola just in time to see Betty yanked back under the truck by two hairy arms. Wally didn't have to think twice about who those hairy arms belonged to. He screamed at Quince. 'Head for that truck – now! Move it!' Quince put his foot down, and 'Lulubelle' thundered down the Boulevard, picking up speed and ripping up the pavement.

Betty struggled with Sitarski, screaming and beating on him. But Sitarski held her tightly, and she knew that she could only last a few more moments. 'Don't fight it, doll! Surrender! We're both Americans, and this is war, so be patriotic and do your part! You're gonna enjoy this, I promise you. You'll feel the earth moving in a few minutes!' Betty didn't have to wait a few minutes – the earth was moving already – moving, shaking and rumbling under the tracks of the approaching M-3 tank!

'Lulubelle' roared toward the panel truck at its top

speed of twenty-eight miles per hour. Quince turned the tank sharply to the right, and rammed the panel truck broadside. The truck flipped over, on to its side, revealing Sitarski and Betty in the street. A shocked 'Stretch' Sitarski looked up and recognized his tank. He let go of Betty and jumped to his feet; Betty dashed down the street, not even bothering to notice who had saved her. She was too frightened to do anything but run. But Sitarski noticed. He spotted Wally immediately. 'You!' he screamed, pointing a threatening finger at his nemesis.

Wally grabbed a ·50 calibre 'ammunition belt and jumped down from the cupola. He and Sitarski faced each other, circling one another like animals. Suddenly Wally swung the heavy ammunition belt wildly over his head, then whipped it into Sitarski's face. Sitarski was knocked backwards, the sharp bullet points cutting through the flesh on his cheek. The Corporal tried to pick himself up, but again Wally cracked him in the head with the belt, and gave him a kick in the balls for good measure.

Quince and Foley had recognized Sitarski immediately, and were watching these proceedings with a bit of un-certainty. 'Maybe we should do something,' said Foley uneasily. 'After all, he's part of the squad.'

Quince considered this, then shook his head. 'Naw. The son-of-a-bitch owes me five bucks! Let him get what's coming to him!'

Wally had knocked all of the fight out of Sitarski, but not all of the cowardice. Sitarski attempted to crawl away, but Wally wasn't about to let him go anywhere. He swung the ammunition belt one last time and brought it down on the back of Sitarski's skull. The Corporal collapsed, unconscious.

Wally's eyes were afire, lit with the thrill of victory. He turned around and saw Betty running down the street away from him. He leaped back on to the tank and again shouted orders to Quince. 'Follow that girl!' Quince followed her. The tank rumbled off, coming up right behind her, but the blood was pounding so hard in Betty's head that she didn't hear the approaching vehicle. Wally leaned over the starboard tank-tracks, extended an arm, and as the tank overtook her, hooked her neatly around the waist and heroically swung her up on to the tank and into his arms. Betty screamed and started beating at him until she realized who it was. 'Wally!' she sighed with the greatest relief she'd ever felt in her life. She threw her arms around him and they came together for a passionate kiss.

Huge tongues of orange flame licked the engine of Wild Bill Kelso's P-40 as he angled it toward the lit section of Hollywood Boulevard. Black smoke intermittently obscured his vision. 'It's gonna be rough!' he screamed. 'Jesus, it's gonna be rough!' The fighter 'plane barely missed hitting a radio broadcasting antenna; then Kelso made one last adjustment to set the aircraft on a course directly parallel over the street. Kelso shoved the landing-gear control lever into the 'down' position, but nothing happened: somehow the control lines had been sheared through! The 'plane was losing power rapidly as it screamed earthward on a long diagonal, and there was nothing left for Kelso to do but grit his teeth.

Wally broke his kiss with Betty when he heard the roaring fighter 'plane. He looked up and saw that the 'plane was going to land right on the street – in fact, it looked like it might hit the tank! 'Get down!' Wally told Betty, pushing her down along the back of the tank. Wally climbed back up into the cupola, grabbed the machine-gun and spun it around, taking aim at the burning P-40.

'Don't shoot,' yelled Quince, 'he's one of ours!'

Wally didn't shoot: he ducked. The P-40 was on a direct collision course with the tank, and Wally dropped down through the cupola hatch. There was no time to run, and if the P-40 was going to hit, well, there was nothing he could do about it now. The P-40 did not hit. It should have, but it didn't, thanks to a last minute manoeuvre by Kelso. The 'plane lifted just over the top of the tank at the last second, missing it by a mere two inches! Then the P-40 hit the street, skidded forward, and ripped through a fire-hydrant. The right wing caught a lamp post which spun the aircraft around, right into the front of the Crystal Ballroom! The cracked water main sent water spraying over everything!

Wild Bill Kelso threw open the canopy and leaped out of his burning cockpit. The back of his leather flying-jacket was on fire too, but it didn't seem to worry him: he simply ran under the water spray and doused the flames. Then his 'plane exploded, showering debris everywhere! The concussion knocked Kelso on to the ground.

Quince drove the tank forward towards the Crystal Ballroom to get a better look at Kelso and what was left of his 'plane. Wally stuck his head out of the hatch, and Betty craned over for a better look.

Kelso spotted the tank and immediately began shouting at the top of his lungs. 'The sub! The sub! Go get the sub!!'

'Are you all right?' Wally called.

'Just get the sub!' Kelso screamed.

'What sub?'

'The Jap sub!!!'

'Where?' asked Wally.

'In the ocean! Off shore from some amusement park!'

Wally couldn't believe what he was hearing. 'The Japs are at Ocean Amusement Park?!?'

Betty turned white. 'Oh my God – that's right near my house!'

'Don't just stand there!' bellowed Wild Bill. 'Get out there and sink it!!'

'Right!' answered Wally. 'Let's go!' he told Quince. 'Move out!'

Just then, Meyer Mishkin pushed through the debris covering the front of the Crystal Ballroom and ran to the tank. 'Wait a minute, kid!' he yelled at Wally, waving the contract at him. 'We've gotta talk business! I'll give you a hundred bucks a week! Just sign here!'

'Forget it!' Wally told him. 'I've got a war to fight!' And with that, 'Lulubelle' thundered down the street, heading west, for Santa Monica and Ocean Amusement Park!

Maxine Dexheimer ran to the unconscious 'Stretch' Sitarski. She, like many others, had been curious enough about the 'plane-crash to venture out into the street. But while the other onlookers gaped at the incredible sight of the P-40 sticking half-way into the Crystal Ballroom, Maxine had spotted the man of her dreams lying in the middle of Hollywood Boulevard. She cradled his head in her arms and kissed him repeatedly, cooing softly. 'My poor, poor baby. It's going to be all right now, I'm here; I'm with you now.' Her kisses revived him and Sitarski awakened with a start.

'My tank!' he screamed. 'That son-of-a-bitch stole my tank!' He pushed Maxine away, and climbed to his feet, trying to get his bearings. Sitarski realized that the tank wouldn't be hard to follow as it had left a trail of ripped pavement in its wake. He followed the trail with only one thing on his mind: revenge. And Maxine followed Sitarski with only one thing on her mind: holy matrimony.

General Joseph W. Stilwell, *en route* to Interceptor Command Headquarters, had spotted Kelso's P-40 going down in flames and had immediately ordered his motorcade to head in the direction of the crash. Now, two minutes later, they arrived on the scene. Stilwell stared from his car window at the carnage in the street, shaking his head at the wrecked cars, smashed windows and littered debris. 'It's a goddamn mess,' he muttered under his breath. The motorcade came to a halt, and Stilwell stepped out of his car, followed by Lieutenant Bressler. His MPs hopped out of their truck and took positions along the Boulevard. Stilwell spotted the wreckage of the P-40 under the fountain of city water, and then laid eyes on Wild Bill Kelso, who was running around near the 'plane, howling like a lunatic. Stilwell shook his head. 'We don't need the Japs,' he told Bressler. Then, Stilwell walked up to Kelso. 'Airman! Are you the pilot of this 'plane?'

Though deranged, Kelso still had enough faculties to recognize a General in the United States Army. He snapped to attention and saluted proudly. 'Yes, sir! Captain Wild Bill Kelso, United States Army Corps, sir! I am proud to report that I am the first American flyer to shoot down a Jap!'

'You shot down a Jap?' asked Stilwell in disbelief.

'Yes, sir! A Zero! I saw the bastard go down! I blew the living hell out of him! Blew him right into the Stone Age!'

Lieutenant Bressler ran up to Stilwell with a soldier carrying a field radio. 'Sir!' interrupted Bressler. 'We just picked up a report that a 'plane went down in the La Brea Tar Pits!'

'That's him!' shouted Kelso. 'That's gotta be the one! I told you I shot him down!'

Stilwell turned to Bressler. 'Was that a Jap 'plane, Bressler?'

'They don't know yet, sir,' came the reply.

'Of course it's a Jap!' screamed Kelso. 'You don't think

I'd shoot down one of ours, do you?'

Stilwell gave him a look. 'I'm not so sure.'

'Forget about the 'plane!' Kelso told the General. 'Get the sub! The sub's more important!'

'A sub? You shot down a Jap sub, too?' Stilwell asked sarcastically.

'No, sir – but I could have! I had the son-of-a-bitch in my sights – I was closing in for the kill – and then I was shot down by fifth columnists! Caught it in the radiator! But it's still out there! You gotta sink it!'

Stilwell turned to Bressler, still curious about the radio report. 'Bressler, what about that 'plane? Any word of a pilot?'

At that moment, six more vehicles full of Military Police arrived, along with City Police cars and motorcycles. They too had come to investigate the 'plane-crash. However, this was the second 'plane-crash of the evening they were investigating: they had just come from the La Brea Tar Pits. Two armed guards ushered Birkhead and Donna out of a police car. Both of them were still covered with tar, and Birkhead was handcuffed. 'I'm getting that old sinking feeling,' muttered Stilwell when he saw them.

Stilwell confronted his aide and his secretary, staring at them with the tight-lipped vinegar expression that had earned him his nickname. There was a very long moment of silence.

'Uh ... good evening, sir,' Birkhead ventured weakly. 'How was the movie?'

Stilwell didn't answer. He continued to stare at his tar-covered aide. After what seemed like an eternity, he spoke. 'Is that tar, Birkhead?' he asked calmly.

Birkhead dropped his head. 'Yes, sir.'

'La Brea tar?'

'I'm afraid so, sir.'

Stilwell looked at his secretary. 'How's your headache, Donna?'

'Awful, sir,' she replied.

Birkhead cleared his throat. 'Sir, I can explain – really, I can—'

Stilwell cut him off. 'Birkhead, is this a long story?'

'Uh, yes, sir . . .'

'Then I don't want to hear it. And as for you,' Stilwell said, turning to Kelso, preparing to place him under arrest – but it was too late for that: Kelso had just slugged an MP and was now revving-up his motorcycle, which had a sidecar attached. Another MP rushed over to stop him, but Kelso kicked him in the chest. Before Stilwell could get out another word, Kelso was zooming off into the night!

'Sayonara, suckers!' he screamed. 'I'm gonna sink that sub!' Whether Kelso actually would or not was a matter of opinion : he was heading inland, due east!

25

When Ward Douglas realized he was going to have a great deal of trouble climbing out of the Jap Trap, he dispatched Macey to round-up some of the neighbours for help. Macey returned with Deke Obens and Sam Frinkhauser, and in a short time, they had pulled Ward, Joan and Scioli out of the open pit.

Frinkhauser, a paunchy, middle-aged pharmacist, now stared with amazement through Ward's binoculars at the Japanese submarine. 'Jesus, there's a Kraut on board too!' he exclaimed, seeing von Kleinschmidt. 'We've got the whole damned Axis out there! What are we gonna do?'

'Only one thing we can do,' answered Ward. 'Sink it!'

'Sink it? How can we do that?' Scioli asked.

'The Army gave me a gun! Let's use it!' Ward motioned the others to the Bofors gun, then pointed to a spot on his lawn. 'Let's move it over there!'

Joan protested loudly. 'Leave it alone, Ward! Let's call the Army!'

'The Army doesn't know what they're doing! If they had any brains, they'd have installed this like I told 'em to! I'll handle this myself! You just get in the house!'

Joan was about to argue, but she decided not to. She'd been arguing with Ward all night, and it had only got her stuck in a hole in the ground. She threw up her arms in exasperation and went back inside.

Scioli suddenly hit himself on the head as he made

a startling realization. 'Jesus, Mary and Joseph! I just remembered I've got two men stuck on top of my Ferris wheel! Somebody's gotta get 'em down!'

Ward turned to his eldest son. 'Macey! Take your bike and get over to the amusement pier!'

'But Dad! I gotta watch you sink the sub!'

'Macey,' Ward said sternly, 'that's an order!'

'Yes, sir!' replied the boy, giving his father the three-fingered boy-scout salute. He then ran to his bicycle which was lying on the front lawn.

'Hold it, kid!' shouted Scioli. 'Come back here a minute!' Macey ran back, and Scioli handed him a key. 'You'll need this to unlock the controls!' Macey took the key, hopped on his bike, and pedalled away.

Scioli and Ward pulled the cement blocks out from under the wheels of the 40 mm cannon, and the four men began pushing it towards the spot Ward had designated. It weighed more than two tons but slowly and surely they began to move it.

Atop the Ferris wheel, Herbie and Claude were firing blindly at the submarine. Fog was obscuring their vision again. 'I know there's Japs on deck,' Claude was saying. 'I just wish I could see 'em!' He reloaded his rifle. 'I wish we had more ammo, too.'

'Just keep shooting,' Herbie told him as he fired his ·44 Magnum again and again. 'We're bound to hit something!'

In fact, Herbie and Claude were coming very close to hitting something. Their bullets were ricocheting off the deck and conning tower, effectively pinning down the Japanese crew. No one had been hit yet, but the chance of such an occurrence was certainly within the realm of possibility. Nor could the Japanese shoot back – they simply could not see where the gunfire was coming from.

Von Kleinschmidt was livid at being in such a power-less position, and didn't hesitate to tell Mitamura so. 'Dummkopf! If you had listened to me and submerged, we would not be in such a helpless situation! The Fuehrer is right: there is no place in the Reich for you yellow swine! Only the Aryan race can ever rule the world!'

Mitamura glared at him. 'You want to know what you can do with your Third Reich, Lieutenant? You can shove it up in your retail orifice!'

Ping! Another bullet hit into the deck, right between them.

Wally Stephans was really enjoying his new role as tank commander. At this particular moment, he was living out the fantasy of every American who has ever been stuck in bumper-to-bumper rush-hour traffic: he was running over cars that were blocking his way! He had given Quince specific orders to destroy as much property as possible on their way to the beach, thus proving the old adage, 'A reformed juvenile delinquent with an M-3 tank does not stay reformed very long.' As they barrelled through an intersection blocked with abandoned cars, Wally spotted a police car with its headlights on. Two policemen were collaring a pair of looters nearby, but Wally decided that this was no excuse for ignoring the black-out. 'Hey, coppers!' he yelled. 'There's a black-out on! You bums are breaking the law!' Wally spun the machine-gun around and blasted the police car. The ·50-calibre slugs emulsified not only the headlights, but the entire automobile. 'Let that be a lesson to you!' Wally told the policeman. He laughed loudly and turned to Betty who was atop the cupola with him. 'How'd you like that?'

'Liked it just fine!' she told him.

It had taken five gruelling minutes for Ward and his neighbours to push the 40 mm cannon into position, and the men were tired. Ward, in his obsessive zeal to sink the sub, had pushed them to their limits and beyond. When Frinkhauser had suggested they rest for a few moments, Ward accused him of being a traitor. After that, Ward's neighbours suffered in silence, afraid to say anything for fear of incurring his stormy wrath.

Scioli came running out of the garage with a shovel and used it to crack open the padlock on the ammunition crate. He handed Frinkhauser a shell, who passed it to Obens, who passed it to Ward. Ward shoved it into the cannon's loading mechanism. Now what? Ward studied the mechanism, trying to figure out how to get the shell from the loading channel into the barrel. It didn't take him long to decide which lever to pull: it was labelled. Ward chambered the shell.

The 40 mm Bofors anti-aircraft gun was designed for a crew of six. There were two seats on either side of the barrel, each with its own sight. These sights were displaced sights, which meant that they did not show exactly what the barrel was pointing at. This was known as a 'parallax' sighting system, and it worked accurately only with distant objects, such as aircraft, which was what the cannon was designed for. No other sighting system was possible for a weapon of this size, for if a man attempted to sight directly down the barrel of this cannon, he would most likely have his head blown off by its tremendous recoil.

Ward Douglas was completely ignorant of all of this. He wrongly assumed that one man could operate the cannon properly, and figured that what he saw in the sight would be what he was firing at. And so, he took his place in the left seat and slowly cranked the barrel around, keeping his eye tight against the sight. The cross-hairs moved across the ocean, and the faint outline of the Japanese sub, now just south of Ward's house, came into view. Ward chuckled to himself as he centred the cross-hairs on the conning tower, totally absorbed in what he was seeing. 'All right, you bastards, just hold it right there . . .' With the final adjustments made, Ward yelled 'Stand clear!!!'

The neighbours stepped back, exchanging glances. They all saw that the barrel of the cannon was aiming point blank at the corner of Ward's house, but they were all afraid to say anything about it.

'Dad . . .' ventured Stevie, but Ward immediately snapped at him.

'Shut up!'

'But, Dad—!' protested Gus.

'Just shut up!'

Now Scioli decided to speak up. 'Ward, I don't think you're gonna hit 'em. . . .'

'I've got 'em right in my sight, goddammit! Now everybody stand clear and shut up! ! !'

Everybody stood clear and shut up. They all put their fingers in their ears, waiting for the inevitable.

Ward stomped on the firing pedal: the blast was incredible! The 40 mm shell ripped a 40 mm hole through Ward's house, passing through one wall of the living-room and out the other through the kitchen and out the back of the house! Joan, sitting in the living-room, was horrified!

The shell whistled through the sky and exploded in the sea, blasting a tremendous waterspout into the air, right next to the sub. The Japanese were sprayed with salt water!

And, because Ward had not thought to replace the cement blocks under the wheels, the recoil from the blast sent the gun flying backwards at an incredible speed, with

Ward still on it! The speeding cannon smashed right through the wall of the garage, causing more rafters to collapse, and the falling debris brought the rolling gun to a halt. Luckily, Ward had put his car on the street after the garage destruction of the afternoon; otherwise, the cannon would have probably destroyed the front end of his Packard.

Scioli and the others ran in, as Ward pushed a fallen rafter out of his way and brushed dirt off of himself. 'Did I get 'em? Did I get 'em?' Ward asked urgently.

'Close, Ward! Close!' said Scioli.

'All right! Let's move this thing back and we'll try it again! Company, push!'

Scioli threw the debris out of the way and the neighbours began pushing. Ward remained sitting on the cannon with his eye to the sight. His neighbours strained: if the gun had been difficult to push before, it was nearly impossible to push now. Scioli joined them. After a few minutes of straining, grunting and groaning, they had been unable to move the cannon an inch.

Scioli threw up his arms in defeat. 'It won't budge!'

'Then do something!' Ward told them. 'We've gotta get it out!'

The men thought about the problem for a few moments, then Scioli came up with an idea. 'I've got it! I can push it out with my "tank"! You just open your garage door and leave the rest to me!' Scioli ran out of the garage and headed for home.

On the sub, Mitamura, von Kleinschmidt and Ashimoto had all climbed to their feet, despite the sporadic rifle and pistol shots which continued to hit into the deck. Mitamura and Ashimoto were trying to get a better look at the Douglas house. Von Kleinschmidt was wet from the water spray, and cursed Mitamura in Japanese, so that he'd be sure to understand. 'So, the American has nothing but a useless shotgun, has he? I suppose that was buckshot which almost hit us!'

Mitamura did not dignify the remark with an answer.

Von Kleinschmidt didn't need one. He drew his Luger and pointed it at the Commander. 'Captain, this insanity has gone far enough! I'm taking command! Order your men to submerge! Now!'

Mitamura stared at him coolly. 'Don't be foolish, Lieutenant.'

'I'm not about to lose my life because of some crazy Jap ideals!' shouted the Nazi. 'Now give the order, or I shall kill you!'

Mitamura did not move. He showed no fear; he simply faced von Kleinschmidt calmly, certain that the German did not have the nerve to pull the trigger. The crew watched with bated breath. None of them made a move to stop von Kleinschmidt – such behaviour would be contrary to the Japanese code of *bushido*, and an insult to their Commander's honour. And so, they waited.

On a darkened street in West Hollywood, 'Stretch' Sitarski continued to follow the path of the tank. His run had slowed to a breathless walk. Despite basic training, Sitarski was in pretty miserable shape. In far better shape was Maxine Dexheimer who was walking alongside him. Sitarski had tried everything to get rid of her. When he had assaulted her verbally, she had told him she loved to hear his voice. When he had threatened physical violence, she had told him fine, she was his to do with as he desired; and when he tried to run away from her, she ran after him. She had, in fact, run him into the ground. True love, they say, makes one stronger.

Sitarski heard a car approaching from behind them. He stepped out into the street and stuck out his thumb. The car whizzed by, not even slowing down. 'Goddamn you, you son-of-a-bitch!' screamed the Corporal.

A little further along, Sitarski heard another car. Again he stuck his thumb out. This time the car slowed down just enough to get a look at the two of them, then speeded up and drove off. Sitarski picked up a rock and threw it at the departing car.

Still further along, they heard the sound of another approaching vehicle. Sitarski was about to step into the street again, but Maxine stopped him. 'Uh, uh, big boy,' she said. 'My turn! I'll show you something I learned from Claudette Colbert!' She was referring to the hitch-hiking sequence she had seen in the movie, *It Happened One Night*. Maxine stepped over to the kerb, raised her skirt and stuck her leg out, showing plenty of skin. And Wild Bill Kelso, in his stolen motorcycle with sidecar, screeched to a halt!

After Kelso had screeched away from the Crystal Ballroom, it had taken him a few minutes to figure out that he was travelling in the wrong direction. Even though he now knew which way was west, he still wasn't sure how to get to the amusement park. Whether Kelso would have stopped to ask directions of Maxine and Sitarski had Maxine not titillated him with a little thigh, no one can say. One thing was certain, however: Kelso had seen Maxine, and liked what he saw. He grinned at Maxine and she winked at him.

'How about a ride?' Sitarski asked, starting to get into the sidecar without waiting for an answer.

'Hold it, soldier!' Kelso told him. 'Just where do you think you're going?'

'I gotta find my tank, goddammit!'

'What tank?'

'The tank that son-of-a-bitch who got egg on my uniform stole, that's what tank!' Maxine was trying to climb into the sidecar with him. Sitarski pushed her away.

'I sent a tank out to get the sub!'

'What sub?' asked Sitarski. 'Where?'

'Where do you think, you chowderhead? In the ocean, that's where! Right near some amusement park!'

'An amusement park?!?' Again Sitarski pushed Maxine away from the sidecar.

'Yeah! You know where that is?'

'Sure I do!' lied Sitarski, climbing in. 'Let's go!'

Kelso didn't go. He didn't want to go without Maxine. He winked at her, and she didn't disappoint him: she jumped into the sidecar, right on top of Sitarski. The Corporal grunted in pain under her sudden added weight, but he didn't get a chance to throw her out – Kelso revved-up the engine and sped off like the wild man he was! Both Sitarski and Maxine hung on to each other for dear life!

Dominic Scioli revved-up his home-made 'tank', pulled out of his driveway, and headed down the hill towards the open door of Ward's garage. He angled into the garage, getting into position to push the anti-aircraft gun. Ward, still sitting on it, called to him. 'Not too hard, Scioli! Just touch it!'

'Okay, Ward! I'm just gonna kiss it – like a baby!' Scioli, however, had not had much experience with infants. He slammed the accelerator pedal into the floor. The 'tank' rammed the back of the cannon at full speed, forcing it out of the garage, and sending it rolling toward the house. The downward grade of Ward's lawn caused the cannon to accelerate, and Ward found himself heading directly towards his own front door!

At this moment, inside the house, Joan decided to open the front door to find out what was happening outside. She found out very quickly. Her face turned white with terror upon seeing the runaway Bofors cannon rolling right at her, and she slammed the door, instinctively assuming that the door would keep the unwelcome guest out of her living-room. She was wrong. The ack-ack gun broke through the door, taking part of the frame and wall with it, and coasted right into the middle of the living-room. It had missed hitting Joan by mere inches! Ward couldn't have cared less – he had a sub to sink. He picked up a lamp from a nearby end table and hurled it through the big ocean-view picture window which he had painted over that afternoon. The window shattered and Ward once again had a view of the submarine. He cranked the cannon around in order to aim, knocking over lamps and furniture with the huge barrel. Joan was shocked. Now Frinkhauser, Obens and Scioli came running in, followed by the kids. 'Reload!!' shouted Ward. Frinkhauser ran outside to get another 40 mm shell.

The battle of nerves between Mitamura and von Kleinschmidt continued. Mitamura had not moved one iota, nor had he spoken a single word to the German since the confrontation had begun. This coolness had only served to rile the Nazi even more. As Mitamura suspected, von Kleinschmidt was afraid to pull the trigger of his Luger. However, the German's rising anger might override his cowardice. Mitamura knew that the time had come to act.

'I'm not going to repeat myself!' shouted von Kleinschmidt loudly, in Japanese, so that the entire crew could understand. 'Give the order to submerge! Now!'

The Japanese Commander's eyes narrowed. There was a moment of extreme tension: he could see that the German's index finger was shaking, starting to push against the trigger. Then Mitamura struck, calling upon his vast knowledge of jiu-jitsu to disarm his opponent. First, he delivered a shattering karate chop to the German's wrist, causing him to drop the pistol. Then, in a lightning-like move, Mitamura grabbed von Kleinschmidt's arm and flipped him neatly over the railings, off the deck and into the cold Pacific. The German hit the water with a tremendous splash and was swallowed up by the black sea. Mitamura stepped over the rail and looked down: there was no sign of the Nazi Lieutenant. He smiled. 'Serves you right, you goddamn Kraut!'

Sam Frinkhauser ran into Ward's living-room with another 40 mm shell. Ward took it from him, placed it in the loading mechanism and chambered it. 'Stand clear!' shouted Ward, as he again put his eye to the sight and his foot over the firing pedal. The others stood clear. Joan was appalled.

'Ward Douglas, don't you dare fire that gun in this house!' she screamed.

Too late: Ward fired, and the blast shattered every window in the Douglas home! The 40 mm shell streaked through the broken picture window towards the submarine. Again, Ward was off target because of the parallax sighting system, and again the shell exploded in the sea, spraying water over the Japanese on deck. The recoil sent the cannon and Ward rolling backwards, smashing through the living-room wall, into the dining-room smashing through the dining-room wall, and into the bathroom. The wheels of the gun were stopped by the toilet, but Ward's momentum sent him flying off the cannon and into the bathtub! The destruction of the wall had ruptured the plumbing, and Ward was doused with water from the shower spigot! Now several sections of the ceilings of the various rooms collapsed, covering Scioli, Joan, the kids and the neighbours with rubble.

Luckily, no one was injured. The startled group rushed into the bathroom to see if Ward was all right.

'Reload!' shouted Ward. Obviously, he was all right.

'Let's call it a night, Ward,' Scioli suggested. 'I think you should go home.'

'This *is* my home!'

'There isn't much left of it, Ward – and what there is, isn't safe. I think you'd better move all your furniture outside and sleep in the yard tonight. Your house is no longer structurally sound ... and neither are you.' As if to prove Scioli correct, the entire house shook: the blast and destruction had weakened the foundations ... but the house held together nevertheless.

'What about the Japs?' screamed Ward. 'What about the Japs?'

The Japs had decided to shoot back. With the windows of Ward's house blown to smithereens, the Japanese could easily see the lights inside. The Douglas home thus became a highly visible target and, with an anti-aircraft gun on the premises, a highly honourable target as well. 'Prepare to fire at that house!' commanded Mitamura. The crew of the deck gun obeyed. They took their positions on the 2·95-inch cannon, dodging the less frequent bullets from the Ferris wheel, and began loading it.

At the same time, a few miles east, Wild Bill Kelso and his passengers were speeding down a street at forty miles per hour. Kelso had just come to an obvious conclusion. 'We're lost, goddammit!' It was Sitarski's fault: rather than follow the trail of carnage left by the tank, the Corporal had convinced Kelso to take a 'short-cut'.

'I say we gotta turn left!' Kelso screamed, loudly so that he could be heard over the roar of the motorcycle.

'No! Keep going straight!' Sitarski told him.

Maxine said nothing. She didn't know where they were, and she didn't care. She was with Sitarski, and that was all that mattered.

'Straight?' Kelso asked.

'Right!'

'Straight or right?!?'

'I said straight, goddammit!!' screamed the Corporal.

'Okay, pal – you wanna go straight, go straight!' Kelso reached down and pulled the pin that connected the sidecar to the cycle. He made a sharp left turn at the intersection, leaving Sitarski and Maxine to fend for themselves in the runaway sidecar! 'Sayonara, sucker!' Kelso yelled as he disappeared into the darkness. Once again, he had lived up to his name.

Maxine and Sitarski screamed in terror. Although the sidecar had only one wheel, at its speed it stayed perfectly balanced. It continued speeding straight ahead at forty miles per hour – and there was absolutely no way it could be steered! The vehicle hit a pot-hole in the street which put it on an angular course, directly towards the crowded loading docks of Lomax Brothers Produce Distributors Incorporated.

Despite the air raid and black-out, proprietor Teep Lomax had ordered his employees to keep working. There were several trucks which had to be loaded with fruits and vegetables tonight so that they could reach their destinations by morning, and Japs or no Japs, Teep Lomax wanted those deliveries made on time. Thus, the loading docks were covered with crates full of tomatoes, lettuces and carrots, as well as live chickens and ducks, all of which had to be shipped.

The speeding sidecar zoomed up the loading ramp and along the dock, smashing through crates of vegetables and knocking dock workers over the side! The sidecar broke through several more crates, and Maxine found herself with a big fat duck in her hands! The sidecar then hit another crate at precisely the right angle to flip Maxine and Sitarski out of it – they went tumbling through space and fell right into the back of a departing open truck loaded with farm-fresh eggs! Their impact broke at least a hundred dozen eggs and gooey yolks splattered over both of them! Sitarski screamed in psychotic rage as he found himself covered with the one thing in the world he hated most. 'Aarrrggghhhhh!!! Eggs!! I hate eggs! I can't stand eggs!!!'

And thus, the adventures of 'Stretch' Sitarski came to an end for the night. Later on, he and Maxine would be picked up by police and returned to where they belonged. Sitarski would be busted to the rank of Private, and eventually be sent to the European theatre. And Maxine would follow him there. But that's another story. . . .

At the top of the Ocean Park Ferris wheel, Herbie and Claude had just run out of ammunition. They both felt completely helpless. Not only were they unable to do anything to the sub themselves, they could not even report it. Then they heard the voice of a young boy yelling at them from below. 'Hey!! Hey you guys!!' Claude had forgotten about his fear of heights in all the excitement, so he looked down along with Herbie and the dummy. They saw Macey Douglas getting off his bicycle. 'Hey!' yelled Macey. 'I'm supposed to get you down!'

'Thank Christ!' replied Claude.

Macey ran to the control box in the electrical shed and unlocked it. He found himself staring at three dozen knife switches, none of which were labelled. Macey gulped. He had no idea what to do. He yelled back at the men on the Ferris wheel. 'Which one do I pull??'

'How are we supposed to know?' screamed Herbie. 'Try 'em all!'

It was the only sensible course of action. Macey closed his eyes and picked a switch. He pulled it, and discovered he had just lit up a concession stand. He tried again: this time he lit up the shooting galleries.

Meanwhile, the Japanese gun crew had loaded their cannon and were now swinging it around towards the Douglas house. They were moving quickly and efficiently now that the gunfire from the Ferris wheel had ceased. As the gun crew were making the final aiming adjustments, Mitamura noticed that the lights on Santa Monica Pier had just come on. He watched with amazement as more bright lights appeared out of the thinning fog. He was not sure exactly what he was seeing.

Macey threw another switch and lit up the entire Ferris wheel!

From Mitamura's angle, the lights suggested the tower of a refinery or chemical plant. He reacted immediately. 'Fire at the industrial structure!' he ordered, pointing at the Ferris wheel. The gun crew immediately swung the cannon back and aimed at the towering lights.

Herbie screamed down to Macey. 'You're getting closer, kid! Try another one!'

Macey tried another one and illuminated the merry-go-round.

The Japanese gun crew made the last adjustments on their cannon, and Chief Gunner Okazaki, standing to the side of the huge weapon, raised his baton, taking command. 'Fire!' he shouted. The gun crew fired. The shock waves rattled the entire submarine, and the 2·95-inch projectile arched through the sky towards the amusement park, as the cannon ejected the hot expended shell-casing into the ocean.

Impact came two seconds later: the shell exploded just south of the base of the Ferris wheel, only a few yards from Macey! Macey dashed away from the electrical shed fast, taking refuge behind the ticket booth of the merry-go-round.

'Oh, God, they're gonna kill us!' screamed Herbie, truly petrified for the first time in his life.

Chief Gunner Okazaki lowered his binoculars and immediately ordered the crew to adjust the cannon half a degree north. 'Fire!' he commanded.

Claude saw the white flash of the explosion from the gondola, and heard it a split second later. 'Oh, Christ! Oh, Christ!!' he screamed, bracing himself for the imminent explosion. This time it landed a few yards to the north of the wheel's base, and blew apart a huge chunk of pavement!

'One quarter-degree south!' Okazaki ordered, planning to place the next shot directly between the previous two. The adjustment made, the Chief Gunner gave the order to fire. Again the cannon belched fire, and again a 2·95-inch shell screamed through the sky towards Ocean Park. Okazaki's calculations were right on target: the projectile slammed smack-bang into the middle of the Ferris wheel's bottom gondola! The impact started the entire Ferris wheel spinning, just like a shooting gallery pinwheel. Herbie and Claude grabbed on to their safety bar and screamed in terror as they began the scariest amusement park ride in history! Their stomachs turned inside out and upside down as they were whipped around twice as fast as the Ferris wheel was supposed to go. And this was only the beginning!

The Japanese gun crew loaded another shell into the cannon. 'Fire!' screamed Okazaki, leaving the gun aimed exactly as it had been before.

Two seconds later, another shell exploded into a lower gondola, blowing it completely apart, but at the same time sending the rest of the Ferris wheel spinning around even faster!

Macey Douglas peered out from behind the merry-go-round ticket booth with wide-eyed amazement. It looked like one terrific ride!

The spinning lights of the Ferris wheel were a blur to the Japanese who were watching with similar amazement.

Again, the Chief Gunner cried 'Fire!' The repeated firing of the cannon had been rocking the sub slightly, and the lateral movement caused a small vibration in the course of this shot. It exploded into the base of the Ferris wheel gantry's north support and completely destroyed it!

The wheel continued whirling around on the single support but without the stabilizing effect of the full gantry, it began spinning off balance, swaying sideways more and more as it slipped further across the now open-ended axle. Herbie swore to himself that he'd never go near an amusement park again, and Claude . . . well, Claude was too nauseous to think about anything.

The movement of the Ferris wheel was now so erratic that the Japanese gun crew could not hold their aim. They repeatedly cranked the gun to and fro, attempting to match and anticipate the wheel's next move, but they were unable to do so.

The wheel's centre of gravity was rapidly approaching the end of the axle . . . closer, closer . . . BINGO! The whirling Ferris wheel dropped off the centre shaft, hit the ground, and rolled straight down the Santa Monica Pier! And Herbie and Claude were riding it! The runaway wheel ripped its electrical cabling out of the ground, pulling a few electrical poles with it, and thus remained lit.

A hushed silence fell over the Japanese as they stared in awe at the incredible sight. The wheel remained on its unerringly straight course, and rolled right off the end of the pier, into the ocean! Herbie and Claude screamed all the way down. Luckily, the electrical line broke just at the last second, so they were not electrocuted when they hit the water.

The Japanese were ecstatic. They jumped joyously up and down, shouting, 'Banzai! Banzai!'

After a few moments, the heads of Herbie, Claude and the dummy broke through the surface of the sea. They trod water, unable to believe they were actually still alive. 'Gee, that was fun!' said the dummy. 'Let's do it again!' Claude grimaced, then shoved its wooden head underwater.

Macey Douglas cautiously approached the pier, rubbing his eyes to make sure that what he had just seen had actually happened. Yes, the submarine was still there, and the two men from the Ferris wheel were splashing around in the water. But would the guys at school believe it? Then Macey became aware of a low rumble behind him. The rumbling was approaching rapidly, and getting more powerful, shaking the very ground he was standing upon. Macey turned, and saw the M-3 tank coming towards him. His sister and Wally were on the turret. 'Betty!' he yelled, waving.

Betty waved back, relieved to see that her brother was all right.

'There's a sub out there!' shouted Macey. 'It sunk the Ferris wheel!'

Wally and the other soldiers had seen it just as Macey pointed it out to them; all of them, that is, except Sergeant Frank Tree. Tree was in a state of semi-consciousness, and had been babbling incoherently for the past twenty minutes, regressing back through boot camp and finally launching into a recital of the Constitution of the United States. After a few minutes of this, Wally had pushed him through the hatch and into the tank, not only for Tree's own safety, but because his discourse was highly annoying. After all, it was not very romantic smooching with your girlfriend while an Army Sergeant was spouting the Bill of Rights.

'Slow down!' Wally ordered. Quince reduced the speed to less than five miles per hour. Wally turned to Betty. 'This is where you get off,' he told her, giving her a good-bye kiss. 'Take cover.' She jumped off the tank and joined her brother. Both of them ran back into the amusement park for safety.

As the tank rolled on to the wooden pier, Wally dropped through the hatch to get at its 75 mm cannon. If he was going to sink the sub, 'Lulubelle's' cannon was the only way he could do it. He stared at its breech with its switches and levers, and scratched his head. He looked to Quince, Reese and Foley. 'Any of you guys know how to work this thing?'

Even as Wally and the soldiers puzzled over the operation of their cannon, the Japanese were taking action of their own. With his binoculars, Mitamura had spotted the tank even before Macey had, and was pleased that at last he would have the opportunity to engage the American Army. He had ordered the submarine into position to fire torpedoes, and now the vessel was turning through the final few degrees that would bring it into that position. 'Ready forward tubes for firing!' he ordered through the ship's intercom. Far below, crew members did exactly that.

'Lulubelle' stopped at the end of the pier. Behind it, the pier's wooden boards had been mangled and cracked by the weight of the vehicle. Inside, Wally and Reese loaded 'Lulubelle's' cannon. The 75 mm shell was so heavy it took both of them to shove it into the open breech. That done, Reese slammed it shut. Wally peered out through the gunner's slit. Now that the submarine was no longer sitting broadside, it made a much more difficult target. 'A little to the right,' he said, and Foley pushed the turret control to the right. 'Whoa!' said Wally after the barrel had moved into proper position. Wally looked at the others, a bit hesitant. The shell had been chambered, the cannon was pointing in the right direction ... was this all there was to it? Wally assumed so. 'Fire!' he cried. Reèse stepped on the firing switch. The cannon discharged a deafening blast. Wally watched as the shell whistled over the ocean and hit into the water just left of the sub. The explosion sent spray over its deck. 'Reload!' he shouted.

Mitamura wiped the salt away from his brow, anxiously awaiting a response from the men at the torpedo tubes. 'Forward tubes ready for firing!' reported the voice over the speaker.

'Fire one!' replied Mitamura.

Torpedo number one was fired. Mitamura raised his binoculars and watched as it hummed along the surface of the water.

Herbie and Claude, still splashing around near the pier, suddenly spotted it. They didn't know what it was, but they knew it was coming towards them, and fast! They swam in opposite directions and the torpedo zipped right between them!

'Jesus!' cried Wally, watching through the gunner's slit. 'They're firing torpedoes!' He climbed up and stuck his head out of the cupola hatch to get a better look. The torpedo missed the pier and ran up on to the beach, right into a lifeguard tower. The projectile blew the wooden tower to kindling! He gasped in awe. 'Jesus!'

Wally dropped back into the tank with tremendous urgency, having seen the fate that might be in store for them. 'A little more to the right!' he told Foley as he again peered at the ominous enemy vessel through the gunner's slit.

Mitamura was giving a similar order. 'Two degrees to port,' he called into the intercom. The submarine turned ever so slightly towards the pier.

'Fire!' shouted Wally.

'Fire two!' shouted Mitamura.

The tank and the submarine fired simultaneously. The tank's 75 mm shell whizzed right over the speeding torpedo, and hit into the water, mere inches away from the submarine. A thousand gallons of water were blown over its deck, and the blast singed the hull. But neither Wally nor the tank crew got a good look at the result of their shot because the speeding torpedo slammed directly into the left front pier post! The incredible explosion blasted the front section of the Santa Monica Pier to splinters, and 'Lulubelle', still intact, dropped straight down into the Pacific!

Once more, the Japanese reacted with joyous triumph, shouting *'Banzai!'* and congratulating one another Mitamura gazed at what was left of the pier through his binoculars. An expression of satisfaction lit his face. He turned to the intercom, speaking loudly so that all could hear. 'This is Commander Mitamura speaking. We have engaged the military forces of the United States of America, and we have inflicted heavy damage. We can now return with honour!' The crew shouted their approval. 'Prepare to dive,' ordered the Captain. The diving buzzer sounded, and those on deck proceeded through the hatch in orderly fashion.

Just as Ocean Park became quiet again, the stillness was shattered by the roar of a motorcycle. Wild Bill Kelso had finally arrived! As he sped through the entrance gate, Kelso saw the sub in front of him. He screamed a crazed battle cry which was even louder than his engine, opened his throttle all the way and zoomed down the pier at ninety-five miles per hour! The motorcycle flew off the end of the shattered pier, through the air and into the ocean, far beyond where the tank had gone down.

As Kelso hit the water, several heads bobbed up from below: Wally, Quince, Reese, Foley and Tree. They had managed to force open the hatches of the tank before it had completely flooded and had swum to the surface. The water had revived Tree, and although dazed and bewildered as to his whereabouts, he was once again conscious and reasonably coherent.

Quince voiced the one question that was on all of their minds. 'Did we hit 'em?'

Wally treaded, trying to see above the water. 'I think so!' he exclaimed. 'It's going down!'

Yes, indeed, the submarine was going down : submerging, as Mitamura had ordered. The deck was bare of crew; all had gone below. But a lone man was swimming towards it, the one man who would see these events to a close come hell or high water ... Wild Bill Kelso! Water began spilling over the deck of I-19 just as Kelso reached the railing. In a moment, Kelso was over it, running towards the main hatch. 'Come on out, ya louzy zipperheads! I'll teach ya to attack the United States of America! I'll show ya what happens to sneaky little wise guys who stab Uncle Sam in the back!' Kelso assaulted the hatch with an unholy vengeance, first trying to kick it open, then grabbing the hatch wheel and turning it. It wouldn't budge. Kelso grunted, summoning all of his strength. The water was up to his ankles now. Once again, he screamed his maniacal battle cry and this gave him the added strength he needed to rip open the hatch! The harsh red light from within illuminated his contorted face, and Kelso dived in head first. The water which was rushing over the deck slammed the hatch shut behind him. As the conning tower of I-19 dropped below the surface, one word could be heard coming from within the submarine, one word which penetrated those thick steel walls, which penetrated the very sea itself . . .

'JAAAAAAAAAPPPPPPPPPSSSSSSSSS!!!!!!!! ! ! '

What happened to Wild Bill Kelso? That, too, is another story. . . .

Epilogue

THE MORNING AFTER

26

Sunday, 14 December 1941
Santa Monica, California
7.20 a.m.

Ward Douglas was nailing his front door back on to his house. All of his windows had been shattered, there were gaping holes in his walls and roof, and the white wooden exterior of his home was charred with black ash. Nevertheless, Ward believed that a house without a front door was not a house at all. Although he would have to call a contractor tomorrow morning, Ward had decided that this was one repair he would make himself. Thus, he was making it.

Ward's front lawn was covered with every salvageable piece of furniture from inside. Scioli had convinced him it would be wise to bring it out there, and the neighbours all pitched in to help.

Ward's furniture was, in turn, covered with a motley assortment of humanity, all sleeping off the events of the previous night. Everyone was there: Wally and Betty, together on the living-room couch; Frank Tree and his tank crew, sprawled out on tables and dining-room chairs; Claude, asleep on the grass; Herbie and his dummy on an easy chair; Stevie, Gus and Macey together in one bed; Joan in another. Even Scioli and the neighbours were there, asleep on other beds: although they all lived nearby, after moving all the furniture outside, they had decided they were too tired to go home. And besides, this was the closest thing to a real block party that the neighbourhood had ever had.

Now, a train of military vehicles pulled up at the

Douglas home. General Stilwell and his entourage had finally reached the end of the trail of destruction. Stilwell stared in disbelief at the sight before him. He climbed out of his car for a closer look ... and perhaps some answers. He was followed by Bressler and the MPs. Birkhead and Donna also appeared, still stained with tar, along with the units that had found them in the tar pits. Even Sitarski and Maxine had been brought along, still covered with rotting eggs and handcuffed to each other, much to Maxine's delight.

As Stilwell and his entourage approached the house, Frank Tree noticed them. He immediately recognized Stilwell, having followed his career for many years. Tree had tremendous respect and admiration for this General. He jumped to his feet and shouted, 'Ten-hut!'

At varying speeds, Quince, Reese and Foley reached the state of attention. Macey, Stevie and Gus snapped to attention as well.

'At ease, men,' Stilwell told them. He spotted Tree's stripes. 'Sergeant, what happened here?'

'Sir, while quelling a riot in our tank last night, I was struck unconscious. My men received a report of a Japanese submarine off Santa Monica Pier from an Air Corps Captain, proceeded to the objective, and at approximately 22.30 hours, engaged the enemy.'

'Damage?' asked Stilwell.

'They sunk both our tank and the Ferris wheel, sir.'

'Casualties?'

Tree pointed to Herbie. 'Just the dummy, sir.'

Herbie stood up with his dummy, which was now missing an arm, and showed Stilwell. As he raised it into the air, two quarts of salt water spilled out of its head.

Stilwell shook his head. 'I don't want to hear about it.' He turned to Tree. 'What about the sub, Sergeant?'

Now Wally stood up and addressed the General. 'I

think we hit it, sir. I saw it go down.'

Stilwell stared at Wally for a moment, noticing the Army tunic over the Navy trousers. 'You? Who are you? And what kind of uniform do you call that, son? Are you in the Army or the Navy, or what?'

Wally cleared his throat. 'Well, not exactly, sir. You see, last night I wore a zoot-suit to the dance at the Crystal Ballroom, only they wouldn't let me in because they changed it to a USO club, but my girlfriend was inside because—'

Stilwell cut him off. 'Is this a long story, son?'

'Yes, sir.'

'Then I don't want to hear about it.' Stilwell took another look at the carnage, then started back for his car.

Ward spoke up, walking towards him. 'Just a minute, General. There's something I want to say.'

Stilwell turned around and faced the man who was obviously the owner of the house.

'We went through a lot last night,' Ward said. 'All of us. For the first time, we came face to face with the enemy, right here in our own backyard. But we all came together, put our differences aside, and carried on in the true spirit of America. I want you to know that no matter what happens, no matter what sacrifices have to be made, we're prepared to carry forward like Americans.' Ward picked up a Christmas wreath out of the debris and shook the dirt off it. The previous day this wreath had been on his front door. 'This wreath is the symbol of Christmas, the symbol of peace. I'm going to hang this wreath on my door, right now, to remind us that no matter what else happens, we're not going to let a bunch of treacherous enemy killjoys ruin our Christmas.'

With that, Ward pulled a nail from his pocket, stepped up to his newly replaced front door and prepared to nail up the wreath. He raised his hammer and gave it a good firm whack.

This good firm whack was all it took – not to put up the wreath, but to crack the one remaining foundation support that had survived the destruction of the previous night! With this support broken, Ward's entire house, with the exception of the repaired front door, slid away from the foundation, right towards the edge of the cliff! The group on the front lawn stared in speechless astonishment while Ward continued hammering, totally unaware of what was happening behind his front door.

The back half of the house slid over the edge of the cliff and seemed to hang there for a moment, as if debating whether or not to tip over and topple the sixty feet to the beach below. Finally, it decided to do so. The house fell, tumbling over and over, breaking apart on the cliff's rocky wall and smashing to pieces on the beach.

Ward adjusted the wreath, admiring his handiwork, and turned to face his public. Upon seeing the looks on their speechless faces, he opened the door – and saw the ocean! Ward's jaw fell open. He walked across his floor to the edge of the cliff and looked down. He stood there for a long, long moment, staring at the house he used to live in, then shrugged and tossed away his hammer. Tomorrow morning he would simply have to call a contractor.

Everyone else turned to the man who was in charge of the defence of southern California, waiting for his reaction, waiting for a statement of importance, a quotable statement, one which they could repeat to their grandchildren.

Major General Joseph W. Stilwell raised his hands in a gesture calling for quiet and calm. He looked at each of their questioning faces. 'I don't want to hear about it,' he told them, then turned and headed for his car.

There was one brief moment of calm before all hell broke loose. This is what happened: Sitarski slugged Wally once before the MPs could stop him, so Wally slugged him right back! Sitarski tried to chase him, but Maxine jumped on his back. Then Quince punched Sitarski in the face for the five bucks he owed him, and the MPs immediately went after Quince! Reese and Foley came to Quince's aid and in moments they were all slugging it out with the MPs! The MPs then began scrapping among themselves, and within ten seconds, everybody was fighting everybody else, whether there was reason to or not!

Sergeant Frank Tree ran after Stilwell. 'General Stilwell, sir!' he called, catching up with him. 'Sir, I was wondering if you might have room for another man in your outfit. I'm only a motor Sergeant, but I'm one heckuva fine mechanic, and if you need someone who knows machinery – or, if you need someone who knows weapons, I know weapons as well as any man in this Army. . . .'

Stilwell looked at him with the expression that had given him his nickname.

'You know, sir,' Tree offered, 'I don't really think 1941 is going to turn out to be much of a year for this war. I've got a feeling that 1942 is really going to be the big one!'

Stilwell took a last look at the pandemonium on Ward's front lawn, shook his head and said, 'It's going to be a long war.' He climbed into his car, and with his entourage behind him, headed east, into the rising sun.

Afterword

For those who didn't know
or have simply forgotten ...

Stilwell was right: it was a long war.
But we won.